Revelation

Also by Carter Wilson

The Comfort of Black

The Boy in the Woods

Final Crossing

Revelation

A THRILLER

CARTER WILSON

Longboat Key, Florida

ISBN 978-1-60809-218-5

Published in the United States of America by Oceanview Publishing
Longboat Key, Florida

www.oceanviewpub.com

10 9 8 7 6 5 4 3 2 1

PRINTED IN THE UNITED STATES OF AMERICA

For Mom

ACKNOWLEDGMENTS

THIS BOOK IS dedicated to my mom, who always reads my drafts, finds all the typos, and says nice things. Huge thanks to my agent, Pam Ahearn, who has been through all the ups and downs with me. Pam, I'm just realizing it's been nearly twelve years since our very first rejection together. And thanks to Pat, Bob, Lee, Emily, Lisa, and all the other fine folks at Oceanview who are putting this book out into the world—I couldn't do any of this without your resources, support, and vision.

As always, I rely heavily on the insights and advice from my critique group. Ed, Dirk, Sean, Linda, and Abe—you keep putting me back on track. Thank you.

None of this would happen without the support and love of all my family. Ili and Sawyer, I love that you come to the coffee shop to write with me; I'm so lucky to be your dad. Jessica, you're all I could ever ask for, and I'm forever grateful for how much you believe in me. Henry, your imagination is inspirational—keep it up. Sole, I truly appreciate your continued support and our friendship.

Dad, I am missing you every day.

I have a hard time sitting in a quiet, lonely room and typing away. Not that I can't do it, but I prefer the buzz of energy around me, even if I shove in earbuds and talk to no one. With that, I want to acknowledge the wonderful Starbucks crew in Erie, Colorado, who gets a visit from me nearly every day. You've made me a lot of doppios over the years, you are always friendly, and you even give me my own little special cup. Now that's class.

Finally, thanks as always to you, the reader. As a reward for your continued support, here is a small token of appreciation: the recipe for my perfect margarita. Perhaps you should make one now and have it in hand as you dive into this book.

2 oz tequila (buy the good stuff)
1 oz freshly squeezed lime juice
½ oz Solerno blood orange liquor
1 Tbsp agave nectar

No salt. Not ever salt.

"God? No one really knows about that. Not truly, anyway. Tell you one thing, though, if there is a god, I hope he has a good sense of humor. Otherwise, I'm screwed."

—Samuel Lowry, convicted serial killer

Revelation

PART I

CHAPTER ONE

Harden opened his eyes to blackness just as something began crawling into his mouth.

He slapped at his lips, bringing a brilliant flash of pain to an injury already there. He turned his head and spit twice into the dark, into the dank space surrounding him, hoping to eject whatever creature was reaching into his mouth. Spider. Cockroach.

More pain, not just from his mouth. His face. Chest. Ribs.

Raging thirst.

Harden struggled to remember, but the real struggle was against the panic, the crushing sense of entombment, of being buried alive.

Focus. Figure out where you are.

He was lying down—that much he knew—with nothing under him except the cold hardness of scratchy earth, the kind that hadn't gone anywhere in a long time. Dead soil.

The smell of sewage. Powerful and close. Was that coming from him?

Eyes shut, then open. Shut. Open. Trying to focus only on *seeing*, but there was only blackness, the kind from the inside of a coffin buried deep in the ground. As he turned his head, Harden finally found what he wanted: a small, watery arm of light somewhere in the distance, as if a fissure just formed in the shell of his cocoon.

That bit of light assured him he at least wasn't blind, but that brought only mild relief.

He had known true horror in his life once before, and in this new darkness he saw himself once again as a seven-year-old boy, crying as he promised his teacher he wouldn't tell anyone. Mr. Kildare had been very insistent on that. Nobody could know what had happened in the storage closet next to room 4A of Owen Elementary School. It would be their secret, their bond.

He sat up and a wave of nausea roiled him, nearly collapsing him back to the dirt floor of whatever room he was in. But he steadied himself against it and gave himself a few seconds to breathe it away. His fingertips found a few small pebbles on the ground. Harden's gaze went back to the shaft of light, and there was no question to him now he was seeing the outline of a door. Maybe the only door in this room.

As he began to stand, pain seared through his rib cage, like someone twisting a butter knife in the gaps between his bones. He gasped and sat back down, remembering only flashes of the beating he took. Fists slamming against him, over and over.

A tooth was loose, dangling, tethered with only a thin string of flesh. His tongue pushed it back and forth. Harden tasted the salty blood for the first time. It made him aware of his desperate hunger.

The last thing I remember is . . .

Coyote.

The girl in the car. *She died with my hand over her mouth.*

Running away.

Coyote found me. Beat me nearly to death. He had . . .

He had a needle.

Harden saw the needle in his mind, the brief gleam of steel before it plunged deep into his flesh.

He felt his arm for a bump. He couldn't find one in the dark, but he felt a spot where his cold skin seemed just a bit warmer. There was a dull sensation of pain there, like the phantom traces of headache.

Wherever this place is, Harden thought, *I'm here because of what Coyote started. What I helped him start. He thinks he's God, and, worse yet, others now think the same thing of him.*

What was it Coyote once said?

The hard part isn't believing in a god. The hard part is choosing the right one to follow.

Taking a deep breath, Harden stood again, exhaling through the pain. He separated his feet, trying to stabilize and orient his sluggish body in the void. There was only the sliver of light on which to focus, but it was something. The light was at ground level, some indiscernible distance away. Harden stuck his arms in front of him and took a step, his body lumbering forward. The tip of his shoe scraped the dirt.

He moved his arms around, feeling for a wall. Nothing.

Another step forward.

The smell of sewage grew stronger. Disorientation consumed him. How big was this room?

Another step.

Now he could make out more faint strips of light, forming a rectangle. It was a door. No question. A small, horizontal slash of light appeared in the middle of it.

Another step. His arms still outstretched, feeling nothing but the weight of darkness.

Another step, and the tip of his shoe plunged into something solid on the floor. Not hard like a piece of furniture. Dense but soft, like a sandbag. Harden lowered to one knee and reached out in front of him, slow and steady, as if trying to pet a skittish dog.

Finally, he felt something. Cold and smooth, like plastic. A lump, then softness. Hair? It felt like . . .

That's a fucking face.

Harden recoiled enough to send him falling backwards, and his tailbone struck hard into the dirt, sending a fresh wave of pain all the way up into his teeth.

"Who is that?" he said. "Who's there?"

Light suddenly flooded the room, piecing his brain and forcing his eyes shut. When he reopened them and looked up, he saw a single, dirt-streaked lightbulb dangling from a thin black cord about two feet above his head. Like the wall in front of him, the ceiling was concrete, its surface etched and scratched with age.

Harden lowered his gaze, and that was when he saw the body.

Derek.

"No," Harden mumbled, pushing himself backward along the floor. "Oh, Jesus, no."

Harden had just been with him. They had had drinks together, celebrating Harden's twenty-first birthday. Emma had been there. So had Coyote. Things had gone so wrong. The girl in the car. The accident. Her eyes rolling up at Harden as she died. When was that? Just last night?

Derek was barefoot, his feet covered in a thin layer of dirt, his jeans and the flesh beneath ripped in three different areas. He was wearing the t-shirt he had bought in the Bahamas on a family vacation, the touristy kind with the phrase *ANOTHER SHITTY DAY IN PARADISE* placed alongside the image of a hammock suspended between two palm trees. The words now mixed with dried blood and gore, and a section of intestine erupted through the fabric, right up through the middle of *PARADISE*.

Derek's head and face seemed untouched, his hair almost defying physics to stay in place. Just below the chin, though, Harden saw what probably killed Derek: a long slice zigzagging the front of the throat. It wasn't a clean, straight cut, but a brutal, jagged rip. Just above the gash on the side of the neck, a simple message appeared in tight black ink.

Andalusian

He heard Coyote's voice in his head.

We have a word for people like you, Derek. We call you Andalusians. They were the first ones killed in the Spanish Inquisition, you know. They were the original doubters.

Harden turned his head to the side and retched, the hot, burning bile scraping like the tines of a fork along his raw throat. "Oh . . . oh, fuck." The smell of his bile mixed with the smell of Derek's body, the stench of the excrement Derek likely expelled in his final moments alive.

Then, for just the tiniest sliver of time, Harden's brain tried to soothe him, convince him none of this was actually real. That it couldn't possibly be, because the contrast of what was happening in this room was far too removed from Harden's normal life. He had just been in Tillman, New York, sleepy home of Wyland University. Graduation was barely a month ago. Things had been . . . well, not exactly *normal*, he supposed. After all, Coyote's experiment had attracted the attention of the FBI, and Harden was slowly being reeled into the investigation. But life had been nothing like . . . like *this*.

Yes, a dream. That must be it, he thought. Maybe Derek was back home in Rochester, spending the summer before going to law school. Maybe Derek wasn't *really* on the floor just feet away from him, his body cold and his exposed, torn flesh crusting in the dry air.

The moment of disbelief lasted one, maybe two blinks of Harden's eyes. Then reality reached into his chest and squeezed his heart until it threatened to burst like an overfilled water balloon. Harden staggered to his feet and turned away from his friend, gasping for air.

He needed to look somewhere else, anywhere. As long as it wasn't *there*.

The room did have a door—dull gray metal with rusted bolts. No handle on the inside, but there was a small frame in the center of the door that looked like it could be some kind of latch. Just large enough to pass a meal through. Harden thought of all the movie scenes with prisoners in solitary confinement. They all had doors like these.

The walls and ceiling were concrete, the dirt beneath him hard, scratchy, and dry.

Harden raced to the door and pushed, but it yielded nothing to him. He slapped the metal until his palms burned.

"Open the door!"

It was the only thing to say, but did he really want that door to open? Who would open it, and what would they do to him once they did?

A weapon. He had to find something to use. Harden turned and scanned the room, and that was when he noticed the small table and chair sitting in a shadowy corner. But that wasn't all there was. There was a typewriter on top of the table.

Harden walked over, his throat burning, trying to keep his gaze away from the body of his friend.

It was a simple folding card table with a spongy green top. The chair was equally utilitarian, a poured mold of cheap white plastic. The typewriter stood out as a retro work of art against a dreary scene.

The machine was old, but shined up as if recently restored. The black keys were perfectly round and displayed bright white characters. The word *Royal* blazoned just above the top row of keys, and a single sheet of paper had been rolled on the platen, waiting for the first words to christen it.

Next to the typewriter was a stack of paper, all blank save the sheet occupying the top position.

In a clear, sharp script, a simple message waited for Harden.

Tell me a story.

CHAPTER TWO

One hour. Two. Maybe three, perhaps as many as six. He couldn't know for sure. But Harden called out until his throat lost whatever moisture it had left, which wasn't much. He screamed to be released, and when that went unanswered, he begged. He swore using every profane word he had ever learned, and then made up a few of his own. He whimpered to be given a single glass of water.

Still, no one came.

He had no watch; there was no way of knowing what day or time it was. No way to call for help. No food or water. No toilet. He only had the table and chair, the typewriter, paper, and Derek's rotting corpse. Harden beat his fists against the immobile door, demanding the body, at least, be taken from the room.

Silence.

Harden didn't cry, but that would come.

All the while Harden kept looking over at the machine on the small desk.

Tell me a story.

It took those hours for him to realize his only way to live was to write. Coyote wanted a story. Of course, not just any story. Coyote wanted to read the story of how he became what he did, from the eyes of his first disciple. How it all happened.

Harden picked at a crust of dried blood on his lip and thought of something else.

Or maybe he wants to see exactly how much I really know.

Harden stared at the blank sheet of paper in the typewriter. He hadn't used a typewriter since he was in junior high—and had never used a purely manual one like this. When he pressed the first key, it did nothing. He pressed harder, and only the slightest ghost of the letter *F* appeared on the page. Then he pressed down hard, and the key released a satisfying *clack* along with a dark purple-blue impression of the letter he wanted to write. He practiced with a few words.

Fuck you. f Uck you fuckity fuck you very mucu.

Harden yanked the page out, crumpled it into a ball, and tossed it into the corner of the room. Then he slid a fresh sheet into the Royal.

He'd decided to give it a page and see what happened. He would tell his story, even if no one ever read it except the man who would probably kill him.

September 1989
I met Coyote in the strange, serendipitous way special friends are supposed to . . .

CHAPTER THREE

I met Coyote in the strange, serendipitous way special friends are supposed to. It was the second day of my senior year, and the air draped over me with the kind of weight only possible in the un-yielding final days of a New York summer. Too hot even for the mosquitoes. As I crossed the quad on my way to my literature class, my face erupted in pain.

It took me a second to process what had happened, but I saw a blue Frisbee on the ground and blood on the back of my hand as I reached for my mouth. I thought the errant Frisbee bloodied my lip, but what it actually did was knock my front tooth out, and I felt the little chunk of bone threatening to jam my throat. I spit the tooth onto the freshly cut grass, followed by a viscous mixture of blood and spit.

Goddamnit. I always liked my teeth.

"Jesus, I'm so sorry."

I was too absorbed to notice him at first. I just stared at the front tooth, which looked like a tiny little tombstone, a solitary tribute to the unknown soldier.

"Oh . . . oh, shit."

The voice was now next to me. As blood dribbled from my lower lip, I turned and saw him for the first time. He was taller than me—something I was unaccustomed to—and he reached out with a tanned arm wrapped in an expensive watch.

"Oh, man," he said. "Your tooth. I can't believe I broke your tooth."

I didn't know what to say. I was pissed off but scared to talk, somehow actually concerned about my appearance with all the blood on my face. Weird, isn't it? But that's what he did to people. He was a guy who made you think about how you appeared in front of him, despite what you were feeling inside.

He touched my face.

CHAPTER FOUR

June 1990

Harden removed the page from the Royal and placed it faceup on the table. He reread it, spotting seven typos, and very much didn't care about any of them. Seconds after he finished reading his work, the solitary light went dark. As before, the room was suffocating in the immediacy of its blackness. The stench from Derek seemed to grow stronger. Panic welled inside Harden.

Breathe. Count your breaths, one, then two. Three, then four.

He closed his eyes, preferring to see the inside of his eyelids rather than the void surrounding him. After an eternity in the dark, he heard a sound. The scraping of metal against metal.

Harden opened his eyes.

The slat in the center of the door opened, bringing with it a brilliant, rectangular shaft of fluorescent light into the room. Then, the partial outline of someone's head eclipsed the beam.

"Put the typed pages by the door. Then turn around and stand in the back corner." The voice was deep, emotionless, and unfamiliar.

"Are you going to let me out?" Harden asked.

A few more seconds.

"Put the typed pages by the door. Then turn around and stand in the back corner." The voice was louder this time. More commanding.

Harden did as he was told. He picked up his solitary page of work and made his way toward the door as the backlit head watched him. Harden noticed an unnatural, Charlie Brown–roundness to the man's skull. He placed the page in the dirt by the door and then made his way back to the far corner of the room, walking along the walls to avoid the body.

"Don't turn around," the voice said. "We're watching."

We are watching. Not *I* am watching.

The slat closed, then Harden heard the sound of a heavy bolt sliding open on the other side of the door. The door opened and more light filled the room. Harden felt the air pressure in the room change as a slight rush of atmosphere rippled throughout the stale cell. He sucked it in and hoped that a bit of fresh air would wash away some of the death stench.

Should he try running? Who knew how many of *them* there were, but this could be his only chance. The door was open. He could run full speed and try to knock over anyone in his path, hoping just to make it outside. He could make it. He could be free. There was a chance.

Or he could end up like Derek.

He squeezed his hands into tight balls, his body shaking with indecision. Listening, he heard a dragging sound, quickly followed by the sound of clanking and a hollow thump. Before he could decide what to do, the door slammed shut, and the bolt slid back into place. Harden turned and stared at the cracks of light. He had missed his opportunity and could only hope there would be another.

The light turned on.

Derek's body and the typed page were gone. In their place was a simple tray of food, a bottle of water, and a red plastic bucket.

Harden yelled at the door.

"I want to talk to him."

There was only silence in return. At one point, he thought he heard laughing. But maybe it was only in his head.

CHAPTER FIVE

"We have to get you to a doctor, man. Let me help you."

I finally chanced some words, mumbling through my fingers.

"It's . . . it's okay."

I don't know why I said it. It wasn't okay at all. This guy just broke my tooth with a goddamn Frisbee.

"No," he said. "It's not. Let's at least go to the university clinic." He said the words with such decisiveness it was hard to argue against it. He called out to whatever kid was supposed to catch the Frisbee instead of my face.

"Jeremy, I'm taking him to the clinic."

Jeremy mumbled something that sounded exactly unlike an offer of assistance. He almost seemed disappointed that my blood interrupted their game, and he picked up the disc and walked off without a word to me.

After I scooped up my tooth and shoved it into my pocket, the guy responsible for my new smile put his hand on my shoulder and walked me along the sloped terrain of the quad toward the center of campus. His hand rested on my shoulder for a while. Normally this would have made me uncomfortable. But not this time. This time it was actually comforting.

He finally released his touch, but only to stick his hand out to me. "Wiley," he said. I offered him my bloodied hand, which didn't seem to give him a second thought. "Wiley Martin. I go by Coyote."

I nodded, then almost asked him why he went by Coyote before I made the connection. Now that I look back on everything, there was much more meaning in Coyote's name than the easy connection to a cartoon character. More than anything, there was something feral about it all.

"Harden," I mumbled.

"Simon?"

I shook my head, then spit a glob of bloody saliva onto the ground. I was thankful to see no other teeth jettisoned with it. "Harden," I repeated. "Harden Campbell."

"Ah, Harden." Coyote shook his head. "Well, Harden, I'm deeply sorry I just fucked up your mouth."

The words *It's okay, no big deal* rose in my throat, but I suppressed them.

"My aim sucks, man. I didn't even see you there. But we'll get you fixed up—whatever you need. I'll take care of it."

"I have insurance," I said. I wasn't actually sure about that. It all depended if the payment was made this month.

"No, no, I'll take care of everything. We'll get that tooth put back in there in no time."

I studied him as we walked. He was one of *them*, I assumed. Wyland University was full of them. The more I looked at him, the more sense it made. Thick rugby shirt. Expensive watch. Styled hair made to look disheveled.

Rich kid.

He would throw money at my mouth, no matter how much it cost. He would buy his conscience clean.

Thank God, I thought. As much as I tired of the constant wealth around me, I was glad it was here now. My dad's threadbare insurance would probably only pay enough to fashion my tooth into a necklace. I would gladly accept Coyote's offer.

The university clinic was almost empty, the suffering flu-ridden masses still months away. After a triage check of my temperature and blood pressure, I was taken back to see the doctor. Coyote, to my surprise, insisted on going with me.

The university physician seemed annoyed at having to do any work. He opened my mouth and crammed some gauze in my gap.

"Got a missing tooth," he said.

No shit, I thought. I dug it from my pocket and presented it to him. He gave it a second's glance.

"Going to have to see a dentist," he said. "You can keep that one as a souvenir. They'll probably make you a new one."

"Are there any dentists here?" I asked.

"Nope," he said, crumbling his fists into the pockets of his pristine white medical coat. "I'll give you some ibuprofen for the pain. They can get you the names of some local dentists up front on your way out."

He scribbled something on a pad and left the room. Coyote shook his head and turned to me.

"You got a car, Harden?"

"No."

"Don't worry about it. Come on."

I followed him out as he strode up to the receptionist. He pulled out a slim leather wallet and placed a shiny platinum credit card in front of her. "Put his bill on this," he said. "And I need the name of the best dentist in town."

I wondered if there was such a thing in Tillman, New York. The receptionist must have, too, because she rolled her eyes as she took his card. She fumbled through a file cabinet and pulled out a sheet of paper.

"Here are all of the dentists in the area," she said, sliding the paper across the counter to Coyote. "One of them has to be the best."

As she rang up my charges on his card, Coyote asked to use the phone. Two calls later he hung up and smiled at me.

"Found a dentist. Don't know if he's the best, but he can see you now. I'm driving."

At that point, I was just along for the ride. Coyote was in charge. Four hours later, I had a repaired tooth and a new friend.

I didn't stop to wonder how long either would last.

CHAPTER SIX

"To the left. Left. *Left.*"

Derek's voice hissed in excited glee. I'm not sure why he was being so quiet. No one could see us up here.

Derek held one handle of the water-balloon slingshot, the black rubber tubing pulled thin and taut as I held tightly onto the balloon itself. Jacob squeezed the other end, snorting laughs through his nose. The lights of our apartment were out, and I could only make out the silhouettes of my two roommates as they stood on either side of our fourth-floor window. Below us, Dilfin Avenue blossomed with collegiate nightlife, punctuated by the late-night staccato bursts of the drunken aimless. We weren't among them. We were drunk, but we weren't aimless. We were aiming, in fact, at a fourth-floor window directly across the street from us.

"Just a sec . . . hang on . . . and *now!*"

I let go. The small blue balloon—about the size of a softball—launched from my grip and whooshed through the open window. I tried to follow its path, but it was damn fast, and I lost it in the darkness of night. Seconds later I heard it slam into the apartment window across the street with a resounding *whomp*. There was a party in the apartment, and we hit our mark perfectly.

Jacob was the first to collapse to the floor in fits of laughter. Derek and I joined him, and we all peered over the windowsill like soldiers scouting from a shallow bunker. The partiers were backlit, so it was hard to make out more than shapes, but pretty soon three or four of them were staring out the window and pointing in our direction. I could see the telltale shape of Solo cups in each of their hands.

"C'mon," Jacob said. "Let's do another."

"Let's give it a minute," I said.

God, this was so stupid, which was maybe why it was so much fun.

We peeked out as more of the partiers came to the window. There were maybe twenty people total in the small apartment, mostly men. One of them, a hulk of a student in what looked like a tight varsity jacket, pressed his face against the window as he scanned outside.

"Okay, another," I said. "Keep low."

Derek and Jacob resumed their positions. I waited and watched. After a few moments, three more partiers across the street had their faces pressed against the window. I quickly lifted myself up, took a fleeting moment to adjust my aim, and fired. As I dropped back to the floor, I kept my focus on the balloon. This time I could see it the entire flight. It was a good shot.

WHAM!

Dead center, a second time. It must have scared the shit out of them, because two of them jumped back and, I can only assume, spilled their beer.

"Holy shit," Jacob howled, collapsing to the floor. "That was *perfect.*"

We hid on the floor and laughed as we finally heard the partiers open their window and yell from across the street.

"Fuckin' pussies! Try doing that again!"

A few more catcalls followed, and then the three of us decided not to risk any more shots for the moment. Jacob reached up and inched the window closed.

"Call that a success," Derek said. He started crawling back to the bottle of tequila a few feet away from us on the floor, and I smiled at the way he and Jacob hid in complete cowardice the same way I did. They were both on the rugby team and could hold their own, but stupid violence wasn't in their nature, at least not Derek's. If someone shot a water balloon at Derek, he wouldn't be angry. He'd want to join in.

Jacob was a little different. I don't think Jacob would ever go looking for a fight, but he would get into one quicker than Derek. He was just stupid enough not to realize when something wasn't worth it. It was an annoying trait, but once in awhile it was entertaining to witness. Derek and I had been roommates since our freshman year, and Jacob shared a house with us our sophomore and junior years. Now, all of us seniors, the three of us shared the rent on a four-bedroom place while we searched for an extra person to cover the cost. We were looking, but not very hard. The extra space was nice; besides, Derek helped to cover my portion of the extra room. It was an above-average place for a college apartment, and the only way I could afford to live there was with a bit of Derek's charity.

Sitting on the floor, Derek poured three more shots and handed one to both Jacob and me.

"To the inauguration of the new apartment," he said, raising his glass.

I swallowed the liquid and felt it tear down my throat. It burned a bit less than the previous two, which meant I was numbing up.

"Salut," I said, pushing on my new tooth with my tongue. The swelling on my lip was almost gone, but the cut on the inside of my mouth was slow to heal. I proudly withstood the sting of tequila.

I started to think about launching another balloon when there was a pounding on the door. Not a knock. A pounding.

"Holy shit," Derek whispered, sputtering a drunken laugh. "They found us."

Jacob took a slug straight from the bottle, not seeming to care in the slightest at the visitor at our door.

The pounding came again, but no voices. I got up.

"Where are you going?" Derek said.

"I want to see who it is."

"Good, you'll be the first line of defense. We'll jump out the window while they tear you apart."

He looked over to Jacob, who said, "I don't give a shit. Open the door. Let's see what happens."

I started walking to the front of the small apartment.

"Seriously, Harden, don't open the door," Derek said. "Could be a whole group out there."

I can't explain why I wanted to open the door. There was something in me that felt like we had to own up to what we did. Not that I felt bad. It was only a stupid water balloon, after all. But if we were going to sit here and hide in the dark, that had to be balanced out with facing a real live person standing at our door, waiting to confront us. I just had a sense that everything would be okay, but that's the kind of drunken thinking that can end badly.

Halfway down the hall, I heard a voice through the door.

"Campus police."

I stopped. *Campus police?* Our apartment building wasn't even *on* campus.

"Harden, don't open the goddamn door," Derek called out.

I turned. "I just want to see."

I laughed as I crept closer to the door, wondering if it would suddenly burst open, knocking out all my other teeth. The thought sobered me just a bit as I cautiously leaned in to the peephole.

My left eye almost touching the peephole, I was surprised to find neither a drunken mob nor the campus police standing in the hall-way. I unlocked the dead bolt and opened the door.

"Hey there, Coyote."

CHAPTER SEVEN

Coyote grinned. It wasn't the same smile I'd seen when I first met him. This one had a touch of snarl to it.

"How's the tooth, Harden?"

Jacob called out from behind me, "Who is it?"

I turned. "Don't worry," I said. "I know this guy." I looked back at Coyote. "Tooth is great. Come on in."

Coyote walked into the darkened apartment with an amused look on his face. I got the feeling he enjoyed unknown situations.

"Were you at the party across the street?" I asked. "Did you see us?"

"No, no," he said. "I was on the street. Saw the whole thing." He walked down the hallway and stood directly in front of the launching-pad window. Jacob and Derek looked up at him from the floor, and I could see Jacob's arms tensing. Coyote turned. "You stayed in the window too long on your second launch," he said to me. "I saw your face in the street light."

That's good eyesight, I thought, forty feet below and all.

I nodded to my roommates. "This is Jacob and Derek." No one shook hands.

"This is the guy who knocked out my tooth," I explained to them.

Jacob looked at Coyote with interest for the first time. "Oh, okay. Right on, man." Jacob was always saying *right on*, which annoyed me mostly because I found myself now saying it on occasion.

"You should've scalped him with the Frisbee," Jacob said. "Harden needs a new haircut more than a new tooth."

"This is Coyote," I said.

"Coyote what?" Jacob asked.

"Coyote is his name."

Jacob cocked his head and asked Coyote, "You Indian or something?"

"No," Coyote said. "It's just a nickname."

"Oh. Right on, man."

Derek remained silent, just studying Coyote as if trying to assess if he was still a threat or not. Coyote walked to our kitchen and opened the refrigerator.

"There's some beer in there if you want one," I said to him. I shrugged to my friends, and Jacob whispered something about the beer being *his*. "And we have tequila over here."

Seconds later, Coyote returned carrying something in his hand. As he came closer, I finally made out a small naval orange that had been rotting in the produce drawer for at least a month.

I said, "Don't eat that. Seriously."

"The problem with water balloons," he said, "is they act more like a grenade rather than a missile." Coyote lobbed the orange up a few times in front of us. "I mean, they're fine if you're going for shrapnel wounds, but they don't give you the impact of a real shelling." He nodded to Derek and Jacob. "Grab the slingshot."

There was an authority to his voice. It wasn't even a commanding phrase, but his tone suggested you could trust him to make the right decision, and the best thing to do was to listen to him. This turned out to be the most powerful thing about Coyote: his ability to sound like he always knew what was for the best. I suspect there are millions of dead soldiers scattered around the world who listened to the same kind of person.

Jacob and Derek rose from the floor, and each of them took one end of the slingshot and positioned themselves on either side of the open window.

I just stood and watched. The party across the street was back in full force, and no one seemed to care anymore about some idiots launching water balloons at them. I knew it was a bad idea the moment I saw Coyote place the small piece of fruit in the pouch and pull the slingshot back. I knew it was a bad idea when I saw Derek and Jacob stretching the rubber tubing to capacity. But I didn't say anything, and that just about sums up the difference between leaders and followers. Followers sit back and watch.

I watched that little piece of forgotten produce rocket out our apartment and absolutely shatter the window across the street. As the splintered glass shards rained down forty feet below, and as Derek and Jacob fell to the floor with fear-tinged hysterics, I sidestepped out of view from the outside world. Not Coyote. He just stood there, plain as sight in front of the window, a tight grin of satisfaction on his face.

In that moment, we found our fourth roommate.

CHAPTER EIGHT

There was no clock, no sunlight or moonlight, no measured time for anything in the cell. There was only one way Harden could loosely keep track of time, which was by writing. As long as he wrote, they paid attention to him, and when they did, he used their interactions with him as a marker of time. He would sit at the desk and write the same amount at a sitting: eight pages. The *click-click-clacking* of the keys would be the only sound in the room, and it always made Harden think of a giant bug tapping at the door with spindly legs, trying to get in. That made him think of the creature that had teased his lips as he had awoken for the first time in this room. Whatever it was, Harden hadn't seen it again. Likely waiting in a crack somewhere for that light to go out again.

Once his eight pages were complete, he'd stack them neatly by the door. Always a moment later, the light would go out, the slat in the door would open, and the same voice would command him to stand in the corner and turn facing the wall. Once he did, the door would open and the pages would be replaced with some kind of food. Harden quickly learned the bucket they had given him was his toilet, and if he left the empty food trays and the used bucket by the door, those would be replaced with fresh supplies.

Eight pages at a sitting. He tried to take the same amount of time per writing interval, though it was impossible to gauge. Mostly, he wrote to the cadence of his hunger, and he was always ready for a new meal by the time his pages were done. He figured it took him about six hours to write eight pages. He would do this for two sequences, then he would try to sleep. Try, because there was no bed, no sleeping bag. Just the clothes he wore and the dirt floor.

In his calculation of time, Harden also had to account for the long, initial chunk of it consumed by his own screaming. Shouting, yelling, storming around the small room, banging on the door. Anything to get the attention of those holding him. This lasted perhaps half a day. There was also a period where he sat silently, shaking in the cool of the loose dirt, wondering if he was being missed by anyone. Wondering if he was due anywhere, if someone would alert the police to his disappearance. Two hours, maybe. And time scouring every inch of the room, every crack in every wall, looking for the slightest of vulnerabilities. An hour, perhaps.

All told, Harden figured he had been in the cell for three or four days. *Three or four fucking days.*

He wasn't built for this. He wasn't a Navy SEAL or Army Ranger. He couldn't go with only whiffs of sleep for days on end, with maybe a thousand calories a day, with no change of clothes, no ability to get warm, and only faint, artificial light to live beneath. Harden wasn't strong like that.

As he lay on the floor in his self-designated period for sleep, Harden was praying for the millionth time that someone was looking for him.

Who?

My dad? he thought. Maybe. But it still might be too soon for him to know something was wrong.

Jacob? No, not Jacob. Jacob is one of them now. He knows exactly where I am. Jacob is probably the one washing out my bucket.

Emma. Hopefully Emma. Oh God, Emma. I hope you're okay.

But mostly Harden figured someone would be missing Derek. Derek came from money, and moneyed students don't disappear for very long. Someone would be looking for Derek, and that might lead them to wonder where Harden was.

That was the only thought keeping his sanity together. He had to believe in something other than his reality.

He tried to find things for which to be thankful, though this was a struggle. The pain in his midsection had subsided, convincing him nothing was broken. His swollen lip was an annoyance, but it was, after all, a minor concern. Whatever had crawled in his mouth hadn't returned. Most of all, he was thankful he was at least alive.

Sleep wasn't coming. Harden rose and prowled the cell again, looking for something—*anything*—new.

It was hard to actually call it a cell, because it wasn't *that* small. He walked the paces again, and again decided it was about fifteen by eighteen feet. Again, he walked every inch of it, scouring the concrete-block walls for any sign of give or wear, finding none. He scratched at the dirt around the edge, hoping he could dig his way to freedom, but the earth was unyielding, leaving him with only bloody fingertips. There were two spots where the dirt separated from the wall by a half-inch or so, but those did him no good. He figured whatever crawled into his mouth was hiding out inside one of those gaps.

The door was just as impenetrable—the metal slat could only be opened from the outside. Where the hell had Coyote found a place like this? he wondered. But each time he asked himself this question, he came to the same conclusion. Coyote didn't find this place. He had it built.

Where?

Only one place made sense. Harden had to be somewhere deep

inside the School of the Revelation. Harden had been inside the School plenty of times, but never heard about a containment facility. Still, it was the only place that made sense. And if he was somewhere deep beneath the School, that meant there were many people wandering around above him. Did most of them even know Harden was there?

Maybe they're all upstairs having a good laugh right now.

Harden stared at his fresh tray of food on the table next to the typewriter, still untouched. It was either breakfast or dinner—he didn't know since the food was always the same. Chipped beef, canned vegetables, and a stale roll. The tray always had a plastic fork, a napkin, a bottle of water, and a plastic vase with a tall, beautiful flower in it. It was an Alstroemeria, also known as the Lily of the Incas. It was the symbol of the Revelation. Coyote told his followers it symbolized the beauty and the fortitude of the movement, but Harden knew the truth. He knew it because Harden himself had come up with the idea.

Every flower has a message behind it, and the Alstroemeria stood for devotion. Coyote liked the message that it sent, so it became the logo of the Revelation. Coyote demanded devotion.

Harden finally ate his food and then stripped naked. He used the bucket, squatting over it to eliminate the previous round of chipped beef. He flattened out the napkin and used it to wipe himself, then he took a small amount of water from his bottle to wash his body. It didn't do much, but it gave him a fleeting sense of being both clean and alert. He shook his clothes—imagining the days-old grime flinging off them—and then dressed again. It was his routine. Routines helped.

He sat back down in his chair and looked at the half-filled page rolled in the typewriter. Writing was also his routine. He didn't know what Coyote was doing with the completed pages he'd submitted and wondered if it was all some kind of exercise in futility, as though the words he set on the paper were just supposed to keep him preoccupied before they sliced his throat as they had Derek's.

As he massaged his left hand before positioning his fingers above the keys, Harden wondered how many words he would be able to put down before he died.

After breaking the window, we all left the apartment with Coyote . . .

CHAPTER NINE

After breaking the window, we all left the apartment with Coyote, hanging our heads low and suppressing our smirks as we walked into the night. A handful of students milled about the broken glass shards and pointed upward, while others were catcalling to the partygoers above. No one knew what the hell was happening, which suited us just fine. It wasn't until we finally turned the corner that I felt a mix of relief and shame. We were too old to be doing such stupid shit, but we were too young to grow up. Looking back, I should have held onto that feeling as long as I could.

The late-night air was the perfect temperature on my skin, like an old thin sweater worn just for its touch. We walked on with no particular purpose other than we were awake and alive, which I guessed would sustain us another block or so.

"I was on my way to Benny's," Coyote said. "That sound good?"

We all nodded. Of all the bars within walking distance of the campus, Benny's was the crappiest. But the bouncers there didn't care how bad your fake ID was, so Benny's was always a good default choice. To save daycare costs when I was young, my mother enrolled me in kindergarten when I was four, lying about my age. So I've always been young for my grade, and seemingly the only college senior still relying on a fake ID to get into bars.

Two blocks and one fake ID later, we were seated in the back corner of the aging establishment. It seemed darker than usual, as if the light from the dusty overheads wanted nothing to do with the place. Jacob collected cash from each of us and returned with two pitchers of beer. I took a sip and immediately knew he bought the cheapest kind he could and pocketed the rest of the cash.

"My girlfriend is meeting us here," Coyote said.

Derek took one sip and then turned to Jacob. "You better have some change left over, because this tastes like piss."

"Calm down," Jacob said. "I'm saving the rest for a couple more pitchers."

"Quality, not quantity," Coyote said.

Derek eyed Coyote. "You a senior?"

Coyote nodded. "Math major."

"That doesn't sound like a lot of fun."

"It's amazing, actually. I just don't know what I'm going to do with it."

I knew the feeling. The uncertainty of not knowing what you wanted to do with the rest of your life was a pervasive annoyance compounded greatly by the sound of time whooshing by.

"You could work for the Pentagon," I said. "Developing weapons. You seem to have a knack."

Coyote smiled. "I hope the broken window won't get you into trouble."

"Oh, we'll make sure your name gets mentioned if we do," Derek said. "You live downtown?"

Coyote took another swig of his beer and shook his head. "It seems as though I'm currently homeless."

The three of us exchanged glances before looking back at him.

"How so?"

"Well, not exactly homeless. But in search of a place. My girlfriend and I got an apartment together this year, but her parents freaked out and refused to pay her tuition until I move out."

"So you left?" Jacob seemed incredulous that an education could be more important than a woman.

"Of course I did," Coyote said. "I can still be over there, can't I? I just can't have all my stuff lying around in case her parents come to visit, which is way too often." He shrugged it off. "I'm staying at the University Inn until I find a place."

The three of us absorbed this information, and I assumed they all came to the same conclusion as me. Or maybe I was just presuming. I think to myself now: What if I hadn't said what I did next? Would anyone else have? Maybe not. God, how different things would have been.

"Actually, we've been looking for a roommate," I said. "Got a nice fourth bedroom in our place, and we could use some help with the rent." I looked at Jacob's face, and he slowly nodded in agreement. Derek's face was expressionless. I think he caught some kind of scent of Coyote that night, some kind of whiff of a predator hiding in the tall grass, stalking.

Coyote acted like I just offered him nothing more than a piece of gum. "Sure," he said. "Why not? I won't be there much anyway. I'll be with—"

Coyote suddenly looked to his left, and my gaze followed his.

"I'll be with her," he said, gesturing to the woman approaching the table.

It was the first time I saw Emma, and I felt immediately pulled back into the ninth grade, where a girl's crooked grin and flashing eyes were enough to make me fall in love. There was just enough light in the room for me to watch her emerge as if out of fog. As she approached, the first thing I noticed was her long hair falling forward over her shoulders. It was a dirty blond with plenty of kinks in it, styled just enough to look messy, giving her a look of happy restlessness. She was small and thin, and she wore faded, tight-fitting jeans and a loose blue top that spilled over her like a rain shower. She looked over at our table with perfect confidence, and, as I imagined her bright green eyes lingering on mine a bit longer than anyone else's, I couldn't help thinking Emma was the type of woman over whom men killed each other.

"New friends?" she asked, giving us all a collective smile.

"New roommates, actually," Coyote replied, grinning. "Gentlemen, this is Emma."

We quickly introduced ourselves. I was the only one who rose from the table.

"Oh," she said to me as I sat back down. "You're the Frisbee guy."

"I am indeed." God, did I sound stupid.

She bent over into my face and placed her nose just inches from mine. "Open up. Let me see."

My skin flushed and I was grateful for dim surroundings. I opened my mouth, and she peered in a bit more. I pointed to my new tooth and prayed like hell my breath wasn't toxic.

"Very nice," she said, putting her index finger under my chin. "They did a good job. Would have been a shame to mess up that smile." She gave me a subtle wink. I closed my mouth and tried to think of something to say, but nothing came.

Jacob tried his best to get her to sit down next to him, but she managed to squeeze between Derek and Coyote instead. Derek poured her a beer.

"So we just met your boyfriend here," Derek said. "And now it seems he's moving in with us." He glanced at me long enough to tell me he wasn't sold on the idea. "Are we taking a big risk?"

She smiled and patted Coyote's arm. "Coyote's a good person. He just has certain needs."

Kind of an odd statement. "Such as?" I asked.

She mulled this over a bit before speaking. "Well, he's the smartest person I've ever met, and he's pretty easy on the eyes, so he has a huge ego as a result. You'll need to tell him how beautiful and brilliant he is every few days. Maybe even more often."

Everyone laughed, including Coyote. "Anything else?" he asked.

"He's got a lot of money," she continued. "And he'll always offer to buy you things. Don't be insulted by it, but don't take advantage of it either. He doesn't ever want to feel like he's buying your friendship."

Coyote nodded, but didn't smile.

"He snores, but he'll probably be at my place most nights, so you won't have to worry about it. And you should pray we don't ever break up, because he can brood like no one I've ever seen."

"That's a pretty accurate profile," Coyote said, and even in the darkness of the bar I saw the tension in his jaw. "Is that all?"

Emma shook her head, appearing to decide whether to continue. She took a sip of her beer, slowly wiped her lips, and then looked directly at him. "Coyote is a man who requires great things to happen to him. He needs to be challenged, and if the challenge isn't there, he'll go looking for it, wherever it may be. Good or bad."

Her honesty startled me, and I looked over at Coyote, who wore no expression whatsoever on his face. Jacob and Derek were silent.

She looked around the room before leaning in across the table, beckoning us all to do the same. Faces hovering close to one another, she whispered to us. "Also, don't expose him to bright light. Don't get him wet. And whatever you do, never, *ever*, feed him after midnight." She flashed a quick grin, grabbed her beer, and leaned back into the booth.

It was a joke, but looking back, comparing Coyote to a Gremlin turned out to be a pretty accurate insight.

CHAPTER TEN

September slipped into October with barely a good-bye. I made it through the first three weeks of classes with a kind of numbness that I blamed on being a senior with no real sense of what the hell I was going to do with my life. It's a disconcerting feeling to be twenty years old and feel like you're running out of time.

Coyote moved in, and it didn't take long to see the evidence of his disproportionate wealth to ours. Expensive clothes, fancy cookware, and a thirty-inch TV that weighed about two hundred pounds and cost, or so he told me, over a thousand bucks. Coyote exuded money like a politician does bullshit. He wore it outwardly but with a sense of comfort and style, so that it buttressed rather than defined him.

Most impressive of all, he had a car. And not some piece of junk, but an emerald-green BMW 325xi. Though Derek and Jacob both came from comfortable middle-class families, neither of them had cars at school. Few students did—Wyland was small and accessible on foot, and there was little in the town worth visiting.

Jacob accepted Coyote like a puppy going home from the animal shelter with a new owner. I think Jacob was attracted to the doors Coyote could open for him, by which I mean he saw Coyote as a vehicle to get laid. Jacob was a decent looking guy with an athletic build, but lacked severely in the personality department, so most weekends Jacob ended up either alone or with some vapid sorority girl who inevitably never saw him again. My guess is Jacob hoped Coyote could help him find a woman like Emma. Stupid, stupid Jacob.

Derek was different. I could see Derek trying to make up his mind about Coyote. He didn't need Coyote's money to help with the rent, and I imagined he secretly would have been content having the fourth bedroom of our apartment sit empty all year. Before Coyote arrived, Derek was the most charismatic one of our group, and, though he didn't date with the fast-food mentality of Jacob, it wasn't because he lacked interest. Girls loved Derek, but he preferred the steady certainty of a monogamous existence rather than the pinball frenzy of weekend hookups. He'd recently got out of a yearlong relationship, and the past few weeks were the longest I'd seen him survive without being in love. Derek was the sensitive one, which is why I think he didn't immediately take to Coyote like Jacob did. It wasn't jealousy. I think Derek was the first to detect that Coyote had something nasty and festering deep inside him.

Coyote was a guy who bought hundred-dollar shirts and never ironed them. He could casually absorb any mathematical concept thrown his way, yet he'd miss an exam because he stayed up late watching old B movies. He was handsome and charismatic enough to attract someone like Emma, but often he didn't even seem to notice when she was in the same room. Coyote circled the periphery of society, around and around, trying to decide if he wanted in or out.

I think Coyote liked me because of my blue-collar background. I had accumulated just enough scholastic and philanthropic achievement in my public high school career to make a ripple on Wyland's application. In the large fish tank of private universities, it was never enough to have beautiful and exotic fish swimming about. You needed a few pebbles at the bottom of the tank to make everything else appear natural.

As the fall days passed, we all settled into a comfortable routine. Coyote spent most weeknights at Emma's apartment, giving the three of us our old lives back for sporadic moments. Those nights were spent watching movies, studying, or, in my case, working three nights a week at the campus library.

Weekends were different. Around Thursday, the slow buzz of the weekend would begin, a faint electric murmur underscoring the excitement of a predictably drunken two days. Coyote was always around on the weekend. Emma seemed to spend time with her own friends on the weekend, and whether or not that was her idea or Coyote's, I never knew. He seemed content going out with the three of us and rarely mentioned her name before Monday.

It always seemed a waste to me. If I had a woman like Emma, I'd dive in deep, never even thinking about coming up for air.

* * *

Friday night frat party.

Wyland University frat houses were thin shells of beer and bullshit that sheltered its residents from any reality of the outside world. Not that I really knew, since neither me nor my roommates had ever been in the Greek system, but I'd been to enough frat parties to form what I believed to be a sound opinion. In my opinion, frats were elementary schools without any teachers and a sack of open sugar left in each classroom.

Going to the party was Jacob's idea. Some girl he met—named *Jen*. For some reason they were always named *Jen*—was going to a Delta Upsilon party with some friends and invited him along. Around ten o'clock, Jacob was busily primping himself in the bathroom while Derek and I were deciding if we wanted to go to the party or find something else to do. Coyote was sitting on the couch, reading *Ulysses*.

"You like that book?" I asked.

"I don't know yet," he said, not looking up.

"You're almost done with it."

"It's actually my third read," he said. "I'm guessing I'll have a better idea after my fifth read if I like it or not." He flipped a page over.

"I had to read it in high school," I said. "I didn't even understand the Cliffs Notes."

Coyote finally looked up. "Sometimes books aren't meant to be understood. It's more a matter of whether or not you connect with them."

"And you don't need to understand it to connect with it?"

"Of course not," he said. "You ever read a haiku and not have a clue of what it meant, but you thought it was beautiful?"

I told him I hadn't, and that ended the conversation.

It was still early, so we spent an hour with a fifth of Southern Comfort and a board game designed by the Mensa Society. Jacob had bought it for some reason, and I loved the fact he was the worst at it. Someone would read a question, and we all had to write down our answers. Whoever got it wrong had to take a shot. After an hour, I was getting pretty drunk, while Coyote's shot glass was dusty dry. It's funny how much harder Mensa questions get with three shots of Southern Comfort jumping up and down on the soft spots of your brain.

We finally emerged onto the sidewalk outside our building sometime after midnight, the night air cool and thick with the invigorating smell of recent rain. I sucked it into my lungs, thinking it would surely clear my head. As I looked up, I noticed the window across the street had finally been replaced. I kicked up the collar of my leather jacket against a light breeze as we headed across campus.

The walk was short—just a straight shot across the South Quad. We heard the party from a few hundred feet away, announced by the thundering of heavy bass from a Run DMC song. The frat house itself was beautiful, an old Victorian, once home to a dean or chancellor back at the turn of the century. I'd been inside it before, though. No dean would have been happy to call it home now, unless he was looking for an insurance write-off.

As we approached the stone steps leading up to the house, I realized we were four men trying to get into a party where the frat brothers were trying to get the odds in their favor. Four more guys wouldn't help their cause. I was wondering how we were going to get in as Coyote walked up to the bouncer at the door.

"Coyote," the massive, pasty guard dog said, nodding his head in approval.

"Big Ben." Coyote extended his hand and the two performed some kind of ritualistic street shake.

Coyote introduced us to Big Ben, who looked down at us while his chest—a delicate mixture of muscle and lard—jiggled beneath a tight black t-shirt. We all nodded back to him, hoping to gain his approval. We all wanted Big Ben to like us so we could go and gawk at drunk girls in his festering house. I was pleased when he said we could.

Passing through the front door, I turned to Coyote and said, "How do you know him?"

"He's a lost soul," Coyote replied. "I seem to attract them."

I had no idea what that meant.

Once inside, we slowly made our way from one crowded room to another, acting like we were looking for someone. In a sense, we were: our goal was to find this mysterious Jen, whom Jacob met at the campus store and insisted was a dead ringer for Elizabeth Shue.

As he looked, I contented myself scanning the room for any girls hanging out in small packs without guys around.

Despite my dislike of frat houses, I loved parties. I loved the feel of the music on my skin, and the smell of sweat from people dancing around me. Things happened at parties like this one. Sometimes good things, other times not. But I always wanted to be around when that something happened.

We found Jen. She looked not so much like Jennifer Jason Leigh but rather like Ferris Bueller's sister, if she was a tramp and ten pounds heavier. Jen liked to smack gum as she drank her beer. She was with two friends, both of whom *were* good-looking, and I could see the hamsters spinning on the wheel in Jacob's brain as he tried to figure out how he could make the shift from Jen to one of the others. He couldn't find the answer, I knew, and I smiled as he wracked his brain with the effort.

The girls bobbed their faces and widened their eyes as we all tried to hear one another. Jen leaned in and spoke closely with Jacob, while her two friends smiled at Coyote and Derek. Once in a while they would turn and nod at me as if requesting their check, and I just nodded numbly back at them. It was okay; I was used to not being the center of attention. I was strong and lean, but couldn't compete with my more athletic roommates. Once in a long while I'd be called attractive, and a bit more frequently someone would say I was cute. I existed in that world just north of plain, and my sense of style did nothing to elevate my status.

The music *thump-thump-thumped* deep into my skin, and wherever there was enough room, girls gyrated to the beats while stiff-collared white boys did their best to keep up with them.

I watched Coyote lead the best looking of the three girls into the fray, dancing close to her in the crowded room. The girl's eyes remained closed as she slithered around the floor, her small frame

seeming to soak in the music through her shoulders and then flinging it out back through her belly button, which was small and tight
against a flat, exposed stomach. Coyote didn't seem to dance as
much as he circled tightly around her like a jackal hovering over a
wounded rabbit, using his hand to occasionally keep her from wandering away. I wondered what Emma would think.

I walked off and looked for Derek, who was in the corner of the
next room trying not to watch Jacob making out with the gum-
chewer. I went up to Derek and pulled him aside.

"He's done better," I yelled into his ear.

Derek nodded. "I don't think he really cares. Better than we're
doing."

I tugged on his sleeve and he followed me as we passed into another, more crowded room. I spotted two coeds giggling together
in the corner of the room, holding their beers like gold ingots. I
realized they were probably freshmen. This could be one of their
very first frat parties.

Perfect.

"Over there," I said to Derek. The music wasn't as loud in this
room, so I didn't have to yell.

"They're like fifteen," Derek said, laughing.

"They're probably freshmen. At least eighteen." I started to feel
lecherous, but it was easy to be scummy when you knew nothing
would likely come out of it.

Derek took the signal and moved forward with me in tow. The
freshmen looked up as we approached. As if connected to the same
invisible puppeteer string, they both dipped their mouths into their
beer cups while turning their eyes up at us.

"Freshmen?" Derek said as he reached them.

The blond one rolled her eyes. "Is it that obvious?"

Derek nodded. "A little. It's okay." He waited until I stepped up to even ground with him. "I'm Derek, and this is Harden."

The blond stuck her hand out. "I'm Laura, and this is Alexis." The brunette smiled. "What year are you guys?"

"Seniors," I said, wanting my voice to be heard. "Fourth year."

Alexis piped in. "Yeah, that's how it typically works."

Okay, so I can be an idiot. I didn't care. Everyone seemed happy.

Our conversation ran the predictable avenue of what we were studying, how they liked Wyland so far, where we were all from, and who we knew at D.U. None of it was particularly interesting, but it all gave us a chance to look one another over, trying to subtly check out each other's bodies, look closely at the faces, and trying to read how much interest there was in each other's eyes. It was an unspoken social contract, and after a few minutes we seemed to have agreed to terms that would allow us to proceed in the present company for a bit longer. Nothing more, but it was a start.

"There you are."

I turned and saw Coyote behind me. The girl he'd been dancing with was nowhere in sight.

"You guys want to get out of here?" He looked at me with excited eyes, as if itching to get into trouble. I very discreetly nodded toward the girls, but Coyote just waved his hand, dismissing me. "Yes, I understand, you're trying to hook up. That's okay, bring them, too."

I withered like a flower under a hair dryer, but the girls laughed, which was a good sign. Derek glared for the briefest of moments at Coyote, then turned to the freshmen. "You guys want to go back to our apartment? Watch a movie or something?" Derek was expert at sounding nonthreatening, probably because he truly was. The girls looked at him, then glanced over at me. They gave me the once-over and then decided I wasn't a threat either. Finally, they eyed Coyote and seemed to see in him the same thing everyone does. A beautiful threat, like a gently waking lion. You feel safe enough at a distance from the lion, and you don't want to turn away; it's just too interesting not to keep looking. Finally, the girls turned to each other before looking back at us.

Laura's voice sounded anything but confident.

"Sure," she said. I noticed the briefest look down toward the floor. "Let's go."

CHAPTER ELEVEN

Harden watched as the spider scurried along the edge of the far wall, occasionally venturing out a foot or so before turning back. This must be what crept into his mouth the first day he woke in the cell. The spider wasn't as big as the creature Harden had imagined, but it was big enough. Rather than being fearful, Harden was happy for the company. He wasn't totally alone.

When Harden stood, his muscles ached with even the slightest movement. His bed was the cold, dirt floor, and every muscle tensed whenever he tried to sleep. It was, he guessed, his fifth day.

He slowly approached the spider, wondering what it would do next. "Hello."

The spider stopped moving as if it understood what Harden was saying. It turned toward him but didn't move forward.

"What did you do to offend the Revelation?"

Harden reached forward, hoping to hold it. He reached out with gentle, probing fingers. The spider seemed willing to oblige in as much as it didn't retreat. Harden never cared much for spiders, but he rarely killed them, and in this case wanted only someone to talk to besides himself. He wondered what a good name for the spider should be.

His fingers crept forward.

The spider lifted one leg slowly.

"Charlotte," Harden said, pleased with the name, as derivative as it may be. He had the briefest of thoughts that perhaps he was going insane, but dismissed them. You needed longer than five days to go crazy, he figured.

Closer. Harden moved his hand toward Charlotte.

Then he saw the marking.

He hadn't noticed it before. The simple red hourglass painted against the jet-black flesh.

Black widow.

Harden yanked his hand back and rose to his feet.

Charlotte bolted, scurrying in a frenzy along the edge of the wall and to the corner of the room. Then it turned inward directly toward the wall and disappeared into some crack so small Harden couldn't see it.

Harden didn't have enough time to consider the one thing he should have done, which was to step on his new friend. And now Charlotte was gone, waiting in the dark periphery. Waiting, perhaps, for Harden to go to sleep again.

Enough. He had had fucking enough.

He ran to the door and started pounding. "Either kill me or let me out!" His fists stung as they connected with the cold steel. He kept hitting and shouting until he grew weary, which was only a matter of seconds. Then, a horrifying thought seized him.

What if they aren't going to kill me or *let me out?*

Maybe he was destined to spend years in the cell, alone, no one to talk to, staying alive on chipped beef and water. But that couldn't happen. People had to be looking for him. There must be search parties. The police must be interviewing everyone, including those at the Church. Maybe even Coyote himself. He wouldn't be down here for years. They'd find him soon.

Still, it had already been five days.

Harden stood and paced the cell, searching the walls and ceiling, poking and dragging his fingertips along the concrete. He looked for any holes, any signs at all, although he had done this countless times before. But there must be. How else would they know when he was done with a few pages of writing?

That's it, he thought.

That's the only control I have. I control when they open that door. And that door is the only way out of here.

Harden sat back down at the typewriter and began writing. After a bit, he would stop and take the pages and stack them neatly. When that happened, the lights would go out, and when that happened, it meant the door would open.

By the time Coyote, Derek, and I reached our apartment, I realized the girls with us were more drunk than I had thought . . .

CHAPTER TWELVE

By the time Coyote, Derek, and I reached our apartment, I realized the girls with us were more drunk than I had thought. I didn't know how many beers they had, but they were loud and excited as we crossed the moonlit night campus.

I looked at my watch as we walked into the apartment. Just after one in the morning. The apartment was empty, which meant wherever Jacob and Jen were, they weren't *here*.

"Nice place," Alexis said, turning on the lights. The apartment wasn't in bad shape, and, except for the still-moist shot glasses and the half-empty Southern Comfort bottle on the table, the place looked almost respectable.

"Where do you guys live?" I asked, though as soon as I did, I realized I already knew the answer.

"East campus," Laura said. "We're roommates."

Of course they lived there—all freshmen were required to stay in the dorms on east campus. Okay, so they were only two or three years younger than me. I don't think that's why I began to feel slimy. As much as I always fantasized about the spontaneous hookup, it was rarely satisfying. I was always happiest in a long-term relationship. I needed someone to take care of, and for that someone to take care of me. For the price of a sincere and gentle touch, my heart was yours, and that wasn't the kind of thing to be found tonight. I got the sense that here was only the potential for awkward and passionless sex with teenagers, and that wasn't something that I wanted. At least not tonight.

Derek and Coyote were the last to enter the apartment. Derek took his coat off and put it on the table before taking the girls' coats as well. He seemed tired, as if he just wanted to go to sleep and brought the girls back here for my benefit. It was probably the truth.

Coyote wasn't tired at all. He bounced around the apartment with a frenetic energy, as if he'd been drinking coffee rather than alcohol. It occurred to me that I never even saw him drink that night; he answered all the Mensa questions earlier, and I never saw him with a beer at the party. No wonder he wasn't wiped out.

I sat on the couch next to the girls and offered them water, but they instead asked for some of the Southern Comfort. Coyote served up shots to all of us but didn't take one for himself. Alexis swallowed hers in a series of painful sips, while Laura downed hers in one gulp. I gulped mine and decided it would be my last drink for the evening. I was just sober enough to realize anything more would make for a miserable morning, if I hadn't already reached that point.

Derek took a seat on the chair opposite the girls and me. He didn't reach for his shot, and I could tell he was also done for the evening. None of us really wanted to party any more, and an awkward tension sloshed about the room.

Coyote was the wildcard. He paced around the room, stopping to stare out the front window for minutes at a time. He never joined the conversation, but his physical presence made him a part of the group, bringing a weird anxiousness to our space. I'd sensed this mood in him before. He was bored and needed to stir up some excitement to make his evening feel complete. But excitement for

Coyote wasn't the same as it was for the rest of us. He needed a challenge.

Coyote turned from the window and stared at Laura. She smiled and flushed, undoubtedly because he was the best-looking one of the lot of us. Her smile slowly faded as his unblinking gaze remained fixed on her chest.

"Catholic?" he finally asked.

She seemed confused, then looked down and fingered the small gold cross hanging around her neck.

"Oh," she mumbled. "Yeah. I'm Irish."

He took a step closer to her. "Are you a virgin?"

"*Excuse me?*"

Derek sat up. "Jesus, Coyote. What the hell kind of question is that?"

Coyote looked dumbfounded. "I'm just trying to figure out if she's actually a religious person or if she just likes to wear a crucifix on her neck for the look."

"I'm not answering that," Laura said. She folded her arms across her chest and leaned back against the couch next to me. I tensed up, scared what Coyote would say next. I didn't do anything to stop him, though.

"No," he said, "you're not a virgin. No virgin would have agreed to come with three strange men to their apartment after a night of drinking."

Derek tensed his jaw. "Knock it off, Coyote."

Alexis finally broke her silence. "It's not like we came up here to fuck you guys."

"And if you aren't a virgin," Coyote continued, "you aren't much of a Catholic. You're a sinner, according to your own faith."

Laura didn't seem to know whether or not he was being serious. "There's always confession," she said, forcing a weak smirk.

I was still focused on Alexis saying *fuck*.

Coyote tilted his head as he took another step closer. "Can you tell me where in the New Testament it specifically permits sinning? I mean, we're all sinners, right? But where does it say it's acceptable to knowingly sin, as long as you confess it afterwards?"

Alexis seemed more annoyed than her friend being accosted. "That's a pretty tired argument," she said. "It's like attacking a vegetarian for wearing leather. Sure, there's a point there, but it's old and obvious."

"Don't take him seriously," I finally said, my words sounding weak and limp in the charged atmosphere. "He's just trying to get a rise out of you."

Derek was much more forceful than me. He stood. "Damnit, Coyote, what the hell's your problem?"

Coyote only shrugged and held up his hands. "No problem here."

Laura said to Coyote, "Tell me what you believe, and I'll give you at least three ways you're a hypocrite."

The room fell quiet. I looked at Laura with a newfound respect. So did Coyote.

"Interesting," he said. "I think I misjudged you, which is something I hardly ever do." He looked at Alexis, who remained silent. "*You* . . . you I have pegged." Back to Laura. "But not you. You don't follow so easily, do you?"

"Follow what?" she asked. Her finger circled the top of her shot glass.

"Anything. You're not a follower. I'm not sure if that makes you a leader, but you're not a follower."

She turned and looked at me. "What's wrong with your friend?"

"I don't know," I said. It was the truest answer I could give.

"Is he always like this?"

"He's never always like anything."

Coyote plopped on the couch next to Laura, who squirmed a couple of inches away from him.

"I think I like you," he said.

"I think you're beyond creepy."

Coyote let out a laugh that reinforced her assessment.

"Coyote," Derek said. "Leave her alone."

"I'm not doing anything. I was just asking Laura about her faith."

Alexis tilted her head toward him but didn't look him in the eyes. "You never answered Laura's question. What do you believe in?"

"Nothing."

"You're an atheist?"

"If you want to call it that."

This surprised me, because I had seen the book on his nightstand. "But you read the Bible," I said.

"Every night. I also read the Qur'an, the Tipitaka, the Torah, the Book of Mormon, and the Satanic Bible."

"The Satanic Bible?" I asked.

"I find it healthy to understand all viewpoints," Coyote said.

It was so easy to dismiss all this as bullshit, and my guess is the girls did just that. But I completely believed Coyote read all these books.

Alexis sat up on the couch. "Laura, let's get out of here."

"I'll walk you home," Derek offered.

"I just want to ask you one question," Coyote said, looking at Laura. "Just one thing. And I want you to be honest with me. Then you can leave."

"I can leave whenever the hell I want," Laura said.

"Sorry, of course you can. Just one question. I need to know."

Alexis tugged on her friend's sleeve. "Laura, come on."

But Laura wanted to answer. It was hard to resist Coyote when he showed an interest in you. "What?" she asked.

Coyote leaned in to her, resting his forearms on his knees. To him, this freshman was the only person in existence in this moment, and the rest of us, only feet away, dropped out of their world.

"What would someone have to do to make you do anything they told you?"

She didn't blink. She didn't look away. And when she answered, Laura's voice was little more than a whisper.

"What do you mean?"

Coyote's tone was soft, his words measured, and he spoke with a therapist's reassuring command. "You believe in ghosts," he said. "You worship a man who may or may not have even existed. You don't even adhere strictly to his teachings." Now Coyote reached out and ran his fingers along her thigh, up and down along her tight jeans. "So, what I want to know is this: What kind of man would it take for you to follow everything he says? What would he have to prove to you?" He leaned in close enough to bite her. "What would he have to *do* to you?"

"That's it." Derek moved toward the couch. I saw Laura's eyes glistening as Derek held out both of his hands. Each girl grabbed one, and he pulled them up. "I'll walk you guys back to your dorm, okay?"

Laura nodded as Alexis oozed hate from her eyes. Derek turned back to Coyote.

"Why do you have to be such an asshole?"

He didn't wait for an answer, and Coyote never gave him one. Within seconds, Derek and the two girls left the apartment, but not before Laura turned back and looked at Coyote with a mix of fear and curiosity on her face, as if witnessing a horrible car accident that she couldn't look away from.

Then I was alone with Coyote.

He stood and stared out the window of the apartment. I looked at him, his hands now shoved in his pockets and his chin touching his chest. His eyes were closed, and I would have almost thought him asleep if I didn't see the grin on his face.

"What the hell was that all about?" It was the only thing I could think to say.

He opened his eyes and turned to me. "Why can't people have a reasonable conversation?"

"Reasonable? Was that some kind of pickup line or something? Because you sounded like a sociopath."

"I'm just honest, Harden. It was a real question, and I truly wanted to know her answer. If that's beyond the capacity for others to absorb or outside of some social convention, that's not my problem." He came over, sat next to me, and poured himself a shot of Southern Comfort, finishing the bottle. It was the first drink I saw him take all evening.

Then he fell silent, and the sound of him breathing stretched for minutes. I felt as I had when he leaned in to Laura: nonexistent.

Then I felt him staring at me. I could see him out of the corner of my right eye. He wasn't moving. Just staring.

I felt my neck grow hot.

"I'm different, Harden," he said. The fresh alcohol on his breath wafted toward me. I grew nervous at his statement. Different how?

"Yeah, Coyote, I kind of gathered that."

"No, Harden, you have gathered very little about me in the short time we've known each other."

"That so?"

Jesus. This was getting weird.

"I like you, Harden."

Oh, God. I didn't need this. I so didn't need this.

I stood and walked toward the window.

"Where are you going?" he asked.

I turned. "Coyote, the question is where are *you* going? What are you trying to tell me?"

He stood. "Are you afraid of me, Harden?"

I took a small step away from him. The discomfort rose in my chest. "I'm not sure *afraid* is the right word."

"What is the right word?" He stepped closer.

I tried to think.

"I don't understand you," I said.

He moved toward me. I couldn't move back any more—the wall loomed behind me. "Of that I'm sure, Harden."

"Okay, you're freaking me out now. I think you should go to bed."

Coyote put one hand on the wall next to my head and leaned in toward my face.

"What are you doing?" I asked. As uncomfortable as I felt at the idea of him trying to kiss me, I also felt unease at rejecting him. Even now, tonight, after all he did, I still wanted his approval. But I wasn't going to let this go any further.

He grinned without showing teeth. "Don't worry, Harden. Trust me, if I was going to fuck you, I would already have done it."

I sidestepped and ducked under his arm, coming up on the other side. "*Jesus*, man."

"Don't worry, Harden, I'm not gay. And I don't think you are either."

"Then what the fuck, Coyote? What the hell are you doing here?" My face was burning. My arms shook. I wanted to leave, but where would I go?

"I'm just trying to share a little."

"Share *what*?" The more I thought about his comment about fucking me, the angrier I became. "And don't ever say shit like that to me again, do you understand me? It's not funny. Jacob would kick your ass if you ever said anything like that to him."

Coyote laughed. "Oh, I don't know about that."

"What does that mean?"

"It means I read people better than most. Jacob isn't all that he seems. And you, Harden . . . you have a vulnerability about you that is unbelievably compelling. It makes . . . makes people want to take advantage of you."

"Fuck you, Coyote."

He ignored me. "But it also makes me want to help you. I want to be your friend. But if that is going to happen, you need to understand me better."

"I don't need your help. Besides, I'm not sure how much more I want to know."

Then he said the most honest thing he ever told me. "I need to consume people, Harden."

That was enough to pause me. "Consume people?"

"Yes," he said, sitting back on the couch. "Consume them. Emotionally. Physically. Sexually. However I can. I feed off people's energy."

I was going to ask him if he was drunk, but I knew he wasn't, which made me start to think Coyote might have some mental issues. "What's wrong with you?"

"If I'm going to help you, Harden, you need to know this."

"Help me with what? I don't need your help with anything."

"Yes, Harden. You do. You're a good person, but you're fragile, vulnerable. I'm not sure where that comes from. Maybe something in your past, but it's there. And me? I use people. It's what I do. I just don't want to do it with you."

This was so confusing. "Emma? You use her, too?"

He nodded. "She takes the edge off, but she's not special. I could fuck anybody with the same result. And, usually, that's exactly what I do."

I started to feel sick. "Takes the edge off what?"

"Other urges."

"Like what?"

"Harden, can't you see it? Can't you see that I don't feel any-thing? Unless I'm in control, I'm numb." He squeezed the edge of the couch cushion. "It's a rush. That control, you know? A rush I can't escape. And a lot of times that rush comes at the expense of others. I like you, Harden. I don't want you to be someone I hurt."

This was edging to the territory of the person warning his loved ones to lock him in a cell before he turned into a werewolf.

"I'm going to bed," I said.

I don't think he even heard me. He wasn't even talking to me any-more. He was talking only to himself. "I'm going to be a great man," he said. "Or I will be a horrible man. But I can't be both."

Then, without a single word more, Coyote stood and walked out of the apartment. I don't know where he went, but I locked the door after he disappeared into the night.

CHAPTER THIRTEEN

Harden couldn't be helpless anymore. He needed to do something, because doing nothing was only resulting in him slowly rotting in the windowless room. He had chosen to do nothing when Mr. Kildare took him into the classroom storage closet as a seven-year-old boy. Worse than the violation itself, Harden had stuck to the agreement. He had never told anyone. He had chosen instead to live a silent victim's life.

That would not happen again. But he was weak from malnutrition. Weak from lack of sunlight. From jagged sleep on a dirt floor with nothing to keep him warm. From his own filth. If he was going to try something, it had to be now. If he waited, he might not even have the energy to peel himself from the floor.

Several hours passed before the light in the cell went out again. When it did, Harden placed the completed pages by the door, walked to the back corner of the room, and stood with his head down like a schoolboy being punished. The slat in the door opened and the same voice he had heard for days stabbed into the small room.

"Pages by the door. Back corner. Turn around."

"Already there," Harden said. It was the first time he had spoken back to the man on the other side of the door, and he hoped his captor heard the fear and weakness in his voice. It was absolutely essential he wasn't perceived as a threat.

You can do this.

Harden took a deep breath, bent his legs into a slight crouch, and listened.

Not yet, he thought. *Wait just a few seconds longer.*

He heard the slat close. The light coming through it vanished.

Now.

Harden spun and bounded toward the door as fast as he could, getting there before it opened. The bolt on the door slid back. Harden pressed his back against the wall next to the door and tried to control his breathing, but the more he tried, the harder his heart pounded. His skin grew hot in the chill in the room.

A wedge of light shot into the cell, widening as an unseen hand pulled the door open.

The silhouette of a man. Bucket in one hand and a tray in the other. The shaft of light widened until it illuminated the back corner where Harden was supposed to be standing.

"What—"

Harden yanked the arm holding the bucket and flung the man as hard as he could against the concrete wall. As he did, he knew his strength wasn't enough. He was too weak, and the man was too heavy. Harden had dreamed of smashing his captor's skull against the wall, knocking him unconscious, but the reality was the man lost his balance for a moment and bumped into the wall as if drunk. Harden released the man's arm and saw him for the first time in the jagged light of the cell.

He wore the mask of a grotesque baby face: red bulbous cheeks and a shiny forehead, with only the smallest of slits for the eyes. Plastic, unblinking eyes. It made a sick kind of sense to Harden. The man was one of the Children. The true followers of the Revelation.

The man dropped the bucket and the tray of food into the dirt.

The sight of the mask made Harden hesitate a moment too long. When he finally charged at the baby-faced man, his opponent was ready, sweeping Harden's legs from under him with a swift movement. Harden collapsed to the floor, and the baby-faced man delivered a painful kick into his already bruised ribs.

"You fucking idiot."

Searing pain shot all the way down Harden's body. He tried to stand, but the man kicked again, sending Harden crashing back to the floor. He used his arms to brace himself, knowing another blow would be coming soon unless he did *something*.

The man's voice was muffled by the mask. "You want to play? I can play all day. No one here is going to help you."

Harden braced himself for another kick, and when it didn't come, he scurried a few feet away and stood.

Baby Face stood between him and the door. The beautiful, wide-open door.

"Now go stand in the goddamn corner."

Harden backed up toward the corner, bumping into the table with the typewriter. As his thigh hit the table, he had an idea.

Baby Face pointed. "Get in the *corner*," he said.

"No," Harden replied.

Baby Face was nothing more than a silhouette; Harden watched as the figure started walking toward him.

"You need a real beating? Is that what you want?"

"I'm not getting in the corner."

Closer. The round head seemed to hover in the dim room like a parade float, growing in size as he trolled up to Harden. Finally, Baby Face was standing just a few feet away, and his heavy breaths were Vader-like beneath the mask. His arms dangled out at an angle over the man's sizable waist, his fists little clenched balls.

"There's no medical care down here," Baby Face said. His voice sounded vaguely familiar, but Harden couldn't place it. "So if I break your face open, it's gonna stay that way. Probably get infected. That what you want?"

"Tell me where I am," Harden said. "Just tell me that, and I'll get in the corner."

One step closer. Harden stood his ground.

Baby Face tilted his head to the left, and Harden imagined a smile behind the plastic.

"You're in the last place you'll ever be."

Harden waited no more. He pivoted and lifted the old type-writer with both hands, then swung in a tight arc upwards toward the shape of the round head. Baby Face began to reach toward him, which is the only reason the typewriter was close enough to con-nect squarely with the side of his skull. The heavy, ancient machine smashed into the mask, crunching plastic and, Harden hoped, the bones beneath it. Harden lost his grip, and the typewriter crashed into the ground. Baby Face collapsed alongside it, where he grabbed his head and gurgled though pooling blood.

"I'm . . . fudding kill you . . ."

Baby Face got to one knee and reached out to Harden, but Harden bolted around him and straight for the bright light on the other side of the room. Straight for the open door.

A hallway. The wash of the overhead fluorescent bulbs momen-tarily disorientated him, but Harden shook it off, reached back into the room, then yanked the door closed. Sliding the gray-blue metal bolt into the slot on the wall filled him with the first amount of hope he'd felt since all of this began.

He turned and looked in each direction, preparing for someone else to come. The hallway was wide and drab, reminding him of a platform area in a subway station. The walls were the same antiseptic concrete block, only these had a coat of gray glaze that reflected some of the fluorescent lighting from the ceiling. The floor was finished in a faded, vanilla linoleum, a smooth and welcome change from the dirt in Harden's room. But if this was some basement underneath the School, he had never seen it before. The hallway was as unfamiliar to him as the cell.

Looking to his right, the hallway extended another twenty feet or so and ended at a closed wall. No other doors. No windows. Just concrete.

To his left, the hall stretched a bit longer, and he saw two doors. One at the end of the hallway, the other on the adjacent wall. Two ways out, Harden thought. Or maybe one way out and another cell. The door along the adjacent wall had a bolt on it, just like the door to Harden's cell.

There were no cameras on the walls or ceiling, at least that he could tell. Harden crept to the end of the hall and leaned up against the door. He paused and listened but heard nothing from the other side.

The door was unlocked, and Harden cracked it open just enough to get the slightest idea of what was on the other side. What he saw was a short stretch of linoleum leading to a flight of wooden steps, leading up.

That's the way out, he thought.

But what was up there? Or, rather, who?

As he pulled the door open a bit more, he glanced back at the second door in the hallway. The one with the slat on it, just like his. He thought he heard something. A soft rapping?

He waited for a moment and listened again.

There. Again. Definitely a rapping, soft and faint, like footsteps in a dream.

Someone's in there.

He shifted his weight as he decided what to do.

Leave, Harden. Just get the hell out of here.

He opened the door to the stairway an inch more and smelled the wood of the stairs. Freedom was close. But he couldn't leave. Not yet. He had one more door to open, the one leading to the cell just like his. He walked back, pressed his ear against it, and listened. No more rapping from the inside.

But he was certain someone was in there. Another prisoner.

Taking a deep breath, Harden squatted in front of the door, slid the metal slat open, and peered in.

The smell hit him immediately. The stale, dead air stench of sewage and rotting food.

"I'm in the fucking corner already!" The scream from inside was horrible. Desperate. Female.

"No, no," Harden whispered through the rectangular slot. "I'm here to help you." The light in the cell was on, but he couldn't see her.

Quick breaths from within.

"Then open the goddamn door and get me out of here."

He slid the bolt back and pulled the door open. He took a half-step inside before his focus shot to the back corner of the room.

The woman was barefoot. Torn jeans. Dirty blue t-shirt, tight around her body. Thick strands of hair fell forward over her left eye like the branches of a weeping willow, and dirt and blood painted her face.

Harden knew her.

CHAPTER FOURTEEN

"Well, hello, Harden."

The comfort of the vaguely familiar voice settled into my ears before recognition did, and all I knew was whoever this voice belonged to, I would be happy to see. I lifted my gaze from my notebook and saw Emma, her hair catching wisps of sunlight from the dusty and filtered rays within the dining hall. I often ate lunch at the Moorhead Hall cafeteria alone to get work done, and any interruptions normally would bother me. Not now.

"Emma," I said.

She carried a tray full of healthy-looking things, colored green, red, and yellow. Outside, the first snow of the year was falling. A collection of melted snowflakes sparkled Emma's hair and her face was a dusty pink from the November wind.

"You here alone?" I asked.

She cocked her head and offered a thin-lipped smile—bordering on a smirk—that was beyond my ability to translate. "I am," she said. "Can I sit with you?"

"Of course." I slid my notebook over but kept it open. I looked down and regretted most of my meal was done. I would sip the hell out of my water, making it last.

"You done with classes for the day?"

I shook my head. "I have a writing class at three."

"What kind of writing?"

"Creative."

She smiled and reached for one of the few remaining fries on my plate. In my twenty-year-old mind, there was something almost sexual about her taking one of my fries without asking. My face got hot. "Are you an English major?" she asked.

"Only because I had to declare a major. Not sure if it's something I want to do with my life."

"Hmmm. Not like your roomies, then? Your life's not already planned out for you?"

I guess Coyote had been telling her about us, because Emma was dead-on with that statement. If Jacob didn't drink his way to failure—liver and/or business—he'd inevitably end up at law school, and then straight to his father's law firm. And all Derek ever wanted to do was teach, so it would be more academics for him—probably a PhD in European History—before settling in as a professor in some liberal arts college. Maybe even Wyland. Sometimes I envied the certainty of their futures. Other times I reveled in the fact I had no clue what I would do after school.

"No," I answered. "I'm currently without any kind of plan whatsoever."

"Kind of like Coyote."

I tried not to think too much about the night he confessed to me his need to consume people. I wanted to dismiss it as narcissistic babble, but I knew it was more than that.

"It seems to me he could do just about anything he wanted," I said.

Emma picked at her food. "You know, he once told me there wasn't a single concept ever explained to him that he didn't fully grasp. Quite the ego."

"That's such an arrogant statement I'm inclined to believe it's true."

She considered this for a moment. "Sometimes I think Coyote might not be the brilliant man we all think he is. He just has to be a little smarter than us for it to appear that way."

I never thought about it that way. She could be absolutely right.

"He'll probably stay in academics," she said. "He likes the campus atmosphere. You ever think about grad school?"

I shrugged. "Sometimes I think about getting a Master of Fine Arts. I like writing, and I'm not half-bad at it, at least according to my professors. Maybe there's a future in it for me somewhere."

"Good for you," she said. She popped a baby carrot in her mouth and spun my open notebook around so it faced her. "Working on something now?"

She surprised me with the move, and my chest tightened as I realized she was about to read the essay I was working on. My instinct was to grab the notebook away from her, which I think is the natural reaction for most creative writing students. But I didn't. I was powerless in front of this girl with three piercings in one ear and none in the other. "It's . . . it's nothing," I finally mumbled.

"Can I read it?"

I hesitated and then nodded, willing the words on the page to rearrange themselves into something good. I had been writing short stories ever since high school, and I believe my college application essay played a big part in why Wyland accepted me. I *was* a good writer, but not a great one, and being only good made me want to set myself on fire as Emma started reading my essay.

I stared at my plate as I listened to her brain absorb my words. I had been on the twelfth page of my story, preferring to write long-hand before putting the finished product on my Macintosh back at the apartment.

Emma looped a strand of hair over her ear and looked up from the page after about a minute. Her irises were olive in the hazy sunlight filtering through the hundred-year-old cafeteria windows. "Harden, this is really good."

"Thanks," I said.

"I mean it. You've got talent."

If she was faking sincerity, I no longer cared. But I think she really meant it. "It's for class," I said. "Actually, Coyote inspired the idea."

"Really? What's it about?"

I thought back to the night with the two freshmen. The question Coyote asked the girl had such a malevolent overtone that it stuck in my head until it culminated with an idea for a story.

"All the major world religions were started when people really didn't know much about anything beyond their own land," I said. "About other societies. About science. Technology. Medicine. I wondered what kind of person it would take in today's culture for him to start a new movement. To get a real following. To get people to do whatever they say. With all the cynicism, doubt, and access to information in modern times, what would this person have to say or do to get people to start following him?"

"Or her," Emma added.

"Or her." I put a cold fry back on the tray. "My story explores a group of friends trying to figure out that problem."

"What does Coyote have to do with this?"

"He . . . it seems he reads a lot of different religious texts, and it just got me thinking." No need to tell her how he berated a drunk freshman about her religious beliefs in our apartment.

"Yeah, he certainly does." Her gaze went back to the pages. "In fact, it sounds like it's him you're writing about."

"That thought crossed my mind," I said.

"He'd be into this, you know? You should show it to him."

"I'm never sure what he'd be into." A dark impulse hit me, an urge to paint Coyote in a bad light in the hope he and Emma might break up and she could be with me. Terrible things, these kinds of urges. I recognized it was wrong, but did nothing to stop myself. "I have a hard time figuring him out."

She didn't say anything.

"Why don't you two ever go out on the weekend?" I asked.

Emma picked at her salad, setting aside a couple leaves of browned lettuce. "It gives us a chance to hang out with other people. We see each other all week." She mulled these last words for a moment, then added, "It also gives us a break from one another."

"You need a break from each other?" This got my hopes up a little.

"Everyone does, Harden."

"Not married people."

She laughed. "God, are you that naive? *Especially* married people. If my parents had taken more breaks, they'd probably still be together."

Mine, too, I considered.

She slipped a slice of tomato into her mouth. "He's a bit intense," she said. "Having breaks definitely isn't a bad thing."

"He does need to channel his energy into something." Do I tell her his confession about needing to consume people? How much does he really share with her?

We sat in silence for a few moments, and this is when I first noticed her scent. Fresh, like a meadow of flowers just washed by rain. It was faint but it was there, and she radiated spring on a dreary November day.

She sipped her water and said, "Actually, Coyote's been more intense than usual lately."

"In what way?"

She hesitated. "Did he . . . did he ever mention anything about something he did when he was younger? A fight . . . with another boy? It happened on a camping trip with his dad."

"No," I said. "Nothing like that. What happened?"

She looked as if she wanted to answer, but she didn't. "It's nothing. It's just a heavy story, and I'm not sure why he told me. He brought it up the other day, and it was just . . . intense." She looked at me as if for reassurance. "Like sometimes I don't know if he's joking about something or not. You know?"

"I know. He has been a bit on edge lately," I said. "When he's at the apartment, he seems to stay up almost all night. I don't know what he does."

"He thinks." Her tone was very certain. "He sits and thinks. Processes. It's like he's working through all the information he absorbed all day to see if he can do anything with it. It's actually kind of creepy."

I couldn't help myself. "You picture yourselves together for a long time?" I thought the question was casual, but, based on her reaction, it wasn't. She smiled and gave me a wink.

"Why? You want to ask me out?" She reached over and the tips of her long, unpainted nails brushed against my own fingertips. I felt hot all over, which meant my face would be about two shades darker than a stop sign.

"No . . . I was just wondering . . ."

"Relax, Harden. I'm just giving you a hard time." She tilted her head and looked into my eyes. "Although I'm surprised you don't have a girlfriend. You're a good-looking guy."

I tried to keep a cool voice through my panic. I wasn't used to receiving compliments from girls like Emma. "I wear my humble origins outwardly," I said, dropping my gaze back to the scatterings of food on my tray. "Which makes me substantially less compelling on a campus like Wyland." This is usually how I reacted to the rare compliment. By insulting myself.

"Girls don't just want money, Harden. But I think you know that. Look at me for a second."

I did, and in that moment I saw ourselves married, waking up wrapped in silky linen sheets late on a Sunday morning. The vision lasted about a second, and it was beautiful.

She studied my face and said, "You're just too shy. Girls like confidence—they want a guy who's not afraid to go after what he wants." She looked a bit longer. "Yes, I'd definitely go out with you."

Wow.

"Likewise," I said, proud of myself for saying it. After that I only offered a nervous laugh. As the moments drifted, I felt my cheeks cool and knew the ruddiness in them had dissipated to normal levels. I detached from myself a bit and looked down at this scene as if watching from the top of the cafeteria. Here was Harden Campbell, transplant from Owen, Pennsylvania, having lunch with a pretty girl, and that was cool. We spent the rest of the meal chatting idly about courses and our plans for winter break, the distant moments of flirting still faintly warm in my chest. She finally stood up and announced she had a dreaded bio class to go to, and as she gathered her purse and picked up her tray, I turned the notebook back toward me and started thinking about the next paragraph.

We exchanged good-byes, and she turned to walk away as I resumed scribbling on the pages. Emma took one step, then pivoted on her heel. I looked up and saw her suddenly leaning over me.

"Your story," she said. "How does it end?"

I ran my fingers through my coarse stock of English-Irish hair, something I did when I didn't have an answer. "I don't know," I finally said.

But I kind of did, didn't I? So I told her my sense of the whole thing.

"But I'm pretty sure it doesn't end well."

CHAPTER FIFTEEN

"Oh, God. Harden. Oh, God."

Emma scampered across her cell toward Harden, hobbling like a dog just clipped by a car. Horror kept Harden frozen. It was her hand, his eyes told him. *Something's wrong with her hand.* It was wrapped in a dirty, blood-soaked gauze.

She grabbed Harden and pulled herself deep into his chest, burying her face in his neck. He could feel her sweat and tears on his skin. He could smell the musk of her captivity.

"They . . ." Her words were muffled and choked. "They cut off my finger, Harden. They *mutilated* me . . . said it would get me to obey."

Oh, God. Oh, Jesus Christ.

"It hurts so much!" She was on the edge of hysterical, and that was going to be a problem. "I don't know why I'm here. Oh, God, Harden. I think they're going to kill—"

"Be quiet," he said, pushing her out an arm's length so he could look at her face. "Emma, we have to leave. Right now. Do you understand?"

Tears streamed from her bloodshot eyes. She nodded.

"They were keeping me, too, and I'm weak. I don't know what's waiting for us, but there's a door just outside the hallway. If we—"

Emma suddenly screamed and pointed to something behind Harden.

He turned.

Another baby-faced man. Not the same one. This one was larger. Same mask, but in the light of Emma's cell, it almost looked Asian. Face of a contorted Buddha. Emma kept screaming as Harden watched Baby Face race toward him and swing at him. A sharp, piecing pain in his side. *Stabbed*, he thought. *He stabbed me.* But when Baby Face pulled his arm back, Harden saw the syringe in his hand.

Emma's screams slowly faded as Harden's consciousness did the same. His last thought before blackness consumed him was whether or not he would ever open his eyes again.

CHAPTER SIXTEEN

The waning days before winter break seemed insurmountable to most students; the hurdle of finals and the anticipation of a long-awaited respite stretched even an hour into a long and twisted trial of patience. Not for me. Christmas was a week away, and going home to Pennsylvania was like a dental appointment. I did it because it was the right thing to do, but not because I wanted to. I was leaving in two days.

As Jacob was fond of saying, winter finally stopped cock-teasing our little town and settled in for a good fucking. It would be like this until April. The icy air wiggled through the cracks of my clothes and snuggled up against my skin with the comfort of frozen metal. Goddamn Northeast. I'd been to Colorado skiing once, and that was the kind of cold weather you wanted. Dry. Sunny. Not here. Here, shitty winters were an industry, and we pumped out the best product in the country.

Thursday night and nothing to do. Derek finished his finals two days ago and had already left for his home in Rochester, which left me alone with Jacob and, for the weekend at least, Coyote. Jacob was here through Saturday, and, with no classes left, had turned our living room into a shantytown of blankets, dirty socks, potato chips, and beer cans. He felt compelled to establish camp and rent the top twenty films in the American Film Institute's Top 100 list. He wanted me to watch *Citizen Kane* with him, but I couldn't do that to Orson Welles. Orson deserved better than Jacob with one hand on a day-old sandwich and the other tucked down the front of his sweatpants.

I came home from my last class of the day and was surprised to find Coyote in the apartment. I usually didn't see him until Friday.

"Hey, Harden."

He was in the kitchen with what looked like enough vegetables to open a farmer's market, cramming fistfuls of them into my blender. Damnit. That blender was one of the few appliances I owned, and I knew he wasn't going to clean it.

"Yes, you may use my blender," I said.

He shushed me as he turned my blender on to the *ice crush* setting and set the contents into a psychedelic whirl. I used the blender to make margaritas and protein shakes. Now it was filled with fucking green Kryptonite.

A few seconds later he turned it off, dipped a wooden spoon into the soupy mix. He tasted it and nodded with pride.

"Pesto," he said. "Want a taste?"

"No, thanks," I mumbled. "You're going to clean that, right?"

He ignored the question.

"You done with finals?" he asked.

"Yup. You?"

"Modern lit tomorrow, but it'll be easy. Let's go out tonight."

This was unusual. "You're not at Emma's?" I don't know if my heart skipped a beat, but there was at least a small palpitation. Did they break up?

"She went home already."

Of course. Damnit. "Sure," I said. "Have anything in mind?"

"Let's go somewhere. Drive away. Get out of town."

"Where?"

"I don't know," he said. "Ask Jacob. He'll have a good idea."

Jacob. Of course Jacob would want to go. I walked into the living room and found him on the floor under his ratty denim comforter with two pillows propped up behind him. He looked up.

"Number twenty, baby," he said, the two-day-old stubble covering his face like black mold. "*One Flew Over the Cuckoo's Nest.*"

"Enjoying it?"

"It's pretty fucked up."

"Yeah, it's no *Singin' in the Rain.*"

"That's number ten. I watched that Tuesday."

"I know. You told me." I looked at the screen and saw Jack Nicholson doing a pretty good Jack Nicholson impersonation. "You want to come out with Coyote and me tonight?"

He propped himself up on an elbow. "Right on. Where you headed?"

"Coyote wants to drive somewhere. Ideas?"

"Doesn't matter to me, as long as they serve Jack and Coke."

"I don't think that will be a problem."

"Cool." Jacob returned to his movie and filth. He would be insistent on taking a half-hour shower before he went out tonight.

I went into my bedroom and tossed my backpack on the twin bed, then looked over at my answering machine. Best thing I ever did was get my own phone line installed in this place. It was a bit of an extravagance, but sharing a line was just too painful. It seemed like every twenty minutes a different *Jen* was calling for Jacob.

No messages on my machine.

"Emma told me you wrote something about religion."

I turned around and saw Coyote in the doorway. He leaned casually against the doorjamb, looking very much like an Eddie Bauer model, wrinkled white button-down shirt, olive pants.

"I did," I said, glad to know Emma had been talking about me. "You inspired me, actually."

"That's what she said. Can I read it?"

I hesitated. Coyote wasn't an easy critic of anything, so I could only imagine what he would think of my writing. If he didn't like something, he never hesitated to tell someone. "I suppose," I said. I navigated to the file on my computer and printed him out a copy—it had grown to nearly thirty pages by the time I had handed it in.

"I'll read it over break. Let's get out of here in a couple of hours, okay?"

It apparently wasn't a question, since he was already walking away as I started to answer. From the living room, I heard a woman in the movie asking a busload of psychiatric patients if they were all crazy.

* * *

I was a good-looking guy in Coyote's car. It was hard not to be. The interior was a mess, but only because Coyote didn't care enough to ever pick up anything he ever placed there; the passenger seat was littered with receipts and food wrappers, and the cup holder contained an eighth-inch of caramel putty that once was a Coke. But the car's sleek black exterior glistened in the icy moonlight, and in the cradling hum of the German engine I felt a part of something special. Or, at least a little extravagant.

We headed south. The small town that lived and died by the matriculation of Wyland faded into the night behind us. There was freedom in this car. We could turn wherever and whenever we wanted, and we had a bunch of hours to still chew up before we could call this a memory. Of course, it only took about a half hour of driving before the excitement wore off and we got bored.

Jacob—whining from the backseat like a four-year-old—kept

asking for different music. He found Coyote's CD organizer and kept asking for Jane's Addiction, while Coyote ignored him and kept playing The Smiths, singing quietly along to Morrissey's suicidal croonings. The trees along the side of the road whipped by us in a measured rhythm as a half-moon rose outside my tinted window.

Montclair was another small upstate New York town, little known except as home to Bradford College, a respected, all-female center for higher education and, if one was to believe the rumors, chock full of lesbians. The stories about Bradford sung like Greek myths. It was said Bradford's small population of straight students craved men with a preternatural ferocity, and a decent-looking guy at a bar on any given night in Montclair could scoop up women as easily as goldfish in a soup bowl.

We drove to Montclair. It was Jacob's idea.

None of us had been there before, and we pulled into a small city garage a block off what looked to be a promising commercial strip. We emerged into the frigid air, and I spotted two bars nestled among a fast-food place, a liquor store, and a pharmacy boasting the quickest prescription-filling time in town.

Both bars were doing a good business, so we chose the first one we came to. It was named Hoolihan's, and it was a typical college-town bar, the kind that was really just a piece of shit but the students would remember for the rest of their lives as the center of the universe. My fake ID wasn't challenged, and we walked in and managed to find a recently vacated table in the center of the room.

"Too many dudes here," was the first thing Jacob said. I was thinking the same thing, but it sounded really stupid coming from his mouth so I was glad I didn't say it.

"You expected all women?" Coyote asked, mulling through a drink menu.

"Better odds, at least."

"They're all morons like us who came here expecting to get blown by some sex-starved coed the moment they walked through the door," I said.

"Nothing wrong with that."

"Except it's all fiction." I glanced at the beer list and found Sam Adams, which was pricey, but I decided to treat myself. A waitress came over and barely said a word as she took our order.

Billy Joel sang about Vietnam as our first beers arrived. After a half hour, Jacob and I were both on our third drink, while Coyote stayed on his first. He was driving, so I knew he'd only have a couple over the course of the night. I wasn't buzzed yet, but would be soon.

After the first hour the bar filled completely, and the ratio of men and women seemed to even out. It was getting more difficult to hear each other, which was good because we were running out of things to say. Jacob started looking anxious, as if he was going to miss out on some great sexual opportunity if he didn't put all his energy into the hunt. He looked around the bar frequently, popping his head up every now and then like a lion peering over high grass.

"How about that one?" he asked, pointing to a young blond talking with a guy who looked to be in his midtwenties.

"Sure," I shouted over the noise. "Tell her boyfriend hello while you're hitting on her."

"No way. That guy's gay. He's playing cover for her."

"Only one way to find out," Coyote said. "Want us to come with you?"

"Nah, I'm all over it." With that, Jacob stood up, checked his fly, and headed in the blond's direction.

I was jealous of his courage, even if it bled into the realm of stupidity. I had a hard enough time approaching girls as it was, and Jacob didn't even blink before talking one up in front of her boyfriend. As much as I often thought Jacob was little more than a ball-chasing Golden Retriever in the body of a college student, I admired his confidence.

"Dollar says he's back at the table in two minutes," I said. "Or at least not talking to her."

Coyote looked on as Jacob wove through the crowded bar toward his target. "I'll take that bet."

Good. Now this was getting fun.

Jacob sidled up to the blond, who flicked her head toward him. She appeared confused at first, and then nodded her head in an impatient manner as Jacob leaned in close to tell her something. Even from our table I could see the guy's knuckles whiten as he squeezed his beer bottle. Then Boyfriend stepped forward and placed his nose inches from Jacob's face, his chest expanding beneath a tight black t-shirt. Jacob straightened and tilted his head, then raised his hand in the universal sign of *take it easy, man*. But he didn't back away.

"This isn't good," I said.

"Clearly not," Coyote said, fixated on the scene. I glanced briefly at him and saw excitement in his eyes. "Maybe we should help him."

Help? I wasn't even sure what that meant. One thing I knew, however, was I wasn't going to lose another tooth, especially not because of Jacob.

Boyfriend pointed over Jacob's shoulder, which I'm guessing was his way of telling him to get the fuck out of there. Then Jacob did something amazing and stupid: he grabbed Boyfriend's raised arm by the wrist and lowered it. Damn.

Things escalated from there. Boyfriend gave Jacob a light shove, and now I could finally hear their voices. The crowd around them quieted down and turned their attention to the scene.

" . . . just trying to make a little conversation, dude." It was Jacob.

God bless him, he was still trying.

"Let's go," Coyote said, rising from the table. Before I could respond, he was already walking away, and I had little choice but to join him. I just hoped Boyfriend didn't have friends of his own.

As we moved in, I could now hear the conversation clearly. An oil stain of people was growing around the two men. Boyfriend had a thick accent I couldn't place, but it made me think of Pacino in *Scarface*, which sounded wholly out of place in upstate New York.

"Maybe you should go to a different bar, *cuca*." Boyfriend's words sounded slurred, and I wasn't sure if he was drunk or if it was the accent.

"Hey, man, it's a free country." Jacob inched up to him so their chests were nearly touching. Jacob had about two inches and maybe twenty pounds on him, but Boyfriend carried the look of a junkyard dog, a creature that would attack anything without concern for its own safety. "Maybe that's not something you're used to, but here in the States we can say whatever we want."

"Stupid fucking American. I'll give you a dollar if you can name any other country in the world."

"Colombia," Coyote shouted out, his Spanish accent surprising me.

Boyfriend jerked his head around and stared at Coyote. I took a step forward, evening my stance with Coyote. I was feeling more confident, at least until I saw two other guys approach the widening circle from the back. I wasn't sure if they were with Boyfriend, but they sure looked like they wanted a piece of whatever was going to happen.

"That's where you're from, right?"

"Yes," Boyfriend said, and for a moment the tension softened in his shoulders. *"Has estado allí?"*

"No. But I know the women there are beautiful."

He nodded. "*Claro*. But we are not there. We are here, and she is with *me*."

Coyote turned to Jacob. "Jacob, she's spoken for. Let's go sit back down and drink the beer we've already paid for."

The woman at the center of all this finally spoke. "I'm not with him," she said, pointing to Boyfriend.

"You see?" Jacob said.

Boyfriend turned to her. "Yes you are, whore."

"Hey, hey, hey . . ." Coyote raised his hands up. "Let's keep this civilized."

I still hadn't said a word. The two guys in the back kept eyeing us, as if sizing up the odds, but Boyfriend hadn't even acknowledged them yet.

Boyfriend turned back to Jacob. "Why don't you do as your little bitch girlfriend says and go back to your table?"

Jacob was twitching. Actually twitching. I guessed the first punch would be thrown in a matter of seconds.

The woman lurched forward and grabbed Jacob by the arm. Holding onto Jacob, she turned to Boyfriend.

"I'm going with him."

Jacob beamed like he'd just won the lottery. But Boyfriend turned his black eyes toward the woman and seized her arm.

"I don't think so."

"Let me go, asshole," she said.

From somewhere behind the bar, a deep voice called out. "Take it outside, boys." I turned my head and saw the bouncer walking our way from the front door. Things were happening fast.

Coyote stepped forward toward Boyfriend. He said, "Can I tell you something? As a friend?"

Boyfriend let go of the woman's wrist, looked Coyote over, and then nodded.

Coyote leaned close into his ear; I watched the man's eyes as Coyote said something undetectable by me. After about twenty seconds, Boyfriend's eyes showed a mix of fear and anger. He turned away from Coyote and told the woman, "Go with them. What do I need with you anyway? *Whore.*"

Coyote stepped back, turned, and gave me a wink. The woman hooked her arm around Jacob, who seemed very proud of himself considering he had actually done very little.

"You four . . . out." It was the bouncer. Our time was up, and Jacob was leaving with a girl.

Coyote pulled two twenty-dollar bills from his wallet and left them on the bar. I went back to our table and collected everyone's coats, and then we all left. Outside, we put on our coats and the three of us stared at the woman. She had her right hand on Jacob's chest.

"I'm Trina, by the way." She reached up and gave Jacob a kiss on the cheek. Jacob apparently couldn't believe his luck, because his normally dopey expression morphed into a mask of borderline catatonia.

"It's Coyote you should be kissing," I said. "What did you tell that guy, anyway?"

Coyote shook his head. *Nothing.*

Trina leaned into Coyote and kissed him on the cheek as well, which brought Jacob out of his euphoria.

"For four hundred bucks I'll thank all of you as long as you want," she said.

A thick silence draped over all of us as we each processed her statement. Only Coyote seemed unfazed.

"Holy shit," Jacob said. "You *are* a whore. I thought that guy was just being a dick."

She took a step back. "I'm not a whore," she said. "I'm an escort. You guys don't have to be such pricks."

I didn't know what to say. I'd never seen a hooker before in real life.

Jacob was shaking his head. "I almost got into a fight over an *escort?*"

I looked at Trina and tried to see the hooker in her. She was young, cute, and had the blue-eyed excitement of a cheerleader making the squad. My heart broke a little bit knowing she fucked guys for money.

She saw her opportunity slipping away, so she put up her hand. "Look, if you guys don't want to party, then I need to get going."

Coyote pulled out his wallet. I froze as I saw him thumb through hundred-dollar bills.

"Dude, what are you doing?" Jacob asked.

Coyote ignored him, handing Trina three bills.

"Here's three hundred bucks," he said. "Let's hit the liquor store for some supplies, and we'll all hole up in a hotel for the night. I don't feel like driving back tonight anyway."

My body started to shake. This was getting *way* out of my league.

"It's going to be four hundred for all of you," she said, taking the money.

Coyote chuckled and offered his best politician's grin. "No sex," he said. "Let's just hang out. I want to ask you some questions."

CHAPTER SEVENTEEN

The motel was three blocks down the street from the bar. We headed there after stopping at a nearby liquor store. Coyote was insistent, though my heart wasn't really into drinking more. Coyote always wanted the people around him well lubricated, and looking back on it all now, it makes sense. You have a lot more power when you're the only sober one around.

The motel dated back to the fifties and hadn't received more than a few coats of paint and, God willing, new bedsheets since that time. There were a handful of similar places around Wyland, and all of them lived and died on university demand. This one seemed to be on the death side of that seesaw.

Coyote checked in, paying forty-three bucks for the night. The four of us walked into a small room reeking of cigarette smoke and disinfectant. Two double-beds and a faded yellow chair with a Rorschach-test stain on the fabric occupied most of the space. I didn't know where to sit so I remained standing, mute, my hands buried deep in the pockets of my old Army jacket.

Coyote removed the bottle of tequila and the four shot glasses he'd bought.

He poured out the shots along the top of the television and gestured for each of us to grab a glass. Jacob fiddled with an ancient heating unit, trying to warm the cold room. His last act before finally giving up was punching it twice on the control panel, then grunting like a confused ape.

"I need to check in," Trina said, her confidence seeming to fade. She picked up the phone next to the bed and asked, "Okay if I make a call?"

"Go right ahead," Coyote said.

She dialed out and lowered her head as she told someone the name of the motel and that she wouldn't be taking any more appointments that night. She answered a few questions with either a yes or no, and then finally whispered "*three hundred*." After hanging up, she grabbed a shot glass and threw the tequila back. "I'm not sure how many of these I'm going to have," she said. "You can understand I don't want to be completely out of control here."

"Of course," Coyote said, downing his own shot. This surprised me a bit, but I was guessing he wouldn't be drinking too much more. I had still never seen him drunk.

Jacob and I drank ours as well. I don't know if I could tell you the difference between a five- and fifty-dollar bottle of tequila, but this stuff was smooth, or at least good enough to make me reconsider not drinking more tonight.

"Who were you checking in with?" I asked. They all looked at me, seeming startled that I finally said something.

"My agency. I always need to tell them where I am."

"So were you at the bar just . . . looking?"

"No. I don't do that. I'm not a street walker."

I could feel my face redden. "I . . . I didn't mean it like that. I just don't know how . . ."

"That guy at the bar—the one you got into it with—he called my agency and asked for me. I met him at the bar, and we were going to go to his place after." She reached into her purse and lit a cigarette, blowing the smoke toward the ceiling. The ceiling seemed used to it.

Jacob said, "So that guy was your John and you blew him off to come with us?"

She sighed. "I've seen him a couple of times before. He pays well, but he's not the most . . . respectful guy out there. He's heavy with the coke. I think he deals it to different campuses. I just wasn't in the mood for his shit tonight, and by the time you came up I was looking for an excuse to get out of there anyway. Life's too short, you know?"

I turned to Coyote. "So when did you learn Spanish, anyway?"

He smiled. "Here and there. I know enough to get by."

Jacob said, "More than that, how the hell did you know where he was from?"

"Lucky guess, mostly. He called you a *cuca*, which they use in Colombia to call someone a pussy."

"And you know that how?"

"I just know things."

He didn't say it to be elusive or arrogant, but more of a surprised statement. As if he thought everyone was like him, sponges soaking up every piece of information and retaining it forever.

"Impressive," Trina said. "And what did you say to him? I was a little worried those boys were going to mess you up."

"It was nothing," Coyote said.

Trina smiled. "Come on."

Coyote shrugged, then stood silently for a few seconds. "Do you really want to know?"

"Of course."

He looked at all three of us, each for a few seconds, before landing his gaze on Trina. She crossed her arms as she smoked, making herself smaller. "I told him I was a stranger in town and no one knew who I was," Coyote said. "I said I had a gun in my car and I would wait for him to leave the bar, and then I would kill him. No regrets. No conscience. I would then just disappear, and the police would never find me. And he would be fucking dead."

"Holy shit," Jacob whispered. "Did you really tell him that?"

"I did."

"You're crazy," I mumbled just a little too quiet for anyone else to hear.

"What made him believe you?" Jacob asked.

Coyote looked at him. "What makes you think I was lying?" He poured four more shots.

"Okay, you're freaking me out now." Jacob took a step closer to Coyote. "Do you really have a gun in your car?"

"I do."

I was the first to consume the second shot.

Trina lifted her glass but did not drink. She just stared intently at Coyote. "What's your name?"

"Coyote."

"Like the dog?"

"Exactly like that."

"So, Coyote, would you have really killed him? Over me?"

"Of course not. I don't even know you."

She seemed suddenly confused, and I filled the silence. "What kind of gun is it?"

"Smith and Wesson M-and-P forty caliber."

"Is that good?"

"Define 'good.'"

Trina finally took her second drink, slamming it back with the skill of someone who had done many shots in her young life. Jacob followed suit, coughing after swallowing it down.

"What am I doing here?" she asked. "You didn't rent a hotel room just to have a conversation with me."

"Why not?" Coyote asked. "What makes you less human that we can't desire to spend nonsexual time together?"

"Because that's not how it works in my world."

"Maybe you need to spend some time in a different one, then."

Coyote's earlier confession came back to me then. About his need

to consume people. This is what he was doing with Trina. He wanted
to control the situation. He didn't want sex—it didn't interest him
if that's what she was paid to do. He wanted to make her vulnerable,
unbalanced. And paying her *not* to have sex did just that.

Jacob fell back into the yellow chair. "I don't really know what
we're doing here, either. I wanted to hook up."

"At the cost of getting all our asses kicked," I said.

"You still can hook up, Jacob." Coyote put a hand on Trina's back.
"You just need to pay for it."

"I'm not paying for it."

"Then we need something else to entertain us." Coyote poured
another round of tequila, but not for himself.

"It's your money," Trina said. "I don't care if we do each other's
nails and watch TV."

I smiled. Something about Trina was growing on me, and I was
glad she wasn't in that bar anymore. When we first came into the
motel room, I had the sinking feeling something regrettable was
going to happen. I didn't want anyone having sex with Trina, least
of all Coyote. Now, although I wasn't sure what we were going to do
in the room, I knew it would be all right.

Trina took another drink, and I sensed that alcohol was a problem for her. Less than ten minutes had passed since she wanted to
be in control, and in about fifteen more she would be far from it.
She swung her hair back. "You wanted to ask me some questions?"

Coyote nodded and thought for a minute. "How old are you?"

"Twenty-six."

"How long have you been an escort?"

"Eight months."

"You like it?"

She put her glass down on top of the TV set, a dribble of tequila
forming a ring around the base of the glass. "Sometimes it's okay,

but it usually sucks. And sometimes it's fucking horrifying."

"How much money you make in a month?"

"Why do you care?"

"I'm paying for your time. You don't like sex with strangers, so you should be happy all I want to do is ask some questions."

She pulled a strand of hair back behind her ear, and the light from the dirty lamp caught her face in such a way I could see how much makeup she was wearing. "Enough to pay my bills."

"How many appointments a day?" he asked.

"One. Sometimes two."

"How much does the house get?"

"Half."

"What's the worst experience you ever had?"

The alcohol seemed to be working itself through Trina's system because her defensive posture started to relax. She sat down on the edge of the bed and crossed her legs, remaining there for a long time. Then: "Third client. Guy from Morgantown. Huge, hairy guy. Probably three hundred pounds. Didn't shower at all, and I was too scared of him to ask. When we were done, I went to the bathroom and threw up."

Coyote remained silent. We all did.

"What about you?" she finally asked Coyote.

"What about me?"

"What kind of whore are you? What would you do for money?"

"I have more money than I already know what to do with," he said. "That makes it difficult to be motivated by it. But I do find it interesting to consider the impact of money."

"Like what?"

He set his shot glass down, and I think I was the only one paying attention to the fact he hadn't refilled it. "I don't know how much money you need," he said, "but you must need a lot in order to start escorting. I imagine I could write you a big enough check to change the course of your life. I wouldn't miss it. My father probably wouldn't even notice."

She looked up and her eyes opened more fully than I'd seen all evening. "You would do that?"

"Of course not. I don't even know you. But it's interesting to think I could."

Her eyes faded. "You're just an asshole, you know that? Is that your deal? You like the power trip?"

"More than anything," he said.

She folded her arms and thought for a moment. "That gun in your car. You ever use it on anyone?"

"No."

"Why do you have it?"

"Just in case."

"You think you could actually kill someone if you had to?"

"Absolutely."

That old motel room became as silent as an abandoned house.

Trina studied him, and I don't think she was afraid of Coyote. In fact, I think she was less tense than Jacob and I were.

Then she said, "You have, haven't you?" She leaned forward and stared at his unblinking eyes. "You've killed before."

I thought she was joking, but I could see in her expression she wasn't. I got the sense Trina had seen the eyes of a monster before, and she recognized the look in Coyote.

Coyote pulled his gaze from her for the first time and stared at the floor. An electric buzz seemed to flow through the room, and my fingers began tingling with an almost painful heat. I became vaguely aware I was holding my breath.

Coyote picked up the bottle and took a swig directly from it, something I'd never seen him do. So much for him needing everyone else drugged but not himself. He put it back and then went and sat down next to her on the bed. Jacob watched them from his chair, and I remained standing next to the bed, frozen.

"Not with a gun."

Jacob's voice suddenly burst through the room. "Bullshit."

"It's true," Coyote said.

"Come on," I offered. "You haven't." I was really hoping it wasn't true. "I have."

"It must have been an accident."

"Sort of."

Trina didn't back away from him. "Tell me," she said. Not *tell us*, but *tell me*.

Coyote leaned forward and placed his forearms on the tops of his legs and interlaced his fingers. Several seconds passed before he spoke.

"I was thirteen. On a camping trip with my dad in Virginia, in one of those state parks that people get lost in all the time, they're so big. It was summer, and the heat was unbearable. I never understood why we had to go camping when it was so goddamn hot. My dad didn't even like camping. Or me, for that matter. But my mom had been dead for years, and my dad was always trying to find new ways to apologize for that. Camping was one of them."

Coyote had told me his mom died in a car crash. I wondered why Coyote's dad had to apologize for her death, but I didn't interrupt.

"We were there four days. Just the two of us. We'd wake up in the morning, my dad would cook something up for us, and we'd spend most of the morning hiking. Fishing in the afternoon, usually. It was boring as hell. I think we were supposed to be bonding, but we always drove back home in silence. We never had anything to say."

Coyote sighed and took another pull from the bottle.

Was all this some sort of act?

He removed the bottle from his lips and gestured if anyone else wanted any, but no one moved. He wiped his lower lip with an index finger and continued.

"One morning my dad wasn't feeling well, so he slept in. I made myself breakfast and headed out on my own. We had an expensive walkie-talkie set, so he could always contact me. I just began walking through the woods, making sure I kept a line in my head on which direction I'd come from. I was just walking. Nothing more. Just walking.

"After about an hour I met another kid. Redhead kid. About fifteen. Pretty amazing I ran into anyone, actually, since I was off-path. He was throwing rocks at a squirrel in a tree when he saw me. After a minute or so, he gave up and started talking to me. His name was Paul, but he said his friends called him Paul. I guess it was some kind of lame joke, but he laughed a lot at it. I remember that. I remember how the patches of freckles bunched up when he laughed at his own stupid fucking joke.

"He was camping with his parents at a site on the other side of the lake from ours, and he'd been walking around by himself all morning. His parents just let him wander off. I mean, he was far away from his camp—much farther than I was from mine—and his parents had no idea where he was. 'How do they contact you?' I asked. He just looked at me and laughed, those freckles bunching up again. 'They don't, Mickey. I just show back up when I feel like it.' He kept calling me Mickey. I don't know why. I told him my name was Wiley, and he just kept calling me Mickey.

"At that point my dad called me to check in, his voice crystal clear over the walkie-talkie. I told him I was fine, and he told me to come back soon. I was thinking about turning back anyway because something about this kid bothered me."

Coyote bowed his head again, like someone on the business end of the confessional booth. He continued.

"I told Paul I had to leave and I started to walk away, but he told me to wait. I asked him why, and then he told me he wanted my walkie-talkie. I didn't understand, because the only person he could call on it was my dad, but then I realized he just *wanted* it. Not to use right then. But to keep. He wanted to take away my fancy Sharper Image walkie-talkie, the one my dad bought just for this trip. I told him no. That's when he tackled me.

"He was heavier and stronger than me, and seconds after he knocked me over, he had me pinned down. He grabbed the walkie-talkie and threw it to the side. After that, he just started hitting me. No reason at all. He had what he wanted. He could have gotten up and left. But he wanted to hurt me. I couldn't move, and he just wanted to throw some pain my way. He couldn't hit the squirrels, so he was going to hit me."

Coyote took a deep breath, and Jacob and I exchanged looks. Was any of this true?

"I screamed," Coyote continued. "Yelling at him to stop, but he wouldn't. He wasn't laughing, but his eyes were wide with excitement. Every time he punched me, his thick, rust-colored hair flung back and forth over his head. His teeth were crooked, and two of them jutted forward, like they'd be perfect for opening cans. I stared at his ugly fucking face as he beat the hell out of me on the forest floor.

"At one point I stopped feeling pain and real fear set in. This wasn't a boyhood fight, I was thinking. I'd had a few of those. This was serious. He was going to keep punching me until either he exhausted himself or I died. One of those things was going to happen in a matter of minutes if I didn't do anything.

"I swung at him, but my arms weren't long enough to reach his face, and he just dodged my swings and dug in with his own fists. Finally, I laid my arms to the side and I found a rock. About the size of an apple, but not round like that. Sharp, like it had just broken off something bigger. I picked it up, and with just the little strength I had left, I threw it at him. It was a great shot. It smashed right in the middle of his forehead. He fell right off me and rolled onto his back."

He paused.

"It was self-defense," I said, my voice sounding weak and soft in the room. Coyote looked up at me.

"It isn't over."

Trina was now looking vacantly at the wall behind Coyote, and I had no idea what she was thinking. I turned to Jacob, and from the expression on his face I could tell he no longer wondered if Coyote was bullshitting.

"The kid was still conscious. He stared up at the trees with a vacant look on his face, a large red knot forming on his forehead. There wasn't any blood. Not yet. No blood. Just a big red welt.

"He didn't move. His arms. His legs. Anything. The only things moving were his eyes, back and forth. I got up and picked up the rock and stood over him. I could taste blood in my mouth. I could hardly breathe from all the punches he put into my stomach, but I was so goddamn full of rage I couldn't walk away. I had to look at him, you know? I had to look at this boy who tried to kill me. As I stared down at him, his eyes finally stopped moving and stared directly at me. He was wheezing from exertion. 'I'm going to kill you now, Mickey', he said. 'Give me a second and then I'm going to kill you.'

"I didn't even wait for him to start moving. I smashed the rock down on his skull, hard as I could. Then I did it again. And again. I pounded his face with that rock until there seemed to be nothing left of his face at all." There was no emotion in Coyote's voice. No remorse. No sadness. Not even the slurs of drunkenness. He took another drink. "He didn't scream or move. He just laid there and died, those stupid freckles painted over with his blood. I knew he was dead the second the blood stopped bubbling underneath his nose."

"Holy shit," Jacob said. Trina didn't move.

Coyote looked up again, his eyes looking at something that was far from this room. "There was something, you know? I'll never be able to explain it, but there was something. The first time I hit him, all I needed to do was call my dad and this kid would've been okay. I had his life in my hands, and I could either save it or destroy it. I had the power to wipe out fifteen years of living, breathing, walking, communicating. Gone. Like that. Animated to lifeless, all based on what I felt like. I didn't have to kill him, but I wanted to. I *wanted* to. I wanted to feel what it was like, not to hurt someone, but to control them on the ultimate level."

"Consume them," I whispered.

Trina finally spoke. "How did it feel?"

He considered this. "Like . . . like swimming in the deepest water. In the water, you can float. Carry things that are too heavy on land. Drift. Fly. Anything. Killing that kid was just like floating. I could do anything, and that was all that mattered."

"Jesus, Coyote," I said. "Please tell me you're making this up."

Coyote said nothing.

"What did you do after?"

"I found the softest spot of earth I could find, and I started digging. Just my bare hands. Took me forever, and I kept thinking how my dad was waiting for me. I got about six inches down, and I put him in there, just covered him up best I could. Dirt, leaves, branches. Anything I could find. We weren't near a path or anything, so I just hoped it would be a while before anyone found him."

"You didn't tell anyone?"

"No. Not even my dad. I washed away the blood, covered myself in dirt, and when I got back to the camper, I told him I fell down a creek bed and got banged up against some rocks. He wanted to take me to the hospital, but I convinced him I was okay. We left for home that afternoon."

Jacob's back was straight as a plank. "Did they ever find him?"

"A few days later. There was a search party, and they found him. I saw it in the newspaper. But no one ever came to question me, and my dad never mentioned it. I'm not sure he'd even heard about it."

My brain was sluggish with that sense of taking one drink too many, but it was Coyote's story that put my world in an uncontrolled spin. "What . . . what did you do after? I mean, that must have messed you up."

"Not as much as I would have thought," he said. "After a few months, I just stopped thinking about it. I mean, every now and then I would, but not every day. But I never felt guilty. Just human nature."

"Human nature?"

He nodded. "Kill. Breathe. Fuck. Laugh. It's all human nature. That kid wanted to kill me, and I wanted to kill him. I just got there first. Simple as that. We're all just animals, and there's really nothing wrong with that."

It took me this long, but this was the moment I realized with final certainty that Coyote was a psychopath. I had many senses about him before, and many of them flirted with malevolence, but now he proved there was something definitively evil inside him. He stood and walked over to the bathroom, where he washed his face and dried it with a thin, faded towel. I looked at Jacob and Trina, but they were off in their own worlds. No one spoke. When Coyote returned, he went around and poured us all shots. He got to Trina last, and he spoke as he handed her another drink. She took it and set it down immediately on the nightstand.

"I don't judge you," he told her. "We all do things society doesn't accept. Do whatever the hell you want, and don't set boundaries on yourself. You're a whore now, simple as that. You won't be forever, but that's what you are now."

Trina's eyes welled with tears, and it was a pitiful sight.

"If anyone mistreats you, you don't have to accept it because they're paying you. Do what your nature tells you to do, and don't listen to anyone else."

Coyote took one last drink, the only one of us who did. On this night, Coyote was the drunk and vulnerable one, and here we saw him as who he really was. The last thing he said before stretching out on the bed and falling asleep was, "If someone hurts you, hurt them back. It doesn't have to be complicated."

CHAPTER EIGHTEEN

Charlotte was back and she looked curious.

Harden lay on the floor, his hair clumped in dirt and dried sweat. He had never felt in so much pain and yet at peace as he did now. The drugs injected into him were wearing off, as was his adrenaline, and though every joint ached with the slightest movement, there was comfort in succumbing to it all. There was a sweet relief in defeat. He floated alone in the middle of the ocean and soon he would slip painlessly beneath its surface.

"Come over here," he whispered. His throat raged for water. He reached his fingertips out, and like a dog, Charlotte obeyed. She crawled closer to him until she reached his hand. The black widow hesitated one last moment, then delicately crept up his hand and along his arm. Harden could feel her, the whisper of her legs on his skin as she glided along.

"Come on," he said. "Do it."

He wondered what it would be like. He assumed the bite would sting, then the area of skin around it would swell and throb. He couldn't remember if a black widow's bite could actually kill a grown man, but in his weakened state and left unattended, he figured there was a fairly good chance of it. How long would he have? Hours, days? There would be suffering, he knew, but then there would be none.

Harden closed his eyes and waited. In the depthless dark behind his lids, he saw shapeless images, like the mucusy bubbles of a lava lamp, floating, coming together, combining and then splitting apart. Then he saw defined shapes. A flash of his father on the day Harden first flew a kite, which harshly dissolved into Derek's torn and discarded body. His lifeless eyes. Then he saw Emma, frightened and screaming, the bandage around her hand black with dried blood.

Emma.

Harden opened his eyes and suddenly he didn't want to die. Well, that wasn't true, was it? He *couldn't* die. He had to help Emma, and she had to help him. She was his only purpose now, and he couldn't just give up.

Little hairy legs on his throat, just to the left of his Adam's apple. He fought the urge to slap at Charlotte, or to move even in the slightest. He was being held captive with the knife point on his throat, and the smallest movement on his part could be his last.

He stilled his mind and waited it out. She would either bite him, or she wouldn't. That was how it would be.

Harden tried to remember what had happened after being injected in Emma's cell. The immediate aftermath was a fog, and all he knew was he woke on the floor back in his own cell with a fresh series of bruises along his abdomen and chest. Kicked, he figured. *Baby Face laid into me good.* The dull throbbing in his ribs seemed a permanent part of his being now. There was also pain on the side of his head. He had probably passed out and knocked his head after being drugged.

The lights went out. The metal door slat slid open.

"In the corner. Turn around."

Harden thought, *I can't move. I can't talk.*

"In the fucking corner!"

Harden spoke through his teeth, moving his mouth as little as he could.

"Wait, goddamnit. There's a black widow on me."

"I will come in there and fuck you up if you don't get in the corner right now!"

"Just hang—"

"NOW!"

Harden counted to three in his head then swatted at his neck. Three swipes, hoping in the dark to knock Charlotte off and onto the floor. He felt nothing, but she could already be elsewhere on his body by now. Maybe down his shirt. He scrambled to his feet and pain shot down from his neck to his toes, not the sting of a spider bite but of the accumulated damage to his body. As Harden tried to find the corner in the dark, he waited for the bite.

Would it be sharp like a doctor's needle, or a heavy, dull pinch?

When he reached the corner, he used his arms to support himself against the walls. No bite, yet.

"Try anything again and we've been authorized to kill you."

"Fuck you," Harden mumbled.

The slat closed. The door opened.

"Don't move," Baby Face said.

He heard a shuffling along the dirt. Then, the sound of a tray—maybe trays?—being placed on the floor. Before he knew it, the door shut again and the room enveloped him once more in stifling darkness.

Harden turned.

Silence.

For a moment, he thought he felt Charlotte on his neck. He didn't move.

The light turned on.

Harden sucked in a breath.

Emma.

CHAPTER NINETEEN

The bus ride home to Owen, Pennsylvania, was everything not expressed in Simon and Garfunkel's *America*. There was no beauty in taking any bus for any kind of distance in the Northeast. It was only something you did as a last resort, when money was tight and you had to be somewhere.

Unfortunately, at Christmastime, lots of other people also had somewhere to be. I squeezed into the last remaining seat next to the bathroom, the morbidly obese woman next to me sleeping across both seats and mumbling profanities as I made her sit up to give me space. We were not destined to be friends.

The bus spat me out near central Owen just after eight in the evening, and nightfall had blotted out the gray, industrial smoke that covered my hometown like a coffin's heavy lid.

My father was waiting for me, and after a single-pump handshake and a "How ya doin'," I collapsed inside his Dodge Challenger, and we journeyed home. Home was ten minutes away, but I wished it to be farther.

Owen was the place my darkest memories nested. Ridge Creek Elementary School was just a few blocks from our house, and I knew we would go past it on our route. It was closed now, but not because of what happened there. I think there just weren't enough kids left in the area to keep it open. That's a good thing.

The worst part is I never told anyone about it. Mr. Kildare told me not to, but it wasn't like he threatened my life or anything. He just made me promise, telling me the others wouldn't understand. I never told my father, as much as the thought of it burned in me every night as I tried to sleep. I had to see Mr. Kildare every day in class for the next three months before he suddenly moved away. He never took me into that closet again. Barely even acknowledged me, actually, which somehow made me feel even more violated.

Sometimes when I was alone, I could smell his meaty breath.

After a while, I went from being scared to tell anyone to being ashamed to tell anyone. That's the horrible cycle of silence.

It wasn't until my freshman year at college that I allowed him back into my thoughts for a brief time. The library where I worked on campus had a LexisNexis database, and I searched his name. Charles Kildare was arrested in 1984 in a small town in Oregon. Still an elementary school teacher, he'd been found guilty on seven counts of sexual assault of a minor. The sentence was sixty years in prison, but he'd only made it six months. Somebody strangled him to death just before lockdown on a Thursday night.

I suppose I should have felt good about how it all ended up, but I didn't. Someone else had to do what I was supposed to do. It was supposed to be my hands around his throat, at least metaphorically. That man had gone on and hurt other kids because I never told anyone. I was a fucking coward, and every time I came back to Owen the memories of it settled on me like a chilling morning mist.

We passed the elementary school, and I stared straight, silently counting. When I reached twenty-two, my dad pulled the car onto the cracked driveway of my childhood home.

Inside, I got a better look at my father. Reston Campbell was an old fifty-two, a man who lived hard for the first thirty years of his life and then paid for it each day after that. He kept his Harley-rider long hair and beard from those days. Most of it was now gray, as was his pallor, giving him a look of someone covered in dust. His craggy face and hard eyes kept any homeless person from ever seeking spare change from him, although he'd probably be one of the first to give it. My father was a beautiful person, but few people, including me, often saw that side of him.

Before I was born, he drank hard, smoked two packs of unfiltered Camels a day, and was a faithful parishioner at any hole serving Jack Daniels. He managed to stay single and carefree—a rarity in working-class Owen—until he met my mother. She was ten years his junior and fell hard for the part-time auto mechanic and aspiring guitarist. I've been told more than once that his talent should've taken him far away from Owen, but he never got the chance. Mom got pregnant, they got married, and I've never heard my dad play guitar.

Having a baby scared the shit out of him, enough so that Dad replaced Jack with Jesus, being born a second time just after my first. No alcohol. No cigarettes. No more aimless nights. He married my mother, found a steady job as a property engineer at a Holiday Inn, and committed himself fully to the Lord, his wife, and his son. Pretty much in that order.

Mom lasted until I was ten, deciding church and family interfered with her ability to get high and fuck other men. She left for California with the assistant manager from the local A&P. Dad got custody, and Mom last sent me a birthday card when I was fourteen. I still think about her and wonder what I would say if we ever see each other again. I'd probably say nothing at all.

"You eat yet?" My dad walked over to the refrigerator and opened the door. Light shone in a solid beam from the inside, having no food to have to pass over. "Don't got a lot. Could order a pizza, s'pose."

"That's fine, Dad. I'll call."

As I ordered, I did my own search of the fridge. It made me wonder if the electricity to power the thing was worth it just to keep a few pops and a jar of mayo cold. Probably not.

The pizza came an hour later. Even though the dinner was informal and barely edible, my father insisted on grace. He reached across the table and grabbed my hands. I could feel the calluses on his leathery palms.

"Bless, O Lord, us and your gifts, which from your bounty we are about to receive, and grant that, healthily nourished by them, we may render you due obedience, through Christ our Lord. Amen."

I mouthed an "amen," which came out as more of a mumble. I picked up a slice and managed to get about half of it in my mouth.

"How's school?"

"Fine," I said. "Busy."

"Busy is good."

"Sometimes."

"Still majoring in English?"

My neck tensed. *Here it comes.*

"Yes," I said.

"How you gonna pay bills with that?"

"I'll figure it out."

He coughed, and I could hear the wet rattle of a thousand consumed cigarettes in his lungs.

"Not a lot of money in that, I would think. Graduation's coming up. Gotta have a plan."

Like you had a plan at my age, I didn't say. I glanced around at the sparse kitchen, the cheap plastic dining chairs, the ten-dollar coffeemaker next to a can of Folgers.

"No," I said. "Probably not a lot of money in it."

I finished off the slice but wasn't feeling hungry anymore. I leaned back in my chair and thought about my writing, about what made me interested in it. I considered the essay on religion I'd turned in, the one inspired by Coyote. It then occurred to me my dad was the person I'd been writing about. Here was a man who found his God late in his life and followed blindly.

"Why did you decide to turn religious?" I asked.

I had never asked the question before, and it just shot out of me.

He let the question sit long enough I thought it would just die there. But then he shot me a glare with his hard brown eyes and said, "I didn't decide to turn, Son. We all have it in us. It's a matter of maturing enough to let it all come out."

"Mom was pregnant, right?"

He nodded. "That's right."

I could tell he wasn't sure where this was headed. Neither was I. We weren't used to talking like this.

"Did it just happen, like all of a sudden?"

"Why are you asking me all of this?"

"I wrote something for a class on a similar topic."

"About me?"

"No. Not you. Just . . . an idea about how religion starts."

He opened up his can of pop and took a few gulps before putting it back on the table.

"Sometimes it takes a man a crisis to find Jesus, Harden. Like Paul on the road to Damascus. He was persecuting the Christians, you know. Putting 'em in jail before Jesus came down and blinded him." He shook his head, as if reliving a memory. "Your mom was pregnant, and we were both living as hard and wild as ever. I was drinking at least a six-pack a day, and your mom wasn't far behind me." He shook his head. "It's a miracle you turned out healthy."

"Yeah, no shit," I mumbled.

"I won't tolerate profanity at my table."

"Sorry."

Dad shifted in his seat and stared at the table. "When I found out your mother was pregnant, I'm ashamed to admit I wanted her to . . . for us to terminate the pregnancy. She refused. The hard truth is if it was up to me, you wouldn't have ever lived."

When a parent tells you they wanted to have you aborted, it flips your stomach enough to push a wad of bile up toward your throat. I forced it back down, but it left a hot burn inside.

"About three weeks after I found out about you," he said, "I went out drinking one night. Especially hard. Small place in another town our band was playing at. Little bar mostly full of steel workers and tramps."

This was the longest conversation we'd had in some time; my dad usually preferred his body language to do the speaking for him. But watching him made me realize he needed to tell me this. He needed to tell me how he found Jesus. Maybe he was holding out hope I would find him too.

"Your mother and I weren't engaged yet, but we were talking about it. We were going to get married and have a baby, and that scared me more than anything. Anyway . . ." There was a long silence as he picked up his unused fork and starting rapping the tines against the tabletop. "I went home with another woman that night. I don't even remember her name. She was filthy, and I went home with her. I . . . I sinned that night. Sinned against what God wanted for us, but I just didn't know it at the time. The moment I . . . you know . . ."

"Moment you what?"

He cleared his throat, decades of regret coming up with his phlegm. "Moment I was finished with her, I saw everything. Who I was. What I was doing. My future in hell. Everything."

"Jesus," I whispered.

"Know you don't mean it like that, Son, but it *was* Jesus. Jesus came to me and told me I had chosen the wrong path in life, but it wasn't too late to change. As I laid on top of that fallen woman, I knew I was under the devil's thumb. And that was a fear more terrifying than any I've ever known. Scared me straight, is what that was. From that moment on, I changed everything. Quit drinking, joined a church, confessed my sins."

"Just like that?"

"Just like that."

"You tell Mom about the other woman?"

"Had to, Son. You can't be a Christian without confession. You can't be absolved of any sins you won't admit to."

"What did she say?"

"She was plenty mad, but I suspect she was sinning as well. She kept sinning long after I stopped, as you know."

"I know."

"Still got married. Still was there to watch you be born." He pushed his chair back a couple of inches. "Sometimes you have to be in crisis to find Jesus, though sometimes you just have to be lost."

I could hear the old wooden clock on the wall ticking behind me, its measured beats counting the seconds of silence between us.

"I think you're a little lost, Harden."

"I'm not sure I'm ready to find Jesus yet, Dad."

He smiled, which surprised me. I never went to church much until Mom left, and then it was every Sunday with Dad. He knew I was never interested, and I hadn't been to church once since leaving for college. I knew I disappointed him, and I expected to hear that lecture again now.

Instead, he said, "That's the beauty of Jesus, Son. Sometimes he just decides to find *you*."

CHAPTER TWENTY

"Jesus. *Emma*."

A gag covered her mouth—a blue bandana wadded up with one end dangling out like the tail of a creature she'd eaten. Hands tied behind her back with a thin nylon rope. Harden desperately worked the knot of the bandana first, and once he freed her mouth he focused on her wrists, trying his best to not bump against the bandaged stump where her finger used to be. When the rope fell to the floor, Emma wrapped her arms around Harden's chest and buried her face just beneath his chin. Her body rattled against his as she sobbed.

Harden didn't know why they brought her to him, but he thought were it all to end this way, at least he would be with her.

Holding her, Harden scanned the floor and said, "There's a black widow in here. She was just on me, and I'm not sure where she went. Keep a look out."

Emma pulled back, and there was almost a smile on her face. "She?"

"Yeah. Her name is Charlotte. It's been pretty lonely in here."

Now a real smile came, only to be replaced by more tears. Harden himself felt a choke of sadness, but he just didn't have the energy to cry.

"How's your finger?" he said.

Emma wiped her cheek with her healthy hand and allowed herself a long, deep breath.

"It hurts," she said. "But I don't think it's infected, at least not yet." She raised her hand, and Harden studied the gauze and tape circled around the stump where the index finger had once been. He didn't know what he was looking for, and he didn't want to look under the tape, so all he said was, "That's good. We'll get out soon and then go straight to the hospital and get you cared for."

"But they can't save my finger. It's gone forever."

Harden nodded.

"Where are we?" Emma asked.

"I have no idea. I was hoping you knew."

"I don't . . . he . . . I met with Coyote. Said he wanted to tell me something. The night after your birthday. Someone grabbed me from behind. I don't really remember." Her eyes welled again. "I woke up in that cell. It seems so long ago."

Harden kept looking at her bandage. "Who did that to you?"

"The men with the masks. They said it would make me obey. Said Coyote had ordered it. They . . . they held me down." She closed her eyes, and with a voice so controlled Harden marveled at her strength said, "They used a bolt cutter, Harden."

Harden tried not to imagine that scene, but the more he tried the clearer the vision became. Baby Face #1 holding her down, pinning her arm to the ground. Baby Face #2 leaning in with the bolt cutters, pincers open wide like a massive crab, going in for the prey.

"Emma, I'm so sorry."

She shook her head, not quite saying *it's nothing*, but rather to stop thinking about her situation altogether.

"What about you?" she asked. "Are you hurt?"

He shook his head and felt guilty they hadn't dismembered him, too. "Nothing like you. They have a plan for me, so they need to keep me somewhat healthy, I suspect."

"What plan?" She nodded at the broken typewriter on the ground. "Does it have to do with that?"

"Yes. But listen, Emma, there's something I have to tell you. You might already know." He reached up and put his hand on her shoulder, craving her warmth.

"What?"

"Derek," Harden said. "They killed him."

"What? Oh, no. Oh, Harden."

"He—his body—was in this room when I first woke up. They took him away after a little while."

Emma sat on the floor, pulled her knees up to her chest, and wrapped her arms around them, pulling herself into as small a ball as possible. Harden sat next to her and put his hand on her back. As he did, he caught a brief scent, so ephemeral he wondered if it was just his imagination. But, above the stench of the cell and their two slowly rotting bodies, he smelled the Emma he remembered. Fresh, like a meadow of flowers just washed by rain. It was the aroma of Emma on the day she sat across from him in the dining hall. And, in seconds, it was gone.

"I don't understand this," she said. "This can't be real. Poor . . . poor Derek."

And that was all she said about Derek, not asking how he died, or if Harden knew who had done the act. Maybe she didn't want to know because the more she asked questions, the less of a bad dream this became. Maybe she could still convince herself she would wake from this. Harden had given up on that fantasy some time ago.

"What do they want from us?" she asked.

Harden shook his head. "I thought I was free. I hurt one of them—hit him in the face with the typewriter. I almost made it."

"You should have kept going. You stopped for me, and that's why you're still here."

"No," he said. "We leave here together or not at all. Do you recognize any of their voices?"

"No."

"One of them seems familiar to me. The smaller one. They want us alive, at least I think. They hurt you, but they treated the wound. Kept you from getting worse. As for me . . ."

"What?"

Harden turned and looked at the typewriter on the floor. He guessed it was broken, but he hadn't tried it. He wondered if breaking the machine had sealed his fate.

"Coyote wants me to write," he said. "He didn't tell me what to write, but each day they come and take out the pages I've finished. I've been writing about how all this started, from the moment I first met him. But maybe that's not what he wants."

"What do you think he wants?"

"I think . . . " Harden lowered his voice. He didn't believe there were any cameras or microphones in the cell after all his searching, but he sure as hell didn't want to be heard. "I think Coyote wants to know what I know. See it from my perspective, as a follower. It's like the New Testament, how all the disciples wrote about their experiences with Jesus. That's what I think he wants. He wants the Book of Harden."

"But you're not even a follower," Emma said. "You're not even a believer."

Harden thought he saw the slightest of movements out of the corner of his eye, and turned his head. He looked for Charlotte, but all he saw was a bare dirt floor leading to a wall behind which she was likely hiding.

"I don't think that matters at all," he said.

CHAPTER TWENTY-ONE

Christmas came and went with little fanfare. Snow fell, but it hardly seems a white Christmas when the only things the snow clings to are wisps of dead front-yard grass and rows of rusted chain-link fencing. Dad put out a plastic Nativity scene in the front yard, and on the day after Christmas someone stole Mary and the donkey. Dad prayed for the thief.

On the morning of New Year's Eve I got my first call in a week; few people knew my home number.

"Hey, Harden."

"Coyote."

"You gotta come back."

"Back where?"

"Wyland."

"You're back at school?"

"I am. And I need you."

We still had two weeks of break left.

"Why did you go back so early?"

His voice became more excited. "Your story. We can make it happen."

I straightened and held the receiver against my ear. The knotted plastic cord twisted around itself like a DNA's double helix.

"What are you talking about?"

"Your short story. 'Revelation.' I read it yesterday, and now I'm back on campus. We can do this, Harden. We can start it all here at Wyland."

I wanted to pretend not to know what he meant when he said *we can make it happen*, but I knew better. I knew Coyote.

"Coyote, it was just a short story for my class. It's fiction."

"It doesn't have to be. The concept is perfect."

I won't say his compliment fell on deaf ears, but I parried it with my usual self-doubt.

"It's nothing original," I said. "It's as old as any idea out there."

"No," Coyote said, "not really. Not the idea of starting it on a campus. Hell, it's the perfect nesting ground. Now get your ass back here and let's figure out how to do this. I can't do this alone." A brief pause, then, "Actually, I could do this all alone. I just don't want to. Harden, come on. I'm bored as hell. This is the perfect challenge."

A perfect challenge. That's how he saw this. "Let me make sure I understand you," I said. "We have one semester left of college, and in that time, in addition to all your coursework, you want to start a religion. Is that right? Because that's what I wrote about, Coyote. I wrote about starting a religion from scratch. A complete, personality-based religion. A following from nothing."

"I know." I could visualize the thousand-yard stare in his eyes. "And I'm the perfect fucking messiah."

He knew it. I knew it. In fact, there was a part of me that believed this was possible.

He added, "Let's look at it another way. You having fun with your pop down there?"

I didn't lie. "Not exactly."

"Then come back up and enjoy the peace and quiet. No one's here. It's cold as bones. It's beautiful."

"I don't know . . ."

"Okay, listen. Give me your address."

"Why?"

"I'm coming to get you. That way you don't even have to take that awful bus back up here. At least you'll get a comfortable ride."

"It's a six-hour drive."

"Then I'll spend the night."

I felt myself on the edge of Coyote's event horizon. He was a black hole pulling me, and I circled right at the invisible edge between drifting into space or plunging deep into his inescapable darkness. I had to admit, there was something alluring about giving in to his gravity, because having direction is something I struggled so hard with on my own. There was really nothing left for me in Owen. It's not like I was spending my days bonding with my dad. He worked ten-hour shifts, and while our dinners together weren't unpleasant, they weren't exactly riveting either. I'm sure he wouldn't mind if I went back a couple weeks early.

"Okay," I said. "You give me a ride, then I'll do it." I gave him my address.

"Great," he said. "See you tonight."

"You're coming tonight?"

"I was planning to. Why, what's the problem?"

"It's just . . . New Year's Eve."

"Oh, yeah. You have plans?"

"No," I admitted.

"Me neither. We'll celebrate in Owen."

Five and a half hours later, Coyote edged his BMW against the curb outside, and as he walked up the sidewalk to my childhood home, I had a strange flash of memory. It was of my mother and how quickly she was walking as she passed for the very last time through our front door.

CHAPTER TWENTY-TWO

Coyote walked into the house with a jackal's smile and a bottle of champagne. I tracked his eyes as he met my father. Not a single wayward glance at the sparse surroundings or my father's rough exterior. Coyote simply didn't give a shit if you were rich or poor. It was your soul Coyote wanted to judge, not your wallet.

As my father gave Coyote's hand a firm pump, Dad gave him the icy stare of a man who had spent many years learning hard lessons about trust. The quickest flick of his eyes and he took all of Coyote in, the perfect hair, the cashmere overcoat, slacks creased to a razor's edge. A second flick to the BMW outside, which beamed in the dirty sunshine. My dad never liked many of my friends, but never because they were too rich; this was a new situation entirely. For all of my father's reestablished faith, he didn't even offer Coyote as much as a glass of water. I think my father saw Coyote for what he was, knowing in ten seconds what I had failed to see after months spent with Coyote.

My father was an exceptional man.

Coyote turned to me.

"We're good to go tomorrow, right?"

"We are."

My father said, "Not sure why you want to leave so early, Harden. You barely even saw your friends here."

It was true, but mostly because I had so few friends here to begin with. My best friend growing up, Tim Johanson, enlisted in the Army the day after graduation and was currently stationed at Fort Hood. I envied his conviction, as much as I disagreed with his choice. Still, he'd have college paid for when he was done with his service, and he had some grand notions of helping to stop the Communist threat, though the world was already letting that fizzle out on its own.

"I've got a project I need Harden's help with," Coyote said. "It's actually based on something he wrote." He gave me a little nod, as if he was doing me a favor by saying any of this to my father. "He's a pretty talented writer, you know."

My father shoved a hand in his pocket and looked me over. "So was Hemingway," he said after a few seconds. "But some cleaning lady still had to mop his brains off the kitchen floor."

* * *

Nothing was more predictable than an eventual clash between Coyote and my father, which is why I suggested Coyote and I eat out for dinner, but my father would have nothing of it. It was New Year's Eve and my last night at home, and I was expected to eat at the house. It had all the elements of a perfect storm, and I counseled Coyote before we went into the kitchen.

"You know, I'm not sure my dad is all that crazy about you."

Coyote opened his eyes in mock disbelief. "Ya think?"

Okay, maybe he had noticed after all. "I think it's just . . . you know." I almost said it was because he was rich, but that wasn't really it. My father didn't like him because Coyote was a predator.

Coyote held a hand up, not needing any further clarification. "Harden, it's fine. It doesn't bother me. I don't need people to like me."

"Just don't do anything to egg him on, that's all I'm asking."

"Like what?"

I exhaled. "Put the champagne back in your car. He doesn't drink. He's a born-again Christian. That might come up."

"No kidding? That's perfect."

"Perfect? For what?"

"For our project. We could bounce some ideas off him."

Oh, *hell* no. "Are you crazy? I don't even want to discuss whatever crazy shit you're scheming until we're in the car tomorrow morning."

"Harden, it's such an opportun—"

"*Promise me.*"

Coyote narrowed his eyes for just a moment, and in that flash I felt the briefest stab of fear. It was barely a mosquito bite, but it was real. "Fine. I won't bring it up."

"Good," I said. "That's all I'm asking."

The small kitchen was a mess of pots, pans, and dirty wooden spoons. In the midst of the chaos, my father was putting the finishing touches on his signature beef stroganoff. I think it was the only real meal he knew how to make, and I was happy he made it on my last night. As much as I wanted to leave home, I was already missing him.

I carried three plates of the stroganoff over and set them on a faded wooden table that had been in our kitchen since Nixon quit. Dad poured us water from the squeaky kitchen tap, throwing a handful of ice chips into each glass. He exhaled with fatigue as he sat down between Coyote and me. Outside the small window next to my right, moonlight bounced off alleyway metal garbage cans.

As I turned to my plate of food, I suddenly realized what was coming next. Goddamnit, how could I not have been prepared for this?

Sure enough, my father said, "Coyote, would you care to say a blessing?" I thought I saw a slight smirk on my dad's face as he asked the question.

Most of my friends would have panicked. Not Coyote. Coyote reached for our hands and lowered his head. He gave my fingers a surreptitious squeeze.

"*Da, quaesumus Dominus, ut in hora mortis nostrae Sacramentis refecti et culpis omnibus expiati, in sinum misericordiae tuae laeti suscipi mereamur. Per Christum Dominum nostrum. Amen.*"

Now my father's grip tightened. Not much, but enough for the tension to flow though me. I looked up. No more smirk.

"Bless, O Lord, us and your gifts," Dad said. "Which from your bounty we are about to receive, and grant that, healthily nourished by them, we may render you due obedience, through Christ our Lord. Also, please show mercy and forgiveness on those who have not yet found salvation through your works and words. Amen."

We dropped our hands.

"No need for Latin at this table, Coyote. We're not that fancy here." He dug into his meat with his knife. "Did you learn Latin in Catholic school?"

No, Dad. Don't open that door.

"No. The small amount I know is self-taught."

"Are you a Christian?"

"Not much of anything, I suppose," Coyote responded. "My dad's a Presbyterian."

Dad let out a grunt and a nod, both of which said that if you're going to be a Presbyterian, you might as well be nothing. Dad was a Methodist.

I wanted to ask someone to pass me something to distract them from the conversation, but the only food on the table was already in front of us.

"And your mother?"

"Dead."

"I'm sorry to hear that," my father said. "You have any siblings?"

Coyote took a bite and spent some time with it in his mouth. He swallowed, then said, "Nope. Only child."

"Harden's not religious either," Dad said. "Most kids aren't, but I can't claim I was a very religious person at your age." He took a sip of his water. "There's still time. Time enough, anyway."

Coyote gave me a pleading look. He was straining against his collar to ask my dad about his religious views, wanting to probe and pry and dissect. I shook my head, and he gave me a frustrated glare. All I wanted was for us to inhale our food and be done with the dinner. But now it felt like I was in a chemistry lab surrounded by beakers of chemicals that threaten to mix and explode at any moment.

I thought we were home free. For the next ten minutes, the beakers remained upright and contained. Most of the conversation passed between Coyote and me, with my dad muttering a few words here and there but otherwise content to keep his gaze on his plate. I asked my dad who he thought was the favorite to win the Super Bowl, and he just shrugged and said, "Don't really care as long as it isn't the pigeons." He meant the Eagles.

Then, apropos of nothing, Coyote recounted how his father had taken him to Paris for Christmas, and how amazing the lights on the Champs-Elysées looked as a rain-snow mix fell heavily on the boulevard. They had stayed at the Ritz.

This brought my dad's gaze up to eye level.

"What does your father do for a living, son?"

"He manages a hedge fund out of West Virginia."

Dad gave a low *mmm-hmmm* and then put down his fork. "Seems he does pretty well for himself to be in the lawn care business."

Coyote seemed startled at first, and then said, "No, actually, a hedge fund is—"

"It's a joke, son. I know what hedge funds are." He tapped the side of his head with one finger. "A small house doesn't mean a small mind."

Coyote's cheeks turned just the slightest shade of crimson, a color I'd never seen on him before. He'd been embarrassed, and even though the transgression was slight, I knew it pissed him off. Something dark came over him that moment, just as the darkness had come the moment he started questioning a couple of freshmen on the couch in our apartment.

Coyote wiped his mouth with the paper napkin and put his elbows on the table.

"Actually, Mr. Campbell, I was wondering if you could give some advice to Harden and me on this project we're working on."

Oh, shit.

"No," I said. "I don't want to talk about this."

"Talk about what?" Dad asked.

Coyote turned to me. "We have an expert sitting right here, Harden. It would be irresponsible of us to not seek his counsel."

"What are you two talking about?"

"Harden wrote a story for school called 'Revelation.' It's the reason we're going back early. It's about religion, and he told me you might have an opinion on the subject."

"Goddamnit, Coyote, I told you not to bring it up."

Dad glared at me. "I won't tell you again to not swear at my table, Harden." Dad kept his attention on me as he spoke. "Now, tell me about this project of yours."

"C'mon, Harden." Coyote's voice had lost a bit of its malevolence, but not all. "You should be proud to share it with your father."

I don't know why I was so nervous. Maybe it was because my dad's vision of God was narrow and complete, and any deviation from his holy path was a quick and harsh tumble to hell. But it was just a stupid paper for lit class. At twenty years old, I still didn't want to disappoint him, although you'd think I'd be used to it by now.

I remained silent, not knowing what to say, and in that space of indecision was enough room for Coyote to pounce.

"Why do you believe in Christ?" he asked my father.

Dad cleared his throat and shot me a sideways glance. "I'm not sure that's any of your business, son, but you can assume I arrived at a point in my life where I needed a spiritual change."

"Exactly. Many people do. It's a human need to turn to something greater for guidance. You turned to Christ. Can I assume you grew up in a Christian household?"

"You can," Dad said. In one of the calmest faces I'd seen on him, he still looked like he wanted to kick the snot out of the punk across the table from him. I just impotently watched, just as I had when Coyote interrogated the hooker in the motel room.

"Just like Harden," Coyote continued. "So if Harden ever hit rock bottom, one can assume he would likely turn to Christ for spiritual guidance."

"I never said anything about hitting rock bottom. But yes, Christ is there for everyone."

"Not necessarily." Coyote softened his tone, but to me it sounded less gentle than patronizing. "Christ is who you knew only because he was there in the background of your life. If you grew up Jewish, I doubt you would have turned to Christ. You would have likely delved deeper into Judaism."

"There's only one true faith, son. If you need salvation, you can only do it through Jesus."

"There's a few billion others in the world who would disagree with you."

"I can't save them all." My dad stood up and went to the freezer.

He pulled out a pint of mocha almond fudge ice cream and took three bowls from the shelf. We all got a scoop, each with a week's growth of ice whiskers.

"What's this got to do with a school project?"

"It's not really a project," I finally said. "Coyote wants to adapt the story I wrote and try it out as an . . . experiment." I gave Coyote a look telling him I wasn't sold on the idea.

"An experiment about what?"

"Starting a new religion," Coyote said. "Not a sect. Not a cult. Not a branch of something else. Something entirely new."

"What in glory's name are you talking about?"

"Two thousand years ago, the mind-set of people was different. People believed in prophecies. People were expecting a messiah. They were superstitious. Their minds were ripe to accept a new belief system and Christianity flourished. What your son asks in his story is if that could happen in today's society—where information is disseminated rapidly and cynicism has replaced superstition. Can you actually get people to believe in something new? To trust their souls to it?" Coyote leaned forward. "And most importantly, what kind of person would you need to be to get those people to follow you?"

Dad turned to me, his spoon frozen in his hand, and the scoop of ice cream intended for his mouth fell back into his bowl.

"*That's* your project? Trying to start a new religion on campus?"

I was about to answer, not knowing what exactly to say, but then I saw Dad's face tighten and his forehead redden, at which point I knew whatever I said wouldn't be heard.

"This is why you want to leave your family and go back to school early, Harden?" He wasn't shouting, but he didn't have to. The bass of his voice shook my bones. "You think it's cute to blaspheme, to challenge the true word of the Lord? What is wrong with you, Son?

And I'm not asking that rhetorically. I really want to know where I've gone wrong with you."

There were so many answers to that question, but the one that came first to my mind had nothing to do with defending my story.

"There's nothing for me here, Dad."

In that moment I saw my father's heart break, saw it straight through his heavy, sober eyes. I never wanted to tell him so much about my abuse as a child as I did in that moment, tell him it was the city of Owen that haunted me, not my dad's house, but that truth would, very likely, leave him in a dark place from which he wouldn't be able to return.

He said nothing back to me, but he didn't drop his cold stare for a few heavy breaths. Then, he collected himself enough to turn to Coyote, and said, "I think you'll get laughed out of school."

Coyote either didn't notice or care about the unraveling of the father-son relationship that just occurred. "Why? A liberal college campus is the perfect location to try something like this. Wyland is full of cerebral, disaffected teens experiencing life outside their homes for the first time. Who better to offer spiritual guidance?"

"Why would they turn to you?"

"Why not?" Coyote wasn't slowing down. "When you needed spiritual help, why didn't you turn to the religion founded by a man who sat under a tree until he discovered pure enlightenment?"

"That's ridiculous."

"Not to four hundred million Buddhists. Or what about Islam? The New Testament was written by mortals and it's treated as divine, but the Qur'an was handed down directly from God to Muhammed, or so the Muslims would tell you. Why wouldn't you turn to that religion instead?"

I felt the hairs on my arms dance with electricity. I could actually envision this turning violent.

"Don't blaspheme the Bible in my house ever again."

"Take it easy, Coyote," I said.

Coyote put his hands up and feigned surprised. "I'm not trying to insult you at all. I'm just saying that, from an objective standpoint, religions all look ridiculous. Look back to ancient Greece, when they had a god for everything. Doesn't it seem like some kind of children's story to have a god of fire, god of water, god of space?"

"They weren't real gods."

"Yet people believe without question that Jesus performed miracles and was resurrected from the dead. To someone not brought up in a Christian home, can't you see how that might seem far-fetched?"

"You are so lost, Coyote. I hope that Jesus finds you, because your soul is in peril."

"No, no, no." Coyote was in his own world now, where only his ideas mattered. This wasn't about emotion; this was strictly point-counterpoint, an intellectual battle to be won. "The point I'm making is that it's innate in human nature to yearn for something bigger than one's self. To believe in something after death, something to give hope to the hopeless. To believe there's a greater purpose than what we can just see and feel in our time alive. It doesn't really matter what outlet a person uses to get there as long as they get there, you see? It doesn't matter what they believe in, so long as they simply *believe*."

"It *does* matter," Dad said. "Because there are correct answers and incorrect ones, and choosing incorrectly has its consequences."

Coyote leaned just a little more over the table, and that slightest extra tilt of his body felt immensely threatening. "Do you *really* believe that the billions of people on this planet who don't believe in Jesus are destined for hell?"

Dad closed his eyes. "Rest in the Lord and wait patiently for him;

Do not fret because of him who prospers in his way; Because of the man who brings wicked schemes to pass."

"Psalm thirty-seven," Coyote said. "Endure pain in life so that you might find salvation."

He opened his eyes. "So you do know scripture."

"I know a lot of things."

"You just don't believe it."

"I don't believe a lot of things."

"That's what faith is for."

Coyote gently shook his head. "Faith is the dregs left when all logic has been consumed."

Now Dad leaned forward and the two men locked in a stare.

"Coyote, you are belittling what means the most in life to me. In my house. At my table, upon which I served you."

My father spoke with so much conviction it took me a moment to realize he just admitted Jesus meant more to him than I did.

Coyote, for a moment, was quiet. I could see in his face a look I'd come to know well. He was at some edge in his mind, looking over into a forest that was both unknown and wild. This was when he made the decision to continue on his path or to turn around. Usually, *almost always*, he continued on. Coyote liked to run wild.

But not this time.

Coyote leaned back in his chair, wiped his mouth with his napkin, and held up both hands, palms forward. "You're right, Mr. Harden, and I'm deeply sorry. I didn't mean any disrespect."

In the following silence, which stretched for a minute until Dad wordlessly left the table and went to go watch TV, I realized this was the start of something. The beginning of my own path, one that, for the moment, seemed to involve me following Coyote into his forest. This forest was darker and stranger than any I'd seen before, and I wasn't sure where the other side of it was. I'd have to follow him in and follow him out, hoping he would protect me from whatever it was he was looking for in there.

Yea, though I walk through the valley of the shadow of death . . .

It was all confusing and more than a little frightening, but there was an excitement to it that I couldn't just ignore. I wanted more, but feared it would end horribly. And doing so meant relying on the guidance of Coyote, who, I knew absolutely, was not the least bit sorry for anything he did. Not about what he did to my father. Not about what he did to anyone.

In this excitement, what I failed to fully consider was it wasn't Coyote's protection I needed in that forest. I needed the forest's protection from Coyote.

CHAPTER TWENTY-THREE

Harden and Emma sat on the dirt floor facing each other, legs crossed, heads bowed more from exhaustion than contemplation. Harden reached across and held Emma's intact hand. He soaked in her warmth, though it reminded him how cold everything else around him was. She had been in his cell for at least a few hours now.

"Tell me something," she said. Her voice held the weary edge of someone drifting in and out of a fugue. "Anything. Just talk to me."

He wanted to talk to her. God, there was so much to say, but more than anything he just wanted to hear her voice. But since they placed her in his cell, Harden realized a truth.

Harden looked up at her dirt- and sweat-stained face, her eyes blazing out against the filth. He slowly shook his head and slowly wrote in the dirt with his finger.

They're listening.

He didn't know how, but they had to be. They might not be watching; Harden didn't know of any cameras small enough that he wouldn't have already been able to find them. But somehow they were listening. There was no reason to put Emma into his cell except to listen to them. Coyote was a master at getting people to talk, to share things they normally wouldn't, and then use all of their own deep truths against them. Harden was convinced Coyote was listening now to see what they would tell each other, to see how much they knew. And, perhaps, what they feared most.

Harden swiped his palm along the floor, scattering the words back to dust. Emma traced fresh words with her fingers in the dirt.

What should we do?

Harden thought for a moment about the question. It was really the only valid question in their lives at the moment. What the hell were they going to do?

He closed his eyes as he pictured Coyote, sitting in some room nearby, straining to hear their words. A thin smile, one of anticipation, would slowly start to creep across his lips, never really forming until he heard what he wanted to. Coyote wanted to control, to form, to shape. Harden had documented so many moments in the rising of the Church of the Revelation that he understood not only what Coyote was capable of, but how much more he wanted. Harden's mistake was not realizing Coyote's thirst would ever apply to those closest to him, but here, in this room of dirt and spiders, Harden now understood it was precisely those closest to him Coyote most wanted to control.

Coyote thinks he understands everything, Harden thought. So the only hope of staying alive meant revealing to Coyote the things he didn't know.

Harden had no idea if what he was now thinking would free him or seal his fate, but it somehow felt right. He needed to poke a stick at the creature in the forest. The one hiding behind the tree with bared teeth. The one watching him all this time.

He opened his eyes and wiped away her words, then scribbled new ones. He could barely read them himself, and could only hope Emma understood.

She peered at the ground and squinted.

When she finished, she looked up and nodded, and in that

moment Harden knew she understood what he was going to do. Emma stood and walked toward the small desk.

"Harden," she said. Her voice was now at normal volume.

"Yes, Emma?"

"No matter what happens to us, I want you to know I will always love you."

The words stirred in him something he couldn't identify. He wasn't sure of the entire mix, but the ingredients of excitement and fear were certainly present.

"I know," he finally responded. "I love you, too, Emma."

It was only moments later that the light in the cell went out, and they came and took Emma away. In her place they left a fresh typewriter, the same style as the first, removing the one Harden had broken.

Harden wasted no time. The story had to continue, because it was the only hope they had.

The campus only showed struggling signs of life; between the bitter weather and the winter break, the snowy sidewalks crisscrossing the quad were cold and lonely, tread upon only occasionally by those who remained behind . . .

CHAPTER TWENTY-FOUR

The campus only showed struggling signs of life; between the bitter weather and the winter break, the snowy sidewalks crisscrossing the quad were cold and lonely, tread upon only occasionally by those who remained behind.

I was no longer on break. I had no school to return to for another ten days, but Coyote was intent on spending our time before classes formulating his plan. His plan to become God.

I didn't completely understand how serious he was until our second night back. Over Italian takeout in the apartment, Coyote said, "It's going to be called the Revelation."

"What is?"

"You know what I'm talking about."

"Your plan?"

"*Our* plan."

"You really want to do this?"

He ignored my question. "No fancy name. Nothing tricky or cute. The title of your story captured it perfectly. Just enough to connote something religious, but nothing in the name should give away what the Revelation is all about."

I bit into a warm breadstick soaked in garlic butter. "And what exactly is this Revelation going to be about?"

"It has no meaning."

"I don't understand."

"That's the whole point—the meaninglessness of it all. It's where you left off in your story."

"I didn't say religion was meaningless."

"*You* argued the difficulties of starting a new religion in modern time. You didn't consider the message, but I say the message isn't important. It's the sense of belonging that drives people to faith. The sense of wanting to believe in something they can't control, which, ironically, is what people need to feel in control. Religion isn't about salvation or enlightenment. It's just about getting the word out."

"But there has to be a word. There has to be something."

"It doesn't matter."

"It *does* matter," I said. "How can the message not matter?"

"Look at Scientology," he countered. "The foundation of the religion is science fiction. Their belief system revolves around a person's *thetan* regaining a state of total freedom. I mean, what does that even mean? It's completely nebulous, but they've ironed it out into a full-blown religion with tens of thousands of members, many of whom are hard-core devotees willing to spend their life savings—or even die—for their belief system."

"What's the point?" I asked. "Why do you really want to do this?"

Coyote plunged a fork into a Styrofoam container of pasta. "To see if I can do it."

"That's it?"

"That's it."

I hadn't forgotten that Coyote was a murderer, or so he had confessed to us. When he smashed in the head of a boy in the woods, he held all the control in that moment. He could decide whether the boy lived or died, and he chose death. What reflection is it on me that, even after all I learned about Coyote, I still wanted to be close to him?

His eyes narrowed in the slightest. "I want to see what it takes for someone to follow someone else. I want to see what kind of people will follow me. Do whatever I ask of them."

"What are you going to ask them to do?" I almost feared the answer, and was a bit relieved when he didn't have one.

"I'm not sure." Though I suspected he was sure, but not yet willing to share.

"And what's your goal?" I asked as I poured some wine into one of the crystal glasses Coyote had contributed to the apartment. Without those, I'd be drinking from either a Solo cup or a Steelers coffee mug. "I mean, how will you know if you've succeeded?"

There was no hesitation. "A thousand members."

"Are you serious? You think you can just make up a religion and get a thousand students to buy into it?"

"No. Not just students. It has to spread, even if just a little. It has to multiply like a virus. We'll have meetings, post flyers, make phone calls, even go door to door if we have to. If I can get a thousand members, I'll know my experiment worked."

"And how will you define a member? If you make them give you money, wouldn't that be fraud or something? You're basically presenting yourself as a faith healer."

"No," he said. "No money. Nothing like that, though I imagine donations will be important at some point. I was thinking a member will be someone who takes an oath. An oath of allegiance."

"Allegiance to what?" As soon as the words left my mouth, I knew the question should have been phrased *allegiance to whom*.

Coyote didn't answer. Instead, he pointed his fork at me. "I want you completely involved. You will be the secretary of the Revelation, and I want you to document every step of the process. I want you to write down everything we do, and help establish the Rules."

"The Rules?"

"We need a gospel. Something that outlines what the Revelation is all about. It needs to be beautifully vague, with just enough words of inspiration to make people think all of it means something. Like I said, it doesn't have to really be about anything, but it's meaninglessness has to be well stated. Like a politician's speech."

"You want me to write a catechism," I said.

He looked at me, as if surprised I knew what that even was. "Yeah, something like that."

"Then you don't want me to be a secretary," I added. "You want me to be an apostle."

"I like the sound of that."

"I know you do."

He looked at me with a slight twinge of threat, as if I looked deeper inside him than was permitted. "What does that mean?" he asked.

I took a large enough sip of the Chianti for it to be a gulp, then choked it down. "This is crazy. You drove all the way to Pennsylvania to bring me back here. At first, I thought you were just bored and wanted some company. Now you're sinking all your energy into this idea that . . . I mean, shit, Coyote. It was just a story I wrote. An idea. A random thought that I wanted to squeeze a few thousand words from."

"Sounds like the way most really good ideas start," he said.

"Maybe," I said. "But I can't tell how serious you are about this."

"I'm completely serious. I fully intend to do this."

"But . . . but if you really want to do what you're talking about, it's going to take a lot of your time."

"I realize that."

"You'll probably have to sacrifice school time to do it. I mean, Christ, a *thousand* members?"

Coyote nodded. "A thousand."

"And what if you can't get your schoolwork done?"

"That's a worthy sacrifice."

"It is?" I had lost my appetite at this point. "I mean, is this all just an ego thing?"

"Yes," he said. "That's a part of it. There's a part of me that wants to see how far I can take this. A part that wants others to follow in a path I've laid out for them." He gave a small smile, the kind usually meant to hide something else. "I want to see if I can get others to do what I want."

"Like me being your secretary?"

"I was hoping you would want to do that. You should be involved. It's your idea, after all."

"But you don't want *me* to be the Messiah."

"I won't be the Messiah. Just a salesman." Coyote had also stopped eating. "You will be the secretary. But I need someone else who can play the role of convert number one. Someone who can be the test subject, because my word won't be enough. It's like those commercials telling you how to make all kinds of money working out of your own home. They need to show you the actors claiming to make twenty grand a month."

I considered this. "Emma?" I hoped he would say no, because I didn't want to see her involved in this. I didn't want to see her as one of Coyote's apostles.

He dismissed the idea almost immediately. "I don't know if she would want to be involved. She's not always so . . . supportive of my ideas."

I wondered what that meant.

"You have someone in mind?" I asked.

"Yes. Of course I do."

"Who?"

Now he gave me a genuine smile. "Someone who has a huge sense of adventure with little regard to consequence."

"Shit, Coyote. You just described yourself."

He shook his head. "Not as smart."

I looked at my half-eaten food and conjured names in my head. It only took a few seconds before I realized about whom he was speaking. I looked up.

"Jacob."

CHAPTER TWENTY-FIVE

Harden didn't know how much time had passed since Emma had been taken from the cell. If he had to guess—which was all he could do—he would say two weeks. He could only base that on his writing.

The words on the paper were the metronome of Harden's existence. He clicked and clacked, and with the mechanics of a decades-old machine and a fading ribbon the letters were born on the crisp white pages. They were reliable. They always came. There was no writer's block in the cell. There were only thoughts, fears, and the punching of ink-laden metal on paper.

A couple thousand words a day, Harden figured. Not a lot, but they were solid. Vibrant. They told the story he was expected to tell. He fed the pages to Baby Face every day, making sure they were as clean as his conditions would allow.

Harden thought it important the reader had little difficulty with his prose.

As he sat on his only chair, he closed his eyes, just for a moment. Watching the swift and flickering sidesteps of imaginary monsters along the inside of his eyelids, he searched for what would come next. There was little left to say, but a well of words awaited him to reach down and scoop them up. He dipped, then pulled. Dipped, then pulled. And then he had them.

Harden opened his eyes and resumed typing. As the words flowed slowly but with ease, he thought that it didn't seem so cold in the cell that day.

CHAPTER TWENTY-SIX

The idea of taping Coyote was an easy one. Innocent, even. He wanted me to record everything that happened so we could eventually shape all of his words in The Book, whatever the hell that was going to be.

I bought a Sony Walkman, a small microphone, and a stack of blank cassettes at the campus store. I thought about making Coyote pay for it—he wouldn't have objected in the least to the request since I could tell him I was doing this all as part of my secretarial duties. Then I decided I didn't want him to know I was taping our conversations. I didn't want him biased. I wanted Coyote to be Coyote, inasmuch as he ever was around other people. Truth be told, I'd rather have a machine that recorded thoughts, but even if such a device existed, I'd probably be too scared to use it with Coyote for fear of what I might uncover. The Walkman was fairly small but not invisible, so I would have to use it with caution if I wanted it to remain a secret.

It was late on a cold and still January night that I almost recorded one of the turning points of my life. Funny how the word "almost" seems to spring up on me like that. I'm an "almost" kind of guy, and I think that's one of my biggest flaws. Coyote was never an "almost" guy. Coyote always just *did*. I always almost did.

That night, I was alone in my apartment, Coyote being out some-where unknown by me, and my other roommates a few days shy of returning for the spring semester. A lonely night. I had the energy to do a lot of things, but my mind kept drifting toward nothingness. I hacked away at my computer for a while, trying to establish my secretarial duties for the Revelation. To me, it was still just a joke, and my efforts to help Coyote organize it were halfhearted.

As I floundered over the words on the screen, I had a sudden urge to crack open the front door of my apartment. Most of the other students were not yet back from break, and leaving the door slightly open might let anyone around know that I was here and bored out of my skull. Opening the door, I figured, might actually summon a friend. It sounds stupid, I know. But sometimes those things work out for me.

That night, it did.

I soon tired of my writing and played a little with my new re-corder, testing the sound quality from different distances. It picked things up pretty well, I discovered. The moment I heard the knock-ing at the door and single word "Hello?" echoing throughout the apartment, I turned the recorder off.

I wonder if I would have listened to that tape if I had kept the machine running that night.

CHAPTER TWENTY-SEVEN

"Emma."

I said her name the way I always heard it in my head when I thought of her. I wondered if she could sense the change.

"Hey, Harden."

She stood in the open doorway but asked me permission to come in. It was possibly the silliest request I had ever heard. I told her to please come in.

I had almost forgotten that, like me, she had returned to campus well before classes began. I wondered why she was here, but I didn't fret about it. Looking for Coyote, probably.

"He's not here," I said.

"I know. I was with him for a while, and then he . . . he went out."

"By himself?"

She shook her head, and the way her hair jostled gave her a devastating sexiness.

"I don't know. He just didn't seem to want to be with me anymore." The words floated at me laced with melancholy. "He's obsessed with this religion thing," she said. I realized I had only seen her once since I had been back, and I hadn't really considered that Coyote would have told her of his plan.

"I know," I said. "It's all my fault, too. I wrote that stupid story."

"If it wasn't this, it would certainly be something else." She walked to the center of the small living room before turning around. "It's all he's been talking about since he's been back."

I shut the door, happy I'd cracked it open, and kind of amazed leaving it ajar actually seemed to work. But now I didn't want anyone else coming over. I wasn't sure what to say next, so I offered Emma a drink. She asked for a beer, but we didn't have any, so I opened Coyote's bottle of Merlot. I decided to join her, and we sat on the couch together as we slowly sipped our wine. There were three cushions on the couch, but the unoccupied one wasn't between us.

"This isn't just some kind of stupid prank, you know." Her cheeks were still flushed from the cold outside. "He's been writing down a whole business plan for this thing. How he's going to do it, who he's going to target. Jacob is going to be his first convert. The one who's supposed to show what happens when enlightenment occurs."

"It's a good choice," I said. "If Jacob can suddenly demonstrate any kind of humanity or intelligence, a lot of people would start believing in miracles."

She laughed feebly before lapsing into silence for some time, lost in thought. When she spoke again, her voice was hardly above a whisper.

"I'm lonely."

Such a simple phrase. But goddamn, did my head start spinning from it.

She turned to me.

"I think I've been playing a role ever since I started dating Coyote. I don't love him. I never have. I've never been myself with him."

"I think Coyote likes to have his friends be exactly as he wants them to be," I said.

She nodded. "For some reason I can't bring myself to break up with him. Not yet, at least. And I think he knows that."

Her words dug at me. "You can do anything you want to."

"With him, that doesn't seem to be true." She took another sip of wine. "Do you really want to be a part of what he's going to do?"

"I don't really have anything better to do."

"That's not a good answer. You're in your final semester of college." She circled the rim of the wine glass with her finger. "I think . . . I think you're scared not to."

"Scared of what?"

"We're all this way with him. I think we're partly scared of missing out, and partly scared of angering him."

I wanted to tell her it wasn't true but I couldn't. It made me feel weak, but at least I now knew I wasn't alone. I *was* scared of Coyote. Yes, some of it was that I was afraid to miss out on what happened in his life; I was, honestly, infatuated with him. Life was more interesting when he was around. Yet I couldn't deny that the idea of defying him gave me serious pause.

"Why did you come here, Emma?"

She turned to me once more, but didn't answer. She tilted her wine glass toward mine and tapped the edges together. The soft chime floated through the room.

"I'm lonely, too," I said. I didn't care how the words sounded. I wanted her to know how I felt, and I think this was the most I could confess, though it was only a fraction of what I wanted to say.

There was a sudden current in the room, and I could feel my hand starting to moisten around the glass it held. Emma put her fingertips on my forearm and started brushing back and forth along my skin. A casual touch, yet electrifying. The heat from her seemed to spread through my entire body. I wasn't sure if her signs of affection were meant the way I wanted them to be, but I was edging at the point of caring. I just wanted her to keep touching me.

I reached out and put my hand on top of hers, stopping it. I didn't mean it as a sign for her to stop what she was doing; I just needed to touch her hand.

She looked at me, and all I could see was vulnerability.

I was looking in a mirror.

In that second I knew what she wanted. It was what I wanted. But I didn't know what things she was wrestling with inside, and I was afraid to ask. Too nervous to even move, as if it would disrupt the moment. There was only one thing I could think of to say.

"Coyote's a good guy."

She stared at me for what seemed minutes, though only seconds passed. Finally, she squeezed my hand and leaned into me.

"No, he's not."

Those three words released us. She closed her eyes as I leaned in to kiss her, and as our lips touched, I thought there was nothing in my twenty years that had ever tasted so good.

CHAPTER TWENTY-EIGHT

It's been so long.

Harden looked up from his typewriter and moved his head slowly back and forth, feeling the muscles seize in his neck. Everything was sore, yet real pain remained suppressed only because fatigue overwhelmed it. Every movement was a chore, and he could only type for a few minutes at a time before he needed to lie on the floor again. Yet true rest never seemed to come; only a momentary shift of his discomfort to other parts of his body gave him the illusion of peace.

He went to the floor now and stretched along the cold, hard dirt. On his back with his eyes closed, Harden put his hand up his filthy shirt and gently stroked his fingertips along his stomach. It had stopped growling weeks ago. He felt along his ribs, over bony ridges he hadn't been able to see since he was a skinny kid. It wasn't that they weren't feeding him, but the food simply wasn't enough.

He was slowly dying.

Harden moved his hand to his face, feeling the weeks-old growth of his beard. He had once asked Baby Face for a razor, but the request was only met with a laugh. Now he was thankful for the hair, for it gave him a sense of warmth. He knew it was only a matter of time before some kind of illness took over his atrophied body.

When that happened, his captors would have to make a decision. Cure him or . . . not.

Which is why he had to type. Telling a story might not save him, but it was his only hope.

With effort, Harden pushed himself up against the desire to melt into nothingness and resumed his position in front of the typewriter. He tongued an old piece of gummed bread around inside his mouth and thought about what he was going to write next.

He noticed the dry, flaking skin on the backs of his hands as he began to type. He brushed off a piece of it, which floated onto the table, becoming, as did all things, just another piece of dust.

The night Emma came over was only the beginning of our relationship . . .

CHAPTER TWENTY-NINE

The night Emma came over was only the beginning of our relationship. We had kissed that night, nothing more. But that hadn't been the end of it. In the week since then, we had seen each other every day, even if just for a few minutes. The first day after, we approached each other with thick uncertainty, neither of us knowing how close to get. The day after, we kissed during a short walk by a frozen pond, the warmth of our lips in stark contrast to the bitterly cold tips of our noses.

"What are we doing?" she had asked.

I thought about that for a moment. "We're deciding what we want."

"So, it's just that easy?"

"Nothing easy about it at all."

She had looked at me, her glowing face bordered by a pink wool hat and the zipped-up top of her parka. "This isn't what I do. Jumping from guy to guy. It isn't me."

"That's good. And I'm not prone to stealing the girlfriends of others."

"You think you're stealing me?"

I shook my head. "No one possesses you, Emma."

"Damn straight."

"But that doesn't make what we're doing any less wrong."

That made her smile tighten and then eventually fade. "So what do you want?"

I only had the truth to offer her. "I want you to break up with Coyote."

She walked a few steps away from me, and her outline was crisp against the snow. She picked up a rock and threw it at the pond, where it bounced along the ice. "Let's take some more time to figure out what I want."

"So you might want him instead of me."

"No, Harden. I don't want Coyote anymore. I don't think I have for some time."

"But..."

She turned, her words steaming from her mouth. "But it seems more complicated than just leaving him. I know that sounds stupid, but that's how I feel. Let's just... take this slowly, okay?"

I took off one glove, walked up to her, and touched her cold, red cheek with the warm palm of my hand. "Whatever you want, Emma. I'm not going anywhere. Maybe..."

"Maybe what?"

"Maybe I could not go anywhere with you for a little bit more."

She reached up and gave me another kiss, and for the moment, I was quite content being a dope.

After that, our conversations grew deeper, along with our passion. We never met at my place or hers, for fear of Coyote showing up unexpectedly. Our radius was limited—neither of us had a car—so we usually met somewhere on campus. On the fifth day we took an innocent walk through the East Quad. Despite the cold, we kept the most casual of paces, as if we were soaking in the sun of a mild summer day. I had been tempted to hold her hand but resisted the urge, unsure if our paths would cross with someone we knew. I wondered if we were walking closer to each other than we would have been a week earlier, or if anything about how we interacted with each other gave off some kind of sign as to what was happening between us. As I considered this, a burst of snowfall surprised us. The flakes were large and heavy, sucking from the area all sound. The silence overwhelmed me, and I felt for a moment a figurine inside a snow globe. I didn't want the moment to end with the inevitability of the flakes in a globe settling to the bottom.

"Follow me," Emma said, not knowing such words were unnecessary. She veered toward the music building and walked down a small flight of steps to a side entrance. Rather than going inside the building, she stopped and pulled me into her. A small metal roof protected us from the snow.

She kissed me first. I returned in kind, allowing myself to melt into her. God, she tasted good. I could stay there forever.

She grabbed onto my parka with gloved fists and pulled me close again. "Don't be infatuated with me, Harden. That doesn't do me any good. I don't want to do this if infatuation is the only reason you're with me."

I wondered where this came from, but I was also very focused on the fact she said *with me*. "I was infatuated with you the moment we met," I said. "That infatuation passed a long time ago. I'm way beyond it."

"I'm not asking you to love me. I just need you to be real, okay?"

"Do I seem anything else to you?"

She shook her head. "No, you don't."

I took her hands from my chest and held them in my own. I wished we didn't have gloves on. "What I feel is beyond infatuation. Coyote is my friend, and I wouldn't be doing this unless I really thought we had something . . . I don't know. Something special." I squinted my eyes in mock pain. "God, that sounded lame."

"Yeah, pretty sappy." She reached up and kissed the tip of my nose. "But it was nice."

"Thank you."

"But you're risking more than your friendship with him."

"What do you mean?"

She squeezed my fingers. "We're both risking more than our relationship with him. He . . . I don't know what he would do if he found out. We both know he's capable of pretty bad things."

She was referring to the redheaded boy in the woods. "He was just a kid then. It was self-defense."

"I think it's still in him."

"You think he could become violent?"

She stared at me for a moment before pulling me in. She kissed me, and either her lips or the cold made me dizzy. Maybe both. After she pulled back, she turned to walk back up the snowy steps.

"I just think we need to be prepared for what could happen if Coyote gets angry." She got up half the steps before she appended her thought.

"Really angry."

CHAPTER THIRTY

Back in the apartment, I slipped a Depeche Mode CD into my player and turned it up. I sat in my room and listened for a while, soaking in the dark melodies. Then, seeking company, I moved to the living room couch and picked up Jacob's *Sports Illustrated*, which showcased Jerry Rice on the cover.

Coyote sat at the kitchen table and poured over a stack of religious studies textbooks. As I stared at him, the music from my room bled into the rest of the apartment.

I think that God's got a sick sense of humor . . .

Jacob and Derek returned to campus within a day of each other. Derek came in the apartment with a bag and a smile. We gave each other a brief man-hug, but he only offered Coyote a vacant smile and a muttered *hey*. Coyote ignored him altogether, and I wondered what would happen to the relationship of these two as Coyote's experiment took shape. Would Derek have a role in it?

Jacob bounded in a day later like a Golden Retriever coming home from being boarded for a week. He was beautiful and stupid, and my urge to pet him was quelled only by my urge to slap him with a rolled newspaper. He gravitated to Coyote immediately upon returning, and Coyote greeted him with a wide smile and a hungry stare. He had plans for Jacob.

It was the night before classes resumed, and after an hour of doing little in the apartment except daydreaming about Emma and listening to Dave Gahan sing about pain, I suggested we all go to Benny's. I hadn't been there in nearly a month, though Benny's changed at the same rate as the Arctic ice shelf. They both were slowly but continually eroding into nothingness, and few seemed to care.

It was good to go back.

Jacob brought the pitchers to the table and asked Coyote a simple question that rattled me.

"Hey, how's Emma doing? When did she get back?"

Her face flooded into my mind. I hadn't thought of her in at least twenty minutes.

"She's been here almost a week. I've seen her a bit. Not a lot, though."

I busied myself pouring beer.

"You guys going to break up?" Derek asked.

"Why would you assume that?"

Derek shrugged. "Just asking. If I had a girlfriend, I'd be all over her as soon as I got back."

"Well, Derek, I suppose that's another difference between us."

Derek forced a laugh and shook his head slightly. "Yup, one of many differences, I suppose."

"Maybe you're interested in her. Is that why you want to know? You want to fuck her, Derek?"

Derek's smile evaporated. "Jesus, take it easy, Coyote. I was just asking."

Then Coyote looked at me over the top of his beer glass and continued his gaze until he set his glass down. There were only two words that were in my head, and they looped over and over in rhythm with my pounding heart.

He knows.

I forced other images into my mind, erasing Emma for fear I was projecting her face through my eyes. I thought of colors, deep ocean blue, lava red, canary yellow. Then yellow made me think of blond, and blond brought me quickly around to Emma's hair, and suddenly I was smelling it, breathing in the fresh scent of her shampoo. Goddamnit.

"What is it?" Coyote asked me.

"What is what?"

"You're staring at me."

"No, I'm not." I could feel myself starting to panic. "I'm just zoning out. I guess I'm tired."

Derek, sitting next to me in the booth, gave me a nudge. "Harden, school hasn't even started yet. What do you have to be tired about?"

I shrugged.

Jacob gulped his beer. "Why did you guys come back so early?"

Coyote shot me a look and a paper-thin smile.

I reached into my coat pocket and quietly turned on my Walkman recorder. It had started to become a habit.

"Harden and I have an idea," Coyote said. "We came back early to flesh everything out."

That was undue credit. Coyote had hardly spoken to me about the Revelation in the past week. That was okay by me. I had been too busy stealing small moments with Emma and dreaming about robbing a bank full of them.

"Flesh what out?" Derek asked.

"An experiment."

"What kind of experiment?"

Coyote pushed his beer glass forward an inch on the table. "The kind that could make us all famous."

We fell into silence as Coyote told Derek and Jacob about the Revelation. The idea was more real since our initial conversations. I was stunned at not only the attention to detail Coyote had afforded the whole scheme, but about the sudden sense of plausibility I had about it all.

Coyote stopped talking after twenty minutes. Derek was the first to speak when Coyote finally raised his beer glass to his lips.

"Are you fucking serious?"

Coyote turned to him. "Have you ever known me not to be?"

Jacob looked star-struck. "I think it sounds awesome."

"Thank you, Jacob. In fact, I have a special favor to ask you."

Before Jacob could inquire further, Derek interjected. "Are you doing this for any kind of course credit?"

"No."

"It's a huge investment of time. What about school?"

"I only need fourteen credits to graduate."

"People are going to think you're crazy."

"Some will, undoubtedly. Others, hopefully, will not. If I fail, then I fail. But I don't think I will."

"But your fake religion makes no sense."

"I don't know," I said, my first words of the conversation. All heads turned to me as I thought aloud about the basic tenets of Coyote's new religion. It was the first time Coyote had shared them with me.

"It's pretty basic," I said, thinking about Coyote's outline for a meaningless faith. "It speaks to the human need for belonging in the most abstract of terms. It involves faith, but it doesn't articulate exactly what the subject of the faith should be. It allows for forgiveness, yet requires obedience. It doesn't judge. It focuses on living in the moment." I felt like I was swimming in Coyote's mind as I considered all the loopholes he had filled. "It's the ideal belief system for the wayward college student. The agnostic masses who want to believe in something, but don't know what that thing is."

In that moment, I realized I had completely endorsed everything.

I was with Coyote, whatever that meant. Despite the man he was, and despite the fact that I was falling in love with his girlfriend, I was too compelled by Coyote's search for greatness to let it pass by me. Inside all of us is a need to be great, and maybe this was actually my chance. I mean, what if the Church of the Revelation actually worked, and I got to be a major part of it from the beginning?

"The Revelation?" Derek asked. "What does that even mean?"

"It means nothing," Coyote answered. "It's vague and has a Christian overtone to it, which is the predominant religion here. And it carries a slight ring of hope. It's the perfect name. It's all about marketing."

Derek shook his head. "Sounds like a self-help book."

Coyote nodded, and I saw his right fist clench and release. "With one difference."

"Which is?"

"The words of a book mean nothing when they're just ink on paper. It's the author you have to believe in, not the message. If the author of a message is believable, the message becomes irrelevant."

Derek squinted as the lights in the old bar struggled for life. "And you think you're believable?"

What happened next still seems only a blur to me, and the tape recording of it does it no justice.

First, Coyote fell silent.

I thought he simply chose to ignore Derek's question, but he didn't. He was preparing himself for the answer. He must have been planning this all along, but the moment was so spontaneous I felt something miraculous was truly happening.

Coyote shut his eyes, his lids squeezed tight in seemingly intense concentration. His hands balled into fists on top of the table. His mouth twitched just enough to make me realize he was murmuring something to himself.

"What the hell are you doing?" Derek asked. When he received no response, we all looked at each other.

"Coyote, you okay?" I reached out and touched his shoulder, but he didn't move. For a second I thought he was having some kind of spell, but his body was so still I couldn't imagine he wasn't in complete control of it.

Suddenly, Coyote's eyes shot open, but all they showed were the whites.

Then he let out a howl.

That's the only way I could think to describe it. He lifted his face toward the ceiling and howled to the heavens. It was primal, emanating from the depths of his gut and releasing with a shock wave through Benny's like a tsunami shattering a small coastal village.

The bar had only about thirty people in it, and all heads snapped in our direction. As Coyote's scream faded in the small room, the only noise remaining was a Zeppelin song trickling out of Benny's tinny wall speakers.

"Call nine-one-one," I said, or at least I thought I said it. I was so scared and confused I might have only thought it.

Before anyone could react, Coyote shot backwards in his chair. I never saw or even sensed his legs moving, and it looked like the chair simply yanked Coyote away from the table. He struggled to maintain his balance, and then he leapt from the chair and jumped on top of a vacant table by the bar's front windows.

Everyone stared at him.

No one spoke.

I heard Jacob say, "What the fuck is going on?"

Coyote—crouched on the table—slowly straightened like a werewolf blooming toward the full moon. His fingertips reached toward the dirty ceiling. Every muscle in his body seemed ready to explode. Then, staring up, Coyote spoke.

"*It is here.*" The voice wasn't his, or at least wasn't the voice I knew to be his. It was deeper. Primitive. He repeated his command, his words peppered out in short, staccato bursts.

"It . . . is . . . here!"

Derek grabbed my arm. "What the hell is he doing?"

"I have no idea," I said.

Jacob then turned to me. "*Help him.*"

"Jacob, what the fuck do you want me to do?"

A few other students shouted something, but I barely noticed. Everyone else was silent, fixed on the crazy man, wondering what he would do next.

The bartender shouted for Coyote to get the hell off the table.

Then something happened that I can't explain. Perhaps I never will, but I know that it did happen. Everyone saw it.

Coyote ripped his shirt open, exposing his naked flesh beneath. He took it off and discarded it to the floor, the sweat shimmering off his body. His muscles were flexed, and every detail of each of them seemed sculpted from a Renaissance artist. He appeared to me as someone I did not know. This was not my roommate. This was a man transformed. He looked both strong and vulnerable, weak and commanding.

He lifted his arms so they stuck straight out and slowly began opening and closing his hands in unison.

Opened and closed. Opened and closed.

His head fell forward and a thick strand of now-damp hair fell across his closed eyes. A long, viscous line of drool dangled from his lower lip. He was in some kind of trance.

Then Coyote levitated.

This I am not making up.

I don't know how he did it, but I will go to my grave swearing that both of his feet lifted a few inches off the top of that dirty bar table. It lasted only a few seconds, but everyone saw it. I know because I heard everyone gasp at the same time.

He levitated, and this parlor trick, more than anything else, solidified Coyote's future. And mine.

His feet crashed back to the table and Coyote collapsed with it, both man and wood crumbling to the floor in a heap. Coyote was a rag doll, his tightened muscles now appearing soft and weak as he laid in an inert mass on the floor. A woman screamed from the corner of the room. I tore my eyes off Coyote for only a second and saw half of the other patrons standing. The bartender seemed frozen in time, his mouth hanging slack-jawed.

No one knew what to do, least of all me. I felt panic rising within my chest. What had to be an elaborate beginning to Coyote's plan was both real and horrifying. Was he having a vision? Or was he truly just acting?

Coyote wiggled about on the floor before finally standing. No one made an effort to help him.

The lights in the bar flickered. I wasn't sure if they had been doing that all along.

I could see what looked like a trickle of blood running down Coyote's chest. Where his wound originated and what caused it I didn't know, but the effect was dramatic. Coyote was beaten, weak, and transformed.

Standing fully erect and his eyes set in a blazing stare, Coyote addressed the onlookers in a booming voice.

"I am ready to understand a new Revelation. None of you are ready, but I can make you so. I must choose."

Derek mumbled under his breath. "Oh my God, he's lost his fucking mind."

Like a dog sensing danger, Coyote flicked his gaze to our table and shot Derek a look that seemed more genuine than acted. He then turned his body and walked slowly to us as everyone else in the bar remained silent. I thought he was going to confront Derek. Derek must have, too, because he pushed his chair back and stood. Coyote walked up to him but quickly stepped around him, stopping instead in front of Jacob. Jacob hadn't moved since his original cry for help moments earlier, and he remained fixed in place as Coyote walked up to him and stood within inches of his face.

I looked at the two of them and couldn't help but feel I was watching a movie. In life, real life, we are so unaccustomed to witnessing the unexpected that when it comes, it transports us to another plane of thinking. It makes us feel special. It makes us want to sustain our feelings of fluttering importance by telling others what we saw, how we reacted, and, as is often the case, what we would have done had we more time to react.

It occurred to me in that split second this was exactly what Coyote was doing. He was giving everyone in this bar a story to tell. This was how he was planting the seed. He was doing something unexpected, and that was probably going to be enough to get something to grow.

Coyote lifted his hands and dipped each of his thumbs into the blood on his chest. Jacob didn't move as Coyote held each side of Jacob's face and smeared a line of blood on each corner of Jacob's mouth.

"You will be the first to hear my message," Coyote proclaimed. "Come with me, and you will learn. Then you will choose others to hear, and they will tell others still." Coyote held out his right hand and offered it to Jacob, who grasped it. "But you will be the first."

Before any of us could react to anything that was going on, a shirtless Coyote and a stunned Jacob left the bar and went into the cold, dark night.

No one saw either of them for ten days.

CHAPTER THIRTY-ONE

Harden woke and smelled urine. The bucket hadn't been collected for the past three meals.

He stretched and rubbed his eyes, hoping to see something different than he always did. He didn't. He sat up and wiped dirt off his face.

It was cold today.

He thought about Emma. He didn't know why they'd taken her back, or what they had done with her. Or why they had allowed them to be together in the first place.

Another game, Harden thought.

He looked around his coffin and practiced not feeling. If he thought too much, he could feel the hopelessness in the hard dirt and concrete walls. If he thought too much, he only felt death.

He missed his father fiercely, in a way he never thought possible. His father's cold and unfeeling exterior was a tropical haven compared to this place. He hated thinking that his father was out there desperate to find his son. Worse, he hated to think his father had no idea Harden was even missing.

He pushed these ideas away and focused on his writing. That was it. Of the little he had, he still had the ability to tell a story, so he clung to it as fiercely as he could.

Harden moved to the typewriter. His joints ached and his stomach growled.

The page was only half filled. He had so much more to say.

He knew where he wanted to resume. It was a good part. He was actually looking forward to writing it, as much as he was able to look forward to anything anymore.

The door opened. Harden turned.

Baby Face stood in the doorway. Harden instinctively began to move to the corner, but something happened. Or, more accurately, something didn't happen.

Baby Face didn't ask him to move. Instead, he said something he had never said to Harden before.

"I want to talk."

CHAPTER THIRTY-TWO

Harden said nothing, and instead, sat back in the chair and lightly gripped its arms. He imagined Baby Face suddenly charging him, and Harden would have to use the chair to fend him off, like a lion tamer. But after a few seconds he realized there was no sudden *anything* about Baby Face. The man wavered ever so slightly back and forth, as if standing on a large beanbag, trying to keep his balance.

His voice was deep, slow, and lazy. "Don't you want to talk to someone, Harden? Gotta be bored by now."

Harden wished he could see the man's face. He'd only seen two Baby Faces since he'd been in the cell. He thought this was the one he'd hit with the typewriter—the slightly larger one—but he couldn't be sure. He wanted to see his eyes, to see if he was what Harden suspected he might be, which was drunk.

A drunk Baby Face could present an opportunity. Also, a drunk Baby Face might turn into something terrifying.

Be careful.

"Your job," Harden said. "Do you enjoy it?"

Baby Face took a step inside the cell and closed the door. Harden didn't hear it lock from the outside.

"I'm not ready to answer your questions yet." A step closer.

"But you're the one who wanted to talk."

"Oh, you'll ask me questions." *Ask* came out as *ashhsk*, and Harden knew he was either drunk or high. "But there are rules involved."

Harden squeezed a little tighter on the top of the chair. "What are the rules?"

Baby Face reached into his back pocket and pulled something from it. It took Harden a moment to see it in the dim light, but once he did, he knew with no uncertainty exactly what it was. It was a surgical blade.

Harden stood and placed the chair in front of him.

"Take it easy," Harden said.

Baby Face held the blade loosely at his side, making no effort to threaten with it. But he didn't need to. He was holding a fucking razor, after all. Bolt cutters for Emma, razors for Harden. And Derek. Derek had been sliced all over, hadn't he been? Maybe with the very same piece of steel on which Harden was now transfixed. This place wasn't a prison anymore. It was a slaughterhouse.

"What do you want more than anything, Harden?"

"To get out of here."

Baby Face shook his head. "Yeah, that ain't gonna happen. Least I can't make that call. So, aside from that . . . what do you want?"

"Answers."

"*Exactly.*"

If he's drunk, he'll be slow, Harden thought. *But don't underestimate him.*

"Kind of hard to carry on a conversation when you're wearing that mask."

Baby Face tilted his head, and just that slight twist behind the smooth, expressionless mask chilled Harden.

"I can take it off."

"Yes," Harden said. "Please."

Baby Face reached up with his free hand and pushed the mask to the top of his head, and for the first time Harden saw his captor's face. He was young, maybe even as young as Harden, but wrinkled layers of fat around the man's small, dark eyes gave him somewhat of an ageless look. Buzzed hair, clean shaven, pasty skin, and a rubbery purple welt from where the typewriter had hit him.

Harden had always figured him at north of two hundred and fifty pounds.

"That's what you did." Baby Face pointed to the welt. "Have to say, I was impressed. Didn't think you'd have the strength. You got me in some trouble, you did."

"Good."

"Not too easy to find typewriters like that and get 'em quick. Big pain in my ass."

So that's it, Harden thought. *He's come here for some payback.*

"What do you want?"

"We're going to have a little chat, Harden. Little *dialogue*."

"About what?"

Baby Face scrunched up his nose, and the words slurred out of him. "Well, I guess that isn't exactly the right way of putting it. I'm going to let you ask me some questions. I'll give you straight-up answers and everything. Scout's honor."

"I doubt you were ever a Boy Scout."

A drunken laugh. "But the catch is, Harden, for every answer I give you." Now he brought the blade up to eye level. "I get a little taste."

The word *taste* brought bile into Harden's throat, and he had to fight off the image of Mr. Kildare and the storage closet.

This will just be our secret, okay, Harden?

Five feet separated the back of Baby Face and the unlocked door, but it felt a mile away.

"What do you mean?"

Baby Face turned the razor over in his hand. "Is that your first question?"

"No, no. I just . . ." He didn't know how to stall, how to tell this sadistic psychopath to stay away from him. Moreover, he didn't want to provoke him. At least not yet. "I suppose I don't have much of a choice."

"We always have choices, Harden."

"What happens if I don't want to play your game?"

"That's question one, and the answer is I hurt you badly. Now get over here."

"That wasn't my question," Harden said.

"You're not the one holding a razor."

Harden took a step back toward the wall. *Think, Harden. You might be weaker than him, but* goddamnit *you have to be smarter.*

"It's not fair," Harden said.

"What's not fair?"

"I want three questions at a time, not just one."

"That so?"

"It's the least you can do."

Baby Face mulled this proposition.

"Fine," he said. "Is that it?"

"No," Harden continued. *Make him human,* he thought. Make a connection. "I want to know your name. Your real name."

"Why?"

"You know mine. Seems fair enough I should know yours."

"You sure do care about things being fair."

"I'm not asking for much."

A small grunt. Almost a laugh, but not quite. "No, I don't guess you are. But maybe I'll just cut you up anyway."

Harden had thought about death a lot since being down here and had even gotten to the point where the idea of being dead sometimes lured him, promising him a warm blanket and an end to his suffering. But the idea of *dying* still terrified him. The process of death. The blade cutting to the bone. The unbearable pain.

"I don't think that would be as satisfying for you," Harden said. "You like games. Okay, let's play games."

Baby Face grunted then cleared his throat, bringing up something horrible into his mouth. He spat it into the dirt.

"Bill," the man said.

"*Bill?*"

This fucking demon's name was *Bill*?

"Yeah. Bill. And that was your second question."

"It *wasn't* a question."

"Your voice sing-songed when you said my name, as if you didn't believe me. That's a question in my book."

"Fuck you."

"You got one more question in this round, Harden. Make it a good one."

Harden took a moment, feeling the walls close in on him. He had about a hundred questions he could think of. Where was he? Were people looking for him? Was Emma still alive? Are they ever going to release them? Harden didn't know which one to ask, or if Bill would even answer truthfully. Or if it even mattered. Harden had the sense he could ask Bill his favorite color and Harden would still end up sliced into pieces, his blood turning the floor into mud puddles.

"Starting to lose my patience, Harden."

"How do I get out of here?"

Bill smiled, then pointed the blade at the door behind him. "Through that door, down the hallway through another door, and up a flight of stairs. There's another door at the top. Go into the room inside, and then it will be very clear to you where the exit is. It's a beautiful day today, too. The fresh air would probably taste like birthday cake to you."

Harden considered the answer, and for a fraction of a second it actually sounded to him like an invitation to leave. Then he realized that his confinement had slowed him mentally. Bill was being literal. Harden wasn't going anywhere, and he just wasted a question.

"Now that's three questions," Bill said. He held up his hand and gestured for Harden to come closer. "Give me your hand."

"What are you going to do?" Harden cringed as he realized he'd asked another question, but Bill didn't seem inclined to debit him this time.

"Cut you. Just a little. Now get over here, or it'll be worse than it needs to be."

Harden looked at Bill, and a sense of peace suddenly washed over him. He would be cut, but Bill didn't seem to want to do anything else to him. At least not anything like he'd been through as a little boy. And if he trusted that Bill's cut wouldn't be bad, Harden would at least get three more questions. Three more questions meant three more answers.

Harden took a step forward, not thinking there was any other choice.

Bill gestured like a shopping mall Santa coaxing a wary toddler. "Little closer now. It's okay."

Harden sucked in a deep breath and took another step. They were close now. Harden could hear a faint wheeze coming through Bill's nose, the distant sound of a rocking chair squeaking in an empty room.

"Give me your right hand."

Harden's arm felt like lead, but he managed to raise it enough to let Bill grasp his hand.

Bill turned it over and studied his knuckles carefully.

"Make it fast."

Bill didn't look up. "Sure thing, boss."

Before Harden could brace himself, the knife flashed, and Harden saw the blade slice across the back of his hand. His flesh zippered open over the ridges of a thousand tiny bones.

Harden screamed and yanked his hand back, then squeezed it with his other hand, trying to apply pressure. He could feel the blood spilling over his fingers, but when he allowed himself to finally look at the wound, it wasn't quite as bad as he'd feared. The cut was maybe two inches long, but it would need stitches. He backed up out of arm's reach.

"See now, Harden? That wasn't too bad, was it?"

Harden resisted the urge to vomit, spitting once on the ground instead. "Why would you want to do that?"

"That your next question?"

Harden shook his head.

"Three more, then," Bill said, his voice calm but far from soothing. He seemed less drunk than before, but maybe that was just because of the suddenness of his brutality.

Harden considered his questions carefully. He knew his questions had to be tactical and unemotional. If he could figure out how to get out of the cell, he could answer most of his own damn questions. He tried not to think of the blood, which was the warmest thing he'd felt since holding Emma.

"Are you alone here, Bill?"

"That's a good one." He switched the knife to his left hand and used his forearm to wipe his nose. "For the moment I am. There're two of us. My partner went out for supplies."

No one else here, Harden thought. Could that really be the truth?

Harden repositioned his footing.

When would the partner be coming back? Was Coyote anywhere nearby? Were they near the campus?

Too many questions, and Harden only had two left before the next slice.

"What would I have to do to get you to let me go?"

This time Bill actually smiled, but there was no humor or warmth in it. Only teeth.

"Got a million bucks?"

"Fuck you. You're not answering my question."

"I certainly am. I would absolutely let you go for a million dollars. Tell you what—I'd even go half that. But short of that, it's not happening. Not worth the risk. How is that not answering you?"

Outwitting Bill wasn't going to work, not because Bill was the smarter man in the room, but because he was the crazier.

"You got one more question. Ask away."

"I'm not sure I want any more answers."

"Oh, come on now," Bill said. "We're just getting started here."

"How long are we going to play?"

"Is that your last question?"

"No. Let me think." Harden tried to make a fist with his right hand and it only brought fresh pain. His skin was sticky slick with blood, and he knew his already weakened state left him susceptible to a wound infection. He had to get out of here. He couldn't get cut again. He couldn't live like this any longer.

The faint sound of Bill's wheezing was the only sound in the room before Harden asked his final question.

"Am I going to die in here?"

Bill chewed on the question for an excruciatingly long time before answering. "Be honest with you, Harden, I don't have a clue what the big man wants to happen to you. He certainly hasn't told us to kill you." He lowered his head but kept his eyes on Harden, and his mouth turned into a crooked wedge. "But he hasn't told me to keep you alive, neither."

"He wants to read what I write, doesn't he?"

"No more questions. My turn now."

Harden took another step back.

Bill furrowed his brow as his gaze burrowed into Harden's torso. "Well, now, I don't want to cut too deep, lest I get into trouble, but it's got to be deeper than the first one. Don't worry, I'll clean you up after. Got some gauze left over that I used on the bitch's stump."

He was the one who used the bolt cutters on Emma. Harden imagined her screaming. The horror in her eyes as she felt the dull metal blades crunch through the bones of her finger. Harden squeezed his left hand into a fist, wanting nothing more than to take the scalpel from him and slice through Bill's eyes with it.

Stay calm. Don't be a threat until you have a real chance.

"Tell me what you're going to do," Harden said.

Bill nodded at Harden's torso. "I'm thinking the belly this time. You lift your shirt and I go in."

"You are a sick bastard."

Bill nodded. "S'pose I could see how you might feel that way."

Bill walked up to Harden. Harden tried to stand his ground but felt his legs retreating. He looked down at his right hand. It was still bleeding, but the flow had lessened.

"Don't you flinch now, hear me? You don't want it worse than it needs to be."

The stench of the man hit Harden. The smell of charred meat in his clothes.

Bill grunted and gestured with the blade. "Lift that shirt."

Nausea roiled Harden. How could he just lift his shirt and allow this animal to slice his stomach? If at least he had some fat to protect him, but he was as lean as a greyhound.

"I don't think I can—"

Bill's eyes morphed into tight slits. "*Goddamnit.* Lift your shirt or I'll go back for a visit with your little girl. Is that what you want?"

"Don't you touch her."

"Touch her? Hell, I ripped her finger out already. That's just the smallest piece of her pie I could take."

Harden resisted the urge to lunge. *Breathe*, he told himself. *Relax. Don't let him be in any more control than he already is. Bill is vulnerable, exactly because he doesn't think he is. You hurt him once, and now he's drunk. He can't even stand straight. Use this opportunity, but don't let him make you mad.*

Harden slowly lifted his shirt. His shrunken, tight belly recoiled even more at the chill of the room. His skin was an almost translucent white. The underbelly of a fish.

"Mmm . . . there we go." Bill leaned over and studied Harden's stomach. Harden could feel Bill's hot breath on his skin.

Without any further warning, Bill raised his hand and flicked his wrist, slicing the top end of the blade along Harden's abdomen. It was done so expertly Harden's first thought was Bill couldn't possibly be drunk, or that it even happened. First, a cold, stinging sensation along his skin, like someone swiped a sharp piece of ice against him. Then incredible, oozing warmth.

Harden looked down. This cut was longer than the one on his hand. The edges of the open wound pushed upwards like dirt heaved by worms. Blood spilled.

A lot of it.

"Oh my God . . . oh my fucking God."

"Yeah, boy. Look at that go."

Don't panic, Harden. It probably looks worse than it is.

Harden grabbed his stomach and blood poured through his fingers. It was so red. The cut was much deeper than he expected.

Bill started mumbling on about something, almost chant-like. Harden tried not to listen. Something about the blood.

Harden felt himself starting to wretch and then sharp pain shot through his belly. If he threw up, his intestines might spill from him.

He fought back the bile.

Bill leaned in toward Harden. Harden feared the knife again, but the man only spoke. His words were whispered through thin lips.

"*Three more questions, Harden.*"

Harden steadied himself.

The blood kept coming.

Through the thoughts of blood and death, Harden realized something: Bill no longer stood between Harden and the door.

I'll never make it.

The door was unlocked. He *knew* it was unlocked.

And Bill's partner was gone.

"*Three more—*"

Harden charged directly into the man's stomach.

It was the second time Harden had attacked him. No matter the outcome, Harden knew it would be the last. This was his only hope.

He had just enough mass and strength to make Bill take a few steps back, but his efforts didn't come close to taking the man out. Instead, Bill bear-hugged him and Harden waited for the knife to slice through him.

Then Bill surprised him. He pushed Harden away.

Harden now stood closest to the door, but he didn't think he could get out before Bill took him down.

Then another surprise.

Bill threw his blade to the floor, where it landed just inches from Harden's feet.

"Pick it up," Bill commanded.

Harden didn't hesitate. He reached down and seized the scalpel, feeling a fresh burst of pain as his stomach contracted.

Harden took a step backwards toward the door, facing Bill. The blade quivered in his outstretched right hand.

"Now things are getting fun," Bill said.

Harden took another step backwards. He was close enough to touch the door, if he dared turn his back on Bill.

"You're so close, man. All you have to do is leave. The door is right behind you. Freedom is just upstairs. It would be so easy—you're the one with the knife, not me. So I'll give you a choice, because, like I said, we all have choices to make. You can either try to make it out of here by being faster and stronger than me, or you can put the knife down and we'll get back to our game."

"Seems like an easy choice," Harden said. The blade felt solid in his hand.

"But here's the rub," Bill said, grinning. "My game will hurt you, but it won't kill you. On the other hand, if you choose to run and I catch you, I'll slice a hundred pieces of skin off you before cutting off your nose and ears. That probably won't kill you either, but you'll wish it would."

"If Coyote wanted me dead, I'd be dead. So I'm guessing if you do that to me, you might be the next one to end up here. And you're too stupid to write your way out."

Bill beamed a big, crooked-toothed smile at this and took a small step forward.

Blood continued to run.

Freedom was *so* close, and the adrenaline in Harden convinced him he would make it. He *could* be faster. He *could* be stronger. All Harden had to do was lock Bill inside. Then get Emma. Then get the fuck out of wherever this place was.

Now is the time, he thought. *It has to be now. I might not make it, but it could be my last chance.*

"I'm leaving," Harden said. "I will use this knife if you try to stop me."

Bill didn't come for him. In fact, he offered a meager shrug and actually took a few steps back into the cell, moving further away from Harden.

"Suit yourself. I'm not going to stop you, man."

Bill now stood far enough away that Harden knew he could make it. He didn't even take the time to question Bill's sudden change of heart. Time to leave.

Harden turned.

That's when he saw the other Baby Face standing just outside the cell door. He was holding something. Small and black, but not a gun.

He pointed it at Harden.

Baby Face pushed a button.

Harden didn't even see the two tiny metal prongs leave the device, but he felt them when they both stuck in his chest.

Then a massive jolt. It was like some huge hand picked him up and shook him like a rag doll.

He crashed to the floor. He looked up and saw the baby mask nodding at him, and Harden realized the man behind it was laughing.

Before he passed out, Harden had the vague sense of pissing himself, but maybe, in fact, it was all the blood.

PART II

CHAPTER THIRTY-THREE

January 1990

The ten days Coyote was gone was both a reprieve and a curiosity. I had no doubt what he was doing was giving a small university town ample time to mold a story disproportionate to the facts. The facts were these: he flipped out at the bar and ran away into the night with a willing accomplice. As the hours and shock value passed, I was convinced he didn't at all levitate. How could he? Still, what I had seen was street magic of the highest caliber, and if I didn't know what Coyote's plan was, I might have even believed he did float above that table. I still don't know how he did it.

And I wasn't the only one wondering what had happened. News of the event scorched through campus, and even the CBS affiliate out of Albany covered the story, the juiciest part being Coyote and Jacob's mysterious disappearance. Charlatan or not, Coyote was a story.

No one seemed to have any contact information for Coyote's father. I was able to call Jacob's home, and his parents didn't seem worried beyond the fact he was missing some school time. *Probably just on a whorin' trip in Manhattan.* That's actually what his dad said to me. A whorin' trip.

Wherever they went, I wasn't too concerned, because I figured the entire purpose of their disappearance was to generate buzz, which is exactly what it did. They would come back when they could make some kind of grand entrance, and that would begin phase two of Coyote's plan.

I remember those ten days clearly. That was when I fell in love for the first time in my life. Not just a little in love. There's no such thing. There is either love or there isn't, and that's something I never understood until Emma.

I read an article once about a group of scientists who did a study on love. They measured the brain patterns of new couples who claimed to be madly in love against long-term couples who claimed their relationship was comfortable but stale. The differences were striking, and the scientists decreed the rush of new love to be as addictive as heroin. In the confines of their lab, these scientists concluded that the high of nascent love is something humans are doomed to chase their entire lives. Heroin or not, in those ten days Emma was all I wanted; I craved her by the second and felt hopeless and lost in her absence.

In those ten days, the frosty air barely registered on my skin. My body was continuously flushed with heat, and at times I wondered if I was getting the flu. But I never got any symptoms apart from my body temperature running hot and my distinct lack of appetite. Emma and I spent nearly every moment we could together: between classes, meals on campus, and the occasional dinner. We had shared several more kisses, but I could tell she was still trying to figure me out. She wondered how far I wanted to take this, and if I really cared for her or was just looking to prolong the excitement and danger.

And what about her? For all I really knew, I was merely a brief rest area on her road to something more interesting. I didn't think that was the truth, but Coyote had taught me that belief can be as spongy as tar on a hot desert road.

The bottom line was I just didn't care. Whatever our subconscious intentions were, I wanted her. More importantly, she wanted me. I wasn't used to that, and it made me guarded, vulnerable, and deliriously happy.

* * *

I lost my virginity at seventeen, but I never made love until I was with Emma. That sentiment sounds like it belongs in a Barry White song, but its triteness makes it no less true.

There was no guilt associated with our physical relationship. She clearly did not love Coyote, or at least not in the way that interfered with what she felt for me. For my part, I didn't distinguish between kissing and fucking. Crass, but true. I had betrayed Coyote's friendship the moment I first touched Emma's lips with mine, and so any further physical and emotional escalation between us left no deeper grooves on my conscience.

She had come over on a Thursday night to watch a movie, and Derek was on the road with his rugby team. Jacob and Coyote were still gone, and it was beginning to feel like they would never return.

The place was ours.

She entered my apartment, movie in hand. No sooner than the door was locked behind her, she attacked me. It was a fierceness of passion I had never experienced. "Let's go to your room," she breathed, flicking her tongue over my earlobe.

I smacked my head into the doorjamb pulling her into my room, but she was nice enough just to laugh a little.

She placed her hands on my shoulders and walked me to the bed, gently nudging me to sit on the edge. As I did, she leaned forward and kissed me deeply as she pushed me all the way down. Her fingers deftly undid each button on my shirt; as she worked her way down, she pulled my shirt open and licked and nibbled every part of my chest. I didn't close my eyes. Rather, I watched her as she explored my body with her mouth, and I moaned as her hair dragged slowly along my stomach, sweeping along my skin with the softness of a feather.

She broke away briefly to stand and pull her shirt off, which she discarded to the floor. Then she was on me again and our skin seemed to melt together.

"Do you have a condom?" she asked.

I nodded, thinking I might have even managed a dopey *uh-huh*. I always had condoms handy. Not because they were needed often, but because that was what you did when you were in college. You kept things in your drawers just because you could. I pictured them in my mind: an unopened ten-pack of Trojans in my underwear drawer, right next to a pack of half-smoked Marlboros from months past that I never threw away.

What happened next seems a beautiful blur to me now. When it was over, she fell forward onto my sweaty chest, and I wrapped my arms around her tiny waist. That's one of those moments you can only cling to with an immediate presence of mind. Try to hold onto it for too long, and it dribbles between your fingers. In that moment, I drank of it.

"I need you," she said. Her words were so soft I wasn't sure I had heard them.

She pushed herself up and stared into me. "I need you," she repeated. "That's not an easy thing for me to say. Do you understand?"

"I do."

"This is good," she said, dragging her fingertips lightly over my nipple. "We are good. I don't know what you want out of this, but I'm beginning to think this could be more than good. This could be something."

"Something," I said. Yes, exactly that.

She looked at me for a moment and I saw her face lose just a bit of its vulnerability. "I think that's enough said for right now."

She started to turn her face away, but I kept it in place with one finger.

"I need you, too."

Her eyes softened once again and she smiled. Then she kissed me, very lightly, as if that gave her back some kind of control she thought she had lost.

After that, we spoke very little, not out of awkwardness but because being together was enough. She dressed and used the bathroom while I pulled my pants back on. I could still smell her hair on my skin, and I hoped it would linger on me forever.

We sat on the couch, her head in my lap, and watched *Big*. I didn't see it when it came to the Tillman theaters about a year before, though I had wanted to. I was expecting a lighthearted comedy, something to laugh with for a while and pass two hours holding Emma. But the movie punched me in the chest. To me, this comedy was a drama, a painful look at the loss of childhood innocence. Emma saw Tom Hanks as a goofy boy trying to figure out how to be an adult. I saw him as an innocent little kid—a twelve-year-old in the movie, but seven in my eyes—whose childhood had been suddenly snatched away in the dead of night, waking up to a world where things were large, dark, and forever unchangeable. In the scene where he's curled up in a fetal position in a cheap hotel room, desperately alone, listening to the cityscape wail of sirens and shouting, I felt myself tearing up. I almost asked Emma if we could watch something else, but I didn't want to have her ask me why. So I closed my eyes and counted to twenty. In those seconds she squeezed my knee. I don't know if she sensed what I was feeling but I didn't say anything. I opened my eyes, breathed deeply, and floated through the rest of the movie.

She left after the movie. I almost asked her to stay but was afraid of her saying no. She kissed me and asked if I wanted to get together tomorrow, and I nearly laughed at the pointlessness of the question.

Thank God she left then. Half an hour later Coyote and Jacob came home.

Jacob walked in first. He was wearing the same thing as when I had last seen him ten days ago, but those clothes—now torn and dirt-covered—were the only semblance to the person I once knew. Everything about him seemed to have changed, not the least of which was his stare, now distant and clouded, as if he were semi-catatonic.

He walked into the room, leaving the door open behind him. He glanced at me briefly and seemed to notice me no more than he would a spider on the wall. Despite the dozens of questions he surely would know I had for him, Jacob beelined it for his bedroom, shutting the door behind him.

"He's the first success of my experiment."

Coyote stood in the doorway.

Unlike Jacob, Coyote was not wearing the same clothes from ten days earlier. A pair of faded camouflage pants sat loosely around his waist and a black t-shirt clung tightly to his chest and arms. I had never seen these clothes on him before, yet their condition suggested they were not recent purchases. He carried no jacket, just a small Army-style duffel bag that looked only half-full. Coyote, from the looks of it, had just come back from some kind of training.

"Where have you been?" I asked. I wondered if he could smell any trace of Emma in here. On me.

Coyote smiled without showing teeth. "Out there, man." He let the duffel bag drop to the ground. "*Out there.*"

"Out where?"

He dropped to his knees and opened the duffel bag, extracting a small box. He opened the box and pulled out a flower. I don't think I had even seen one like it before. The petals were a soft white, like the fading light from a movie projector. Along them, a series of maroon sprinkles lined up like a trail of marching ants in formation. He went to Jacob's door and knocked on it. I heard it open, followed by the muffled sound of Coyote's voice.

"Put this in water."

The door closed, and then Coyote went into his own bedroom and shut the door. They were gone as quickly as they had reappeared, and it wasn't until March that I found out what had happened to them.

CHAPTER THIRTY-FOUR

MARCH 1990

"He's starting to scare me," Emma whispered, pretending to look at the books on the shelves. "He's really losing it."

I stood close to her, probably closer than I would have if we were more in public. But it was late at night and we were well hidden in the stacks of the library where I worked.

"I don't understand why you don't break up with him."

"It's not that easy."

"Yes, Emma. It is that easy."

She took a book from the shelf and gazed aimlessly at its spine. "You don't understand. It's like he's teetering on the edge of something. I don't want to do anything to push him off."

"What are you afraid of?" I asked.

I feared even our faintest whispers could be heard across the whole of the library.

"I don't know."

"It wouldn't be worse than him finding out about us." In a way, I almost wanted him to find out. Coyote, the person everyone admired and feared, wasn't in total control for once. *I* was sleeping with Emma, and nothing he could do to her or me would erase that. It was a morsel of knowledge I savored.

She turned her head and looked at me. There was a sad desperation to her expression. "He *can't* find out about us, Harden."

"But what if he does?"

"Harden, he *can't.*"

And I thought, *Why are we always so afraid of what Coyote knows?* But I didn't say it, because I already had a vague sense of the answer.

Coyote was going to hold his first Revelation meeting the following night. It wasn't going to be so much a meeting, I suppose, as a recruitment seminar. He was going to start his experiment in earnest, and he wanted me there. I was the secretary, after all.

"Do you know what he's planning for tomorrow?" I asked.

She shook her head. "I hardly even see him anymore."

"He told me he's going to talk about where he and Jacob went in January."

"As if I even care at this point," she said.

I was more curious than Emma. Neither Coyote nor Jacob had spoken about their ten-day absence. Despite repeated questions from me—and Derek, to a lesser degree—they spoke very little at all. Whatever had happened to him, Jacob was Coyote's boy now. Coyote had brainwashed my once happy-go-lucky roommate, leaving him a quiet and intensely serious shell of the roommate I knew. No more school. No more rugby. Gone were the alcohol-infused weekends, the stories of sexual conquests, the snack-riddled movie marathons on the living room floor. Or perhaps Jacob was a gifted actor, willing to sacrifice his friends, his personality, and his education for whatever it was that Coyote needed. But whatever he was doing, it seemed to be the first time Jacob took pride in his work.

Coyote and Jacob often left the apartment in the middle of the night, not coming back until late morning. Neither of them went to class, and both were informed both by phone and mail that the enrollment deadline for classes had passed, and neither would be graduating in June.

They didn't care. They weren't at Wyland for diplomas anymore. And all of it for some stupid experiment. It was an incredible waste, and I think that's what fascinated me most.

"You're not curious?" I asked Emma.

"The whole thing is so sad. I don't even understand it. But I don't want to be a part of it."

"People are talking," I said. "There's a buzz going around about tomorrow."

A couple of weeks ago, Coyote and Jacob had become a bit more social. They started walking the campus, making connections with lost friends. Naturally, everyone wondered what had happened to them, and both were happy to tell any eager ear about how they discovered something wonderful. Many people had heard about Coyote's famous "levitating" incident at Benny's, and this only served to fuel interest into the nature of their mysterious discovery.

"Come to the Lincoln next Wednesday night," Coyote would tell the curious. "Nine o'clock. I'll tell you all about it."

I reached out and lightly stroked Emma's arm with my fingertips, a bold public move, even deep in the deserted stacks of books. She smiled.

"You need to break up with him," I told her.

"I will. I just need a little time."

She rarely saw Coyote, as he spent most nights at our apartment now. In my mind they were already broken up, but it wasn't official. Official meant she would talk to him, tell him they were done. Official meant I could date Emma openly, even if that caused tension around my apartment. The truth is, I think Coyote had gotten what he wanted from Emma and wouldn't even flinch at being dumped. Coyote moved on with predatory purpose, discarding bones that no longer had meat on them. But Emma sensed something more. She picked up on something that gave her pause, told her breaking up with Coyote might have more significant consequences. I was frustrated and wanted it over with. She was cautious and treaded lightly.

Turned out, she was right to be afraid.

She must have been reading my thoughts, because she reached out and lightly squeezed my forearm. "I want *you*."

"And I want you to have me. *Only* me."

"I know," she said.

"Do you?"

She loosened her grip. "What do you mean?"

It was time for all the unspoken thoughts to pour from me. "I think I . . ." I closed my eyes again. Tight squeeze. Open again. "No, I know that . . ." Just put it out there. How can it be wrong to say it if it's the truth?

"Emma, I . . ."

I didn't say it. It would be too painful if it just died a slow, silent death in the space between us.

Then she kissed me. As she pulled back, she pushed her fingers up into my hair.

"I love you, too, Harden."

I felt a hundred pounds lighter at her words, and I vaguely remember reaching out and touching a shelf of books, steading my balance. We walked from the stacks, and my hand grazed her thigh as we turned the corner.

Everything was okay. It would all work out. Emma and I were together, and that's all that mattered in my little world.

Then I saw him.

The bouncer from the frat party. Coyote's friend. Big Ben.

He wasn't looking our way at the moment, but that doesn't mean he didn't notice us. My skin grew cold as I looked at the floor and walked away from Emma. The rest of the night, as much as I tried to repeat Emma's words in my head, four other words replaced them.

What had he seen?

CHAPTER THIRTY-FIVE

The Lincoln was an old, single-screen Baroque-style movie theater in the downtown area of Tillman, a fifteen-minute walk from campus. It used to be a playhouse around the turn of the century, but I guess they converted it to a movie theater once the talkies changed the course of entertainment for sleepy towns around the country. Nowadays, the Lincoln showed mostly indie and arthouse flicks, and did a pretty good business from what I could tell. The owner also rented it out for events, and Coyote had chosen it for his recruitment seminar.

The Lincoln could hold over four hundred people.

On Wednesday night the theater was looking particularly ominous: the dimmed lights took the polish off anything that could gleam and the air was still and thick. The silence absorbed everything around it. I was backstage, watching the place slowly starting to fill.

Coyote put a hand on my shoulder.

"Take notes, Harden. Take notes tonight, that's all you have to do."

I looked down at my notepad, which he had instructed me to bring.

"Notes about what, exactly?"

"Everything."

"Where am I supposed to be? Back here, or—"

"In the audience. First row. Write everything down. I want a record."

"Why not just tape it?"

"No video. No audio."

He walked away, and I took a seat in the first row, my pen resting on the notebook in my lap. I knew I couldn't transcribe everything that was said, so my goal was to get the general outline of what happened, filling in the blanks later. I spent a few minutes warming up by writing the conversation I just had, and the words came out smoothly and easily. I was ready to write what Coyote wanted, not because he ordered it, but because I had the sense that it could be an interesting story. Maybe it could even be a book someday. Or, perhaps, evidence.

When nine o'clock came, I looked around and found the theater half-full. Surely Coyote was disappointed, but I was amazed. Over two hundred people came here on a Wednesday night to hear what he had to say. I took note of a man sitting two seats to my left. He caught my attention because he was taking notes as well, and I wondered if he was a reporter. He looked too old to be an undergrad, but maybe he was a grad student, or perhaps a professor. He jotted away on a small pad, looking around every so often to see if anyone was watching him. He caught me staring at him and offered me a small nod, prompting me to nod back. We suddenly had this fragile bond, and I wondered why he had come here tonight. I wanted to ask him but neither my self-confidence nor our distance allowed it.

Seconds later Coyote took the stage, and that's when things started getting strange.

CHAPTER THIRTY-SIX

"I'm not going to waste your time here tonight."

Coyote wore a simple white t-shirt that hung on the outside of faded jeans, but his presence was as commanding as a battleship captain in full regalia. I don't know how he did it—maybe this is what charisma was all about—but you just wanted to keep watching the guy to see what he would say or do next.

"I'm not going to tell you things you already know or promise you something that can't be delivered. I'm not going to sell you anything, and I'm not going to preach a gospel of false hope." Coyote turned gently to the different areas of the theater as he spoke, his hands reaching out with an air of inclusiveness.

"What I *am* going to do is tell you about a recent journey of mine and what I learned from it. What I learned is something you will all want to learn. I want you all to be able to finally *see*."

Pretty hard sell, I thought. But I was hooked enough to have to keep reminding myself to take notes. My shorthand was nonexistent, but I scrawled well enough to get most of it. I looked up at him from time to time, catching his expression and his focused gaze as he singled out people from the crowd with his eyes. He was making a connection one person at a time.

"Some of you may have heard what happened to me at Benny's a couple of months ago, and perhaps that alone is the reason you're here tonight. You want to know what really happened. Did I

actually levitate off that table? Did I really hear a voice?" I heard
a small snicker from someone behind me, which Coyote ignored.
"I can't answer those questions, because I simply don't remember.
But there are those who were there that night, and they can tell you
what they saw. There are eleven people who will swear my feet left
the table that night, if just by a few inches. I can't tell you. I don't
remember any of that. All I know is something tore open inside of
me that night. Something wonderful."

Where was *this* going?

"I left that night with my friend Jacob. I didn't know where we
were going or what I was supposed to do, but I knew he was supposed to come with me to witness what I was to witness. He was
supposed to become as I now *am*, and, after ten days together, he
was. That journey wasn't easy, but I know my goal is to teach what
we have learned to anyone who is willing to listen. Anyone who is
willing to *become*."

Okay, now you're being too vague, I thought. *You need to start being
specific if you're going to keep their patience.*

Then he did just that. "We spent ten nights in the woods, about
eighty miles north of here. We had no food or water. You might be
strained to believe this, but it's true. We spent the nights sleeping
on the cold, hard dirt, in temperatures that should have killed us.
But we survived. During the day, I sat with my friend, and told him
every thought flooding into my mind. I had thoughts I had never
experienced before, and I thought them in ways completely new to
me. It was difficult for me to explain them to him, but he studied
my every word, trying to see what I saw."

I chanced a look behind me to see if Jacob was still by the door,
but he wasn't. I shifted my gaze down to the faces of those behind
me, and not one person looked at me. I wouldn't say they were transfixed on Coyote, exactly, but they were all looking at him. Some

probably thought he was full of shit, maybe even most of them. But the theater was silent, and no one had left.

"On the sixth day, what happened to me at Benny's also happened to Jacob. His mind opened to a potential he could never before conceptualize. On that day, Jacob also *became*."

A man's voice came from the crowd. "I don't believe you."

Coyote smiled, and I had seen that exact look before. It wasn't a smile you wanted to be on the other side of.

"It's your right not to believe, as much as it's your right to leave here and miss the rest of what I have to say. Disbelief is, in fact, the greatest ally of belief. You cannot have one without the other. You need to doubt, because without it, you cannot *become*. Will you stand, please?"

"Why?" the man said.

Now everyone looked at the heckler, including myself. He was our age, wearing a baseball hat and faded Skynyrd concert tee, and he slouched deep in his seat as if it were his living room couch. I wondered why he'd come tonight.

"Because I want to show you something."

His friend next to him poked him and gave him a nudge. Finally, with a nervous smile the student stood and, in an odd gesture, turned his baseball cap backwards over his moppy hair, as if it might get blown off otherwise.

"Close your eyes," Coyote said.

"I thought you wanted me to *see*." A few people around him snickered.

"You will. Close your eyes."

With a shrug, the student closed his eyes and dug his fists deep into his baggy jeans.

Five seconds later he was screaming.

It was horrifying. This man, this student, suddenly screaming as if being torn open by massive, invisible jaws. He clawed at his face and grabbed his hair. No one tried to help him, because it all ended as quickly as it had started. He just stopped, and when he did, I could hear his frantic panting and wheezing. Then he turned to his left, threw up on his friend, and barreled out down the aisle and through the back doors, into the night. The friend, now covered in a thick slime of vomit, shouted *fuck* at no one in particular and followed his friend.

I didn't know what to do. I had never seen anything like it. Not even Coyote's levitation trick matched this. I witnessed this with two hundred others, as if we all had been watching a grisly car accident together, and yet I'm not even exactly sure what it was I saw. A wave of chills ran through me as my brain unconsciously replayed the sounds within me. I turned back to Coyote, and the sudden silence of the room encompassed me.

"I just showed him something he wasn't ready to see, and I doubt he'll be back." Coyote offered a slight shake of the head. "Please understand this is new to me, and I'm still learning. I truly didn't know he would react so negatively."

I struggled to write down as much as I could. Was that guy a plant, paid by Coyote to do what he just did? It seemed the only real explanation to me. But how did he throw up on command? How was he able to seem so completely terrified? I wished Emma were here; I felt an overwhelming need to talk to her.

"I haven't spoken to God, in case that's what you're wondering. I'm not sure at all there is a God. I haven't spoken to anyone except myself, a side of me that waited inside an untapped part of my brain my whole life. We all have it." His words were slowly paced, his rhythm almost hypnotic. No one said anything. No one objected to what had just happened. No one else left the room. "Think of your brain as a tunnel, and your life of learning a slow dig through it, scooping out spoonfuls of dirt as the tunnel slowly expands. Far down your path, beyond miles of coarse dirt and rock, lies an opening. A chamber." He paused for a sip of water, and I could discern the faintest beads of sweat on his forehead. "Inside this chamber are things almost inconceivable, treasures nearly beyond comprehension. Most people dig and scoop their entire lives and never come close to this chamber. I, however, broke through that final wall two months ago, and Jacob soon after. I can show each and every one of you how to reach it."

I transcribed this whole speech, my pen writing as fast as my hand would allow. I could feel the air around me still even more, as if I were the only one in the darkened theater.

"But I won't."

I looked up and saw Coyote smile.

"I don't want all of you, and I don't need all of you," he continued.

I saw a few people to my left exchange glances. I would call them confused, but I don't think that word does it justice.

"I don't want to start a cult. I want to start a church. A church of people who believe in themselves more than anything else, and have the ability to do exactly that. I want to share what I've learned, because I believe the . . . the *revelation* both Jacob and I have discovered is a key to advancing humankind." Another smile, this one with a painful wince. "I know that's an arrogant statement, but it's true. Do I think we're the only ones in the world who have discovered this? No, of course not. But we've discovered it for a reason, and we must use our new knowledge with responsibility. I must seek those who can be trusted with this new knowledge. These new powers."

"What powers?"

The voice came from my left. It was the man I had spotted at the beginning of the evening—the only other one I could see who was also taking notes.

Coyote looked down at him, his gaze cutting a jagged swatch through the struggling light.

"Are you a reporter?"

"No."

"Yet you're taking notes."

"As is he," the man said, pointing to me. I was suddenly conscious of a room full of eyes on me.

"He is *my* secretary," Coyote said. "His job is to record all of this."

"For what purpose?"

I could see Coyote calculating.

"For me."

Now everyone was eyeing the man, waiting to hear what he would ask next. The people immediately around him shifted their bodies away from him, as if any moment Coyote would make his head explode.

"I want to know about the powers," he said.

"You want them, don't you?"

"I suppose I would want to know what they are first."

Coyote turned his back on us, took a few steps away on the stage, and turned around again. He brought the microphone up very close to his mouth, so his voice was gravelly and distorted. He was pushing his luck here with his showmanship, but he hadn't yet turned into a carnival barker.

"I will show you something," Coyote said. "I will show all of you, because unopened minds need a push. A nudge. Something to get them prepared for further levels of advancement. Without that stimulus, those minds never grow. But I will only show you once. That is all. Afterwards, many of you won't accept what you have seen. But some of you, maybe even just one or two, will believe and will have taken the first small step to revelation. *You* are the people I am interested in."

With that, Coyote looked up and gave a nod to the projection room. I turned and looked up, seeing Jacob's face only for a moment before it disappeared back into the darkness of the small room.

The red velvet curtain behind Coyote began to rise, looking like a wall of lava creeping back up into the mouth of a volcano. When the curtain completed its journey, the projector from Jacob's lair shot out a bright white beam, illuminating the screen behind Coyote.

Coyote didn't turn to watch. Instead, he watched us.

CHAPTER THIRTY-SEVEN

A crisp image came to life on the screen. It was the cover of the *New York Times*, dated back in January, during the time Coyote and Jacob had been missing. Slowly, the shaky camera zoomed out from the paper and pointed up to the man holding it. Coyote's face filled the screen, his cheeks and chin coated in a week-old beard. He looked both exhausted and elated. He was outside somewhere. A forest.

I realized they had shot this during their ten-day exodus. They must have purchased a video camera along the way because I had never seen either Jacob or Coyote with one in the apartment. Jacob, it seemed, was the cameraman for this production.

"This is because people need proof," the Coyote on the video announced. I could see the frost of his words ghost around him as he spoke. "Dismiss it if you want. Believe it if you want. All I ask is you open your minds and your eyes, and you take in what is possible." With that, Coyote gave a brief nod to the camera, telling Jacob that he was *ready*. Jacob zoomed out a bit more and panned the camera a few degrees to the right, revealing a large tree in the foreground. It was large and old, rising at least forty feet out of the ground.

Suddenly the camera wobbled and it became clear Jacob was setting it down on a makeshift tripod. Then Jacob came into view, his clothes tattered and filthy, his skin gray and sallow, his hair showing the believable effect of sleeping outdoors in the dirt. The two men looked at each other, and then Coyote reached out with his right hand, which Jacob grasped.

Then, they closed their eyes.

What happened next did so without much fanfare, which only added to the spectacle. Jacob and Coyote stood there, eyes closed, hands locked, facing that old tree.

The camera started to shake.

Then the tree started to move.

The tree itself—so deeply rooted into the depth of the forest floor—started to shake. Just a little, at first, but within seconds the shaking tuned violent. Birds scattered to the sky as smaller branches snapped and rained to the ground. The rumbling grew, like a thousand buffalo stampeding toward them. Then the earth around the base of the tree heaved upwards and the tree itself—this massive life form, which had probably been growing for decades—began to slowly lift from the ground.

Its tangled roots ripped through the soil and became exposed to sunlight. They looked like an unearthed nest of snakes, white and vulnerable, writhing in protest. Rocks and dirt scattered, and above the din in the video I could hear birds screeching to each other, raising the alarm for something they couldn't possibly understand. Coyote and Jacob remained completely still.

The tree hovered above the hole beneath it, its roots barely touching the ground, the weight of the tree apparently supported by nothing other than the thoughts of the men standing before it. The tree levitated as Coyote had: impossibly, yet without question. On the video, Coyote gave a nod and opened his eyes. The tree crashed to the earth, where it briefly stood upright before falling backwards, crashing through smaller trees before bringing forth a concussion of soil as it smashed into the forest floor.

Coyote turned to Jacob, who was now bent over the earth, and asked him if he was okay. Jacob nodded, opened his eyes, and then immediately dropped to his knees and dry heaved, his empty stomach revolting but producing no fruits of its labors. He crawled off-camera.

A tight shot of the fallen tree followed, accompanied by a slow pan out, revealing a profile shot of Coyote, who, on the video, seemed to be something beyond what he once and ever was. His face seemed frozen in time as he stared at something far in the distance, beyond the forest, beyond anything.

The video stopped. The curtain fell almost immediately. Coyote stood there on the stage and looked at us—at *me*.

I hadn't taken a single note. The lights in the theater grew but remained dim.

"Underneath your seats are pads of paper and pens," he said.

There was a ruffle of noise as everyone checked.

"If you're interested in learning more about what I have learned, I want you to write down your name and phone number on the first sheet." Coyote paced back and forth on the stage like a caged animal. "On the second sheet, I want you to write down the most terrifying thing you have ever seen. Not in a movie. Real life. Tell me the memory that still haunts you the most."

He paused, as if considering what to say next.

"I will only choose a handful. You'll be contacted. Don't try to contact myself or Jacob directly."

The lights exploded to full intensity. Without saying anything else, Coyote walked off the stage.

CHAPTER THIRTY-EIGHT

I sat there for a moment and watched. Some people got up and immediately walked out, but I was surprised to see most of them actually writing on the notepads. I reached down and found the pad and pen under my own seat and looked at that top blank page for a moment.

What is the memory that still haunts you?

I knew immediately the answer to that question. But I had never as much as breathed a word of it to anyone, much less written it down. Maybe this is where and when I finally did that, told the world—really, just Coyote—what had happened to me. I wouldn't sign it; hell, I'd even disguise my handwriting. If I wrote it out, would there be a weight lifted off me?

I stared at the blank pad. I flipped past the first sheet, with no intention of writing my name.

Fuck it, this will be good for me, I thought. *If anything real comes out of this bizarre night, let it be this message in a bottle.*

I scribbled as fast as I could.

I was molested by my elementary school teacher when I was seven. It happened in the school. The storage closet. The memory that haunts me most is his breath on my neck.

I stared at the words and soaked them in. Seeing them didn't have the impact I expected. I felt neither better nor worse for having written them. I just felt empty.

I tore the page off, wadded it up, then put it in my coat pocket. On the way out of the theater, I found a trash can full of similar crumpled sheets and added mine to the pile.

Outside, the cold air slapped my face and gave me a rush that I needed after whatever the hell I had just watched in *there*. I had either watched something truly phenomenal or a very elaborate con job. My gut said the latter, but my desperate hope was for the former. Don't we all want to be part of something truly special?

"Harden."

I turned and saw the man who had spoken up in the meeting. He stood in a heavy overcoat still holding onto his notepad and pen. He took a step forward and extended his gloved hand to me.

"Mike Barrillo."

I shook his hand and said nothing. How did he know my name?

"Wiley is your roommate, correct?"

Again, I didn't respond. I hadn't heard anyone say Coyote's real name in some time.

"Can we talk for a couple of minutes?" he asked.

"About what?"

"I'm intrigued by your friend." A decades-old streetlight threw off an orangish glow, the light impeded by an old warehouse that, until recently, housed a nightclub but now sat empty. We stood in the building's night shadow, which made everything feel even colder.

"Many people are," I responded, not knowing what else to say.

"How long have you known him?"

"Who *are* you? And how do you know my name?"

"I need to know more. That's why I came tonight."

"You didn't answer my question."

"Look, Harden. I'll give you a little bit of info, if you give me some."

I paused. "Maybe."

Barrillo did a quick glance to his right and left. Who was he worried about hearing us?

"I'm not a student," he said.

"Yeah, I figured."

"I know. Probably obvious, huh?"

"Are you a reporter?" It wasn't inconceivable that Tillman's tiny local paper might bother with a human interest piece on Coyote.

"In a way." He nodded at the notepad in my hand. "I suppose in the same way you are."

"I was only there taking notes."

"So was I. In your case," he said, pointing a thick finger at me, "you were taking notes for Wiley. In my case, I was taking notes for someone else."

"Who?"

"Your turn," he said, shifting his tone. "How long have you known Wiley?"

"Only since last August."

"And how long have you known Jacob?"

"Couple of years more."

"And Jacob has known Wiley as long as you?"

"As far as I know."

His eyes widened a fraction. "Why do you say that? You think it's possible they've known each other longer and kept that a secret from you?"

I didn't think that at all. Still, I don't know why I had answered like that. "No," I said. "But Coyote's life is built around secrets, so one more wouldn't surprise me. My turn."

"All right," Barrillo said.

"Why are you here?"

"I've been asked to collect information on your friend Wiley."

"You said that already. By whom?"

Even in the shadow of the old theater, I could see Barrillo shifting his eyes back and forth in the dark. He reached inside the pocket of his jacket, and in a momentary rush of senseless panic, I thought he was going to pull a gun on me. Or a knife. But when he held out his hand I saw instead a dark leather billfold. Barrillo flicked it open and extended his arm so his hand trespassed into the streetlight. Something glimmered, and I could see it was a shield of sorts. A badge.

"Harden, I work for the government."

"Government?" I looked down to the badge, but it had already disappeared back inside Barrillo's coat pocket.

"I work for the FBI. Desk jockey. Securities fraud. I was pulled out of that for a while to work on this. Wiley caught the attention of somebody high up. It has something to do with his father."

"What does his father do?"

Barrillo gave me another crooked grin, but not one that gave any sense of comfort.

"He really does keep secrets from you, doesn't he? Wiley's father is one of the biggest crooks of his generation."

CHAPTER THIRTY-NINE

I didn't go back home, at least not immediately. I only spent a few more minutes with Barrillo, telling him I didn't have time to talk, and maybe we could set up another time. Truth was, I freaked out. I mean, I had no idea if the man was even telling me the truth, and if he was, did I really want to chance Coyote walking out of that theater and spotting me talking to an FBI agent, one who was trying to bust his father?

I burrowed my hands in my coat pocket, put my face down out of the direct path of the bitter wind, and went straight to the library where I worked. It was nearly empty. I chatted up Margie who was working and told her I needed to use the LexisNexis database, to which those of us who worked at the reference desk had login access.

I needed to find out about Alastair Martin, Coyote's father.

The only time Coyote had ever mentioned him was when he told us the story about killing that boy in the woods. I barely had an impression about his father other than he seemed nice enough to take his son camping and buy fancy new walkie-talkies from Sharper Image. But I learned much more of him from a two-year-old *Business Week* profile of the man. He was both new and old money, the old coming from generations of West Virginia coal-mine operations. The new came from speculative venture-capital investments in a variety of start-ups, none of which I had ever heard of. All of the companies had long since folded after being sold by Alastair for high profits based on prospectuses, that, the article insinuated, were nothing more than high-quality fiction.

Another article had the acronym RICO only four words away from Alastair's name. RICO was the fancy term for racketeering. Racketeering was the fancy term for being mobbed up.

Back in the apartment I wrote and wrote. Neither Coyote nor Jacob had returned, so I locked my bedroom door, sat at my computer, and transcribed all of my notes from the evening, adding to them the detail of the video and also every bit of my conversation with Mike Barrillo. When I was finished, I saved the file under an innocuous name and password-protected it. Then I saved a copy to a floppy drive and placed that under my mattress.

I chanced a call to Emma. It wasn't likely Coyote was over there, but if he was, I could just say I was looking for him. I had to talk to her, and, in fact, had been wanting to all night but needed to get my thoughts down before I lost the clarity of the evening's events. She sounded sleepy, and I looked down at the clock on my computer and realized it was after midnight.

"Hi, baby," she said. With that one word I knew she was alone. "How was it tonight?"

I told her everything, start to finish. When I finished, she asked me a slew of questions about the video and Coyote, none of which I felt I had any kind of good answer to.

Then she asked more about Barrillo. "Do you think he really was an FBI agent?"

"I have no idea. Why would he be someone else?"

"I mean, Coyote's barely ever mentioned his father to me. It just seems so unreal." Then she paused. "All of this does, really."

"Emma, when you see him, don't tell him about the FBI, or that I went digging around about his dad."

"Of course not. And, Harden, you know I hardly see him anymore.

We're basically broken up."

But not broken up enough to let our relationship be public, I thought.

"I know," I said. "It's just that . . . there's some really weird stuff going on, and I don't know how it's going to end. I just want to control this part of it, okay? I want to . . . to control *something.*"

I heard the front door to the apartment open and close.

"Gotta go," I whispered. "See you tomorrow?"

"Of course, love." The phone disconnected.

She called me *love.*

* * *

I walked out into the living room and found Coyote sitting on the couch, reading the Old Testament. Coyote was a different man now, and there was no longer a casual air between us.

"Where's Jacob?"

"I don't know," he replied, briefly looking up at me. "Where did you go after the meeting?"

I felt a brief rush of panic. Had he seen me with Barrillo?

"Came here," I said.

He mumbled something that sounded like dismissive agreement.

"That was . . . pretty amazing," I said. He looked up again. "At the meeting. How did you do that thing with the tree?"

Coyote slowly closed the Bible after dog-earing the page he was on.

"How do you think I did it, Harden?"

His gaze bored into me, and I wondered what it was he saw.

"I don't know. It looked pretty real."

"What makes you think it wasn't real?"

At that moment Derek walked in. His entrance startled me, but I welcomed it. Derek was the only thing normal happening in our apartment.

"Hey," he mumbled, setting his backpack down. He had probably been with a study group. Exactly what I should have been doing, instead of watching a circus performance, being interrogated by the FBI, researching Coyote's father at the library, then secretly transcribing every moment of all of it. I suddenly yearned for homework.

"Derek," Coyote said. "You weren't there tonight."

He stared down at Coyote. "I heard about it."

Coyote smiled. "Really? From whom?"

"Another guy from the lacrosse team was there. I saw him afterwards. Told me all about it."

"And what was his impression?"

"He thinks you're trying to scam people."

"Scam? I didn't ask for money."

"Not yet," Derek said. "I told him it was all a big joke, anyway."

The smile faded in an instant. "Derek, I can assure you that what I am doing is not a joke."

At this point, Derek would normally have shrugged off Coyote and gone to his room. This time, however, he took a step toward him. "Look, I don't really give a shit what you do, okay? You pay your share of the rent and you're hardly ever here, so what more could I ask for?"

"Exactly," Coyote said.

"But you pulled Jacob into this stupid thing of yours. He's dropped out for the semester and he's off the lacrosse team. The kid is walking around here glazed-eyed and distant, and that's when I even see him. Half the time I have no clue where the hell he is." His voice grew louder. "His parents are calling me wondering what's going on, and I can't tell them anything because I have no fucking idea. All I know is that he's not graduating this semester because of you."

Coyote stood.

"He's his own man, Derek. I don't make decisions for him."

Derek took another step forward. "Yes, Coyote. *You do.* You know you do."

"You place too much significance on me."

I saw Derek squeeze his fists before he turned to me. "Tell him, Harden. You've known Jacob longer than him. Tell him how Jacob's thrown away his life because of this stupid experiment Coyote is trying. You've seen the changes. Everyone has."

It was true. Everything Derek was saying was true. While I had never put much stock in Jacob, he at least was someone who had stayed on the path on which he was supposed to be. His life was written for him, and after school he would pass the bar and work for his father. He used to talk about that path all the time. Now that path was overgrown with weeds, and Jacob had strayed far into some other territory.

My momentary silence seemed to enrage Derek further.

"What the fuck, Harden? Are you so far up Coyote's ass that even you don't see what's going on?"

Coyote placed a hand on Derek's shoulder, but the gesture didn't seem a peaceful one. It was more like he was holding his prey down so he could get easier access to its neck.

"What do *you* think is going on, Derek?"

That was when Derek hit him. It happened so fast my mind barely registered what happened. I thought Derek was pulling away to storm out of the room, but instead he took a step back and swung impossibly fast with his right hand. His knuckles connected with Coyote's jaw—a perfect hit—making a sound like a hardbound book slamming against the top of a wooden desk.

Coyote didn't go down. How he didn't, I have no idea. He absorbed the blow, which reeled him back a few steps before righting himself again.

I don't think I had ever even seen Derek angry before. Of all my friends, he was always the most forgiving, willing to give anyone a second chance. Girls invariably described him as *nice* and *sweet*, and, despite his size and his aggressiveness in his athletics, I could never have imagined him in a fight. And yet he just threw the first punch.

"Derek," I managed to say. "What the hell?"

Derek held up his fists and kept his gaze on Coyote, but directed his words at me. "Yeah, Harden? What do you want to tell me? You want to be on his side for all this? Are you brainwashed, too?"

"Take it easy, Derek," I said.

Coyote remained silent, his arms dangling loosely at his sides, his hands not even balled into fists. I could see a sizable welt blooming on the left side of his face, but he didn't reach up to feel for blood. He stood there in a defenseless position, yet there was nothing passive about his look. It was a look I would never want directed at me.

"*Take it easy?*" Now Derek was shouting, not at Coyote, but at me. "Why am I the only one who sees that nothing good has happened since he moved in here with us? Don't, Harden." Derek held up a finger in my face, and for a second I panicked that I was next on his assault list. "Don't let him do this to you."

"Do what?" I asked. Yet I knew the answer. I knew exactly what he was talking about, and I cursed myself that I couldn't react in the moment, like Derek, and bring to light all the things I knew were bad in our apartment. There was evil there. Coyote was a devil, as much as the devil actually existed among us. He was there to change and corrupt, and he would not be satisfied until he had taken as many of us with him as possible.

Derek turned back to Coyote. "I want you out," he said. "Jacob, too, if he's still too caught up in your shit to know what's good for him. I'll pay for your rent until the lease is up, but I want you out now."

Coyote stood still for a few moments and then he cracked his mouth just enough to expose a bloody half-smile.

"Yes, Derek. I think that's a good idea."

CHAPTER FORTY

Things were happening fast.

After Derek told Coyote to leave, Coyote did just that. It took him perhaps all of thirty minutes to casually pack his possessions and take them to his car, choosing to leave many of his things behind. Derek stayed in his room, and I remained in the living room, watching a bruised and smiling Coyote make trip after trip to his car.

"You really going?" I asked him.

"It was time anyway, Harden. I need more space."

"Space for what?"

He didn't respond until he had come back for another load of his belongings.

"There are going to be many of us," he said. "There has to be for all of this to work. It's not just Jacob and me. We need a place of our own."

Then he left for his car. When he came back for one last load, he set down two armfuls of designer clothes on the couch next to me.

"You can have these." I eyed the clothes and knew just this pile was worth more than everything I owned altogether. "You could use a new look, Harden."

"You don't need them?"

"I have what I need."

I still couldn't decide if I was relieved or disappointed he was moving out. "Where are you going to go?"

"Emma's, of course."

The words sucked the breath out of me. I hadn't even considered that was where he would go, but of *course* it would be.

"Do..." What I wanted to ask was, *Do you know she wants nothing to do with you?* But I didn't. "Does she know you're coming over?"

"No," he said.

The thought of Coyote sleeping in the bed next to her angered me, and I felt impotent to do anything about it. Would she really let him stay there?

"See you around, Harden." He held out his hand, and as I always did, I took it and offered a pump. "I don't know if you still want to be involved, but I need you. You know that, don't you?"

"I don't think you really need anyone, Coyote."

He smiled and released my hand. "If that were true, I'd be a much different person." He handed me his apartment key. "But I definitely don't need this anymore."

I took it and squeezed it in my palm.

Coyote headed for the door, and I called out after him, wanting to know one more thing.

"How many people wrote on their pieces of paper? At the meeting?"

He turned. "A hundred and twenty-four."

"You read them all?"

"Yes, of course."

I was glad I had thrown mine away.

"Why did you ask them to write that? The memory that haunts them most?"

His look was one of disappointment, as if I had missed the easiest question on a test. I hated that I actually cared about letting him down. He let out a sigh before answering.

"Because, Harden, in my experience, those who are haunted are the most vulnerable."

"Vulnerable to what?"

"To everything."

CHAPTER FORTY-ONE

I saw Emma the next day. We both had midmorning classes on the same quad, so we met behind the music building in what had become one of our many rendezvous points. I had managed to call her the night before, right after Coyote left, to tell her what had happened and that Coyote was headed to her place. I barely slept during the night, tossing about in an impossibly warm bed, wondering what was happening at her place.

I arrived first, trying to look like I always loitered behind the back of the music building once the temperature dipped below thirty. Emma arrived after me, wearing a wool cap and a forced smile. Something was wrong.

"Hi, baby," I said, hoping I was misreading her. I wasn't.

"Hi." Her voice was flat. Not a good sign.

I wanted to reach in and kiss her, but we didn't do that in public. There was always a wall between us like that, and I hated that I was becoming used to it.

"What is it?"

She took a deep breath and exhaled a fog.

"We broke up."

Are you kidding me? She couldn't have told me better news.

"Did you tell him—"

"I didn't say anything about us, Harden."

"Then why did you—"

"We had sex last night."

Cold air burrowed through my thin jacket like maggots on a corpse, and I could feel the chill eat me from inside out. My stomach tightened to a tiny ball.

"Emma. I . . . I don't know what to say." What I wanted to say was that those simple words just broke my heart.

"Let me finish, Harden. I'm so sorry."

Now she started to cry, and yet I wasn't even sure if I could hold her. I wasn't sure I wanted to hold her, and I hated myself for that.

"He . . ." She struggled to talk through her tears. "He came over. I let him in. I . . . I didn't want him there, and we got into a big fight. I told him he couldn't move in and he flipped out. Afterwards . . ."

"Emma, you don't have to tell me."

"I need to, Harden."

What she didn't understand was I wasn't ready to hear any more, but I had to. It was what I was supposed to do.

"After the yelling, he wanted to have sex," she continued, wiping more tears from her reddened cheeks. "I told him I didn't want to, that he was crazy. But he . . ."

My breathing stopped. "He *what*, Emma?"

"He was really angry. I thought if maybe I had sex with him, he would calm down. I . . . I was scared."

"*What?*"

"He's different, Harden. He's changed, even since a week ago. He . . . I think he wants to hurt Derek. For real. I had never seen him like he was last night."

So why the hell did you fuck him? I wanted to shout. But I couldn't. Goddamnit I couldn't, and it was killing me.

"What happened, Emma?"

"I slept with him. It was horrible and angry and . . . ugh, I don't know. Afterwards I regretted it and I cried. Then I broke up with him. I can't be around him anymore."

"He raped you," I said. I wasn't even aware I had said this aloud.

"He didn't rape me, Harden."

I jabbed a finger at her. "He wanted sex. You didn't. You feared for your safety, so you finally agreed. Is that right?"

"It's more compli—"

"*Is that it?*"

My words stopped her short. She stood silent for a moment before nodding almost imperceptibly.

"You need to call the police," I said.

"No, Harden. Let it go. I'm okay. It was my own dumb mistake."

Rage suddenly consumed me, and it wasn't all directed at Coyote. *Yes*, a part of me said, *it was your own dumb fucking mistake, Emma. You are an intelligent, strong woman, yet you let this animal have his way with you to calm him down, but then you still broke up with him. Didn't that just enrage him more?*

But my true rage was focused on Coyote. Being with Emma had pushed me past a threshold I had toed my entire life. I was in the world of passion now, and I wanted to embrace every facet of it. As much as she had brought about the beautiful side of passion in me, I now tasted the darker side of it.

I wanted to kill Coyote.

"What . . ." I tried to remain calm and supportive, but struggled. "What happened when you told him you were breaking up with him?"

She stopped crying. "He smiled. He was perfectly calm. All he said before he left was, 'I think that's a good idea, Emma.'"

CHAPTER FORTY-TWO

It was late and the library air was onionskin dry.

Nightshift, eight to midnight. I enjoyed working the evening hours. No one bothered me much, and, aside from having to deal with a handful of administrative duties, I was free to do my classwork.

I pushed the book-laden wooden cart through the stacks, shelving the discarded volumes of information back into their dusty homes. I was in the most desolate of the stacks when I heard the soft pattering of feet on industrial carpet. The library was closing in less than fifteen minutes, and I hadn't seen anyone else in at least that long.

I was in the middle of the stack, the ends fifteen feet from me on either side. I turned my head in both directions and saw no one.

I put the book up on the shelf, close to where it was supposed to go.

I listened.

Nothing.

I wanted to peer through the stacks, but the old metal shelves had a solid backing, preventing me from seeing through to the other side.

Libraries are funny beasts. In the right moment, it's hard to think of a more calming and more meditative place. In the wrong moment, at those times when silence is a scream without the noise, there's nothing quite as unsettling as the sound of tens of thousands of books not being opened.

This was one of those times.

Then I heard the noise again. Someone was close.

Whoever it was, they weren't pulling books from the stacks. That sound is unmistakable, and I heard none of it.

Whoever it was just stood there, listening to me, as I listened to them.

I looked at the next book on my cart. It didn't belong in this aisle. Next one over.

I pushed my cart forward. My hands clung to the old wooden edges smoothed over by hundreds of palms before mine. I felt a thin sheen of sweat beneath my fingers.

I reached the end of the aisle and pushed the cart out into the open, turning it toward the next row of books. The one where someone waited for me.

I turned in.

No one.

The aisle was empty. Just books and their stillness.

Then something appeared at the end of the stack.

A person. Hands at his sides, arms tight with tension. Blocking my exit. He wore a mask.

It was the mask of a baby face. Eyes squinted. Mouth stretched into the smile of a carnival barker. Head disproportionately large, as if the baby had drowned. Cheeks bulbous and obscenely red.

He didn't move.

I froze.

Then movement behind me.

I turned.

Another baby-faced person blocked the other exit from the

aisle. I hadn't even heard him approach, yet he stood only feet behind me. Close enough to touch me. I could hear this one breathing beneath the plastic of his false face. Shallow and sweaty breaths.

I grabbed the fattest book on my cart, holding it in both hands in front of me, like a shield. I could swing it pretty hard, but it probably wouldn't do much good. If the library was empty and they came here for me, I was shit out of luck.

Nothing made sense, but in that moment, nothing had to.

I was scared as hell.

Then one of them started laughing.

It was the one farthest from me. His smiling plastic face remained frozen as the muffled laughing rumbled beneath it.

Then he took his mask off.

Coyote.

"Wow, you should have seen your face, Harden."

Relief didn't exactly wash over me. I held onto the book.

"What the hell, Coyote?"

The other one was laughing now, too. This one, however, kept on his mask.

Coyote walked toward me.

"I came for a visit." His laughing had eased into a simple lilt of pleasure in his tone. "Had these back at the house." He held up the mask. "Figured I'd give you a little scare."

"You did," I said.

"I can see that."

"Harden, this is Ben."

I turned around and the other man finally removed his mask.

I knew Ben. Big Ben, the frat-party bouncer. The one who had seen Emma and me in these very same stacks.

I wondered what was coming next.

Coyote put a hand on my shoulder. "Haven't seen you in a while, Harden." Coyote squeezed my skin a bit too hard. When he touched me, I thought of him touching Emma. Of forcing himself on her. I wanted to hurt Coyote for what he had done, but I knew I wouldn't just start swinging at him. Why couldn't I be that kind of man?

I pushed his hand off. "Been busy. Some of us have graduating to do." I tried to control my voice. I heard the fear in my words. Fear and anger.

"Ah, yes. That."

"Yeah, *that*."

"The place is shaping up," he said. "You should see it again."

Coyote left our apartment a month earlier. Jacob and Coyote, as expected, found a place on their own, a sprawling old Georgian that was once home to Sigma Chi before their local charter was revoked as a result of a pledge getting drunk, climbing halfway up the chimney before getting stuck, and subsequently dying. The house henceforth sitting empty, Coyote landed a good deal to rent it out.

It seemed a good place for Jacob and Coyote. And yes, others joined them. There were about twenty of them, all men. I didn't know what exactly they did over there. I had only visited once.

"I will if I get a chance," I said.

"How's Derek?"

"Okay, I guess. He's not in the apartment much. Has a new girlfriend."

"That so?"

"Yup."

"So you're alone there?"

"I suppose. It's not like we rented out your rooms."

"That sounds very lonely."

I shifted my gaze to Ben. Had he seen or heard anything that day in the library? Did he know anything about Emma and me?

Ben's eyes remained flat and dull. A weak smile lounged on a weaker chin.

"It's okay. I have a lot of work going on right now, so it makes things a little easier, actually."

That seemed to satisfy him for a moment. Truth was, Emma came over to the apartment all the time.

"I miss you," Coyote said. Big Ben took a deep breath through his nose. The aisle seemed to close in on me.

"I can't imagine you missing anyone," I responded.

"But I do. We're not as close as we once were, and that makes me sad."

"Sad?"

"You were supposed to be the secretary of the Revelation."

"And how do you know I've given that up?"

He seemed surprised by my answer. "But how can you document what you're not involved in? What you've written so far is great. I need more, though. I need *you*."

I glanced over at Ben, who took the slightest step forward toward me. "I'm still involved," I said. "Not too hard to follow your activities."

"Yes, I hear you've been asking about me."

My fingers dug a little deeper into the spine of the book in my grip.

"Trying to stay informed."

"And what have you heard about the Revelation?"

It just hit me then how much more formal his tone had become, almost professorial. He was fully immersed in the role he was now playing. Or, perhaps, he had finally found his true self.

"That you have a handful of people living with you now—"

"Children," Coyote corrected, nodding at Big Ben's mask.

The idea of his followers being called *children* disgusted me.

"Handful of *people* in the house," I continued. "More around the campus."

"Two hundred," Coyote said. "And not just here. All around New York."

"*Two hundred?*"

"You see? You need to be closer to the action."

"How did you get so many?"

Coyote shrugged as if getting hundreds of people to follow him was something that should occur without effort. "Two or three people are all it takes to start, just as I had expected. They are transformed and then want to tell others about it."

"Transformed into what?"

"Into something they weren't before. I'm the medicine for whatever ails them. They have no idea if I'm a placebo or not. All they know is that they feel better."

"Even though it's all in their minds?"

He chose to ignore this.

"So these people," he said. "My *Children*. They start talking to other people. Spreading the word. It hasn't changed in two thousand years, Harden. Most people they talk to think they're crazy, but a few are curious. They want a new way of looking at their own lives. They want *more*. They come to our introductory sessions. They see the video. They meet *me*. Some join. Most I never see again. It's just a matter of numbers, Harden. Percentages."

"Just like that?"

Coyote shook his head. "Nothing is just like that. Don't think I'm not spending every waking moment dedicated to my cause."

I didn't think that at all. I knew what kind of fanatic Coyote was. Truth was, I was monitoring Coyote's group as closely as possible without throwing myself into the middle of it. Coyote wasn't the only one who wanted me taking notes.

Mike Barrillo had become my new friend. He worked out of the FBI's Albany field office, and I contacted him soon after the night we first met. I told him I wanted to help, but it had to be on my terms. I wasn't going to be a part of Coyote's group, but I could try to keep tabs on what he was doing the best I could.

I sent Barrillo all the notes I had taken for Coyote so far. Then I scouted around a little more. I talked to people who had seen Coyote or Jacob. I asked about what they were up to. I did everything short of talking to Coyote himself, because Coyote was dangerous.

Coyote was good at a lot of things, but more than anything he was good at reading people. I was afraid he would be able to sense what I was up to. He would find the tape recorder on me as I probed him for details. He would look into my eyes and sense I was trying to bring harm to him. When that moment happened, there was no telling what he would do to me.

I wanted to hurt Coyote and avoid him all at the same time, and those two things could not coexist. I had to embrace one and release the other.

"You're still my friend, aren't you, Harden?" His hand was suddenly on my shoulder again. The veins in his forearms wormed visibly beneath his skin.

"It's about consumption, isn't it, Coyote? Your need to consume. Emma. The boy in the woods. The hooker. Now this, right?"

He kept smiling.

"Getting people to do whatever you want," I continued. "Whole groups of them. That's the ultimate consumption, isn't it? It's what you think will make you great."

"You can be great with me, Harden. Isn't that what you want? I thought you were with me."

"I need to graduate. That's the only thing I'm focused on."

He tilted his head. "You're jealous I chose Jacob and not you. Aren't you?"

This rare lack of perception surprised me.

"What do you want from me, Coyote?"

"I don't want you to be like Derek," Coyote said. "I want us to be close again."

"It's all bullshit, Coyote. Right now, here, can't you admit to me this is all bullshit? It wasn't very long ago you read my essay and came up with this plan, which was nothing more than a mental exercise for you. Just admit to me this is a game, and nothing more."

Coyote released his grip and shot a glance at Ben before focusing on me. "I know how this all started, Harden. But it's real. You were meant to write that essay to spark everything. I was meant to be the leader I've become."

"It's all parlor tricks," I said.

"No, Harden. It's all *belief*. You should see the kind of progress we're making."

"Progress?"

He nodded. "We're moving in directions you never thought of, Harden."

"That I believe."

"I'd really like you to be with us."

"As opposed to against you?"

Now he took a step closer and I could smell him. Leather and dried sweat. His stubble was a couple of days old and looked rough as sandpaper. "What is it, Harden?" He was whispering now. "Why do you hate me?"

Then I said it. I wasn't expecting to, but it came out with nothing to stop it.

"You raped her."

In that moment I expected him to hit me, and even bent my

knees and shifted my footing, preparing for a fight. But all he did was smile.

"Harden, I have no idea what you're talking about." Then he backed up, and as I straightened, Ben walked in front of me and put his meaty paw on my chest.

"Take it easy," he said. His hand was massive, and it felt like he could squeeze his fingers and rip my heart out with little effort.

Then Coyote laughed, and Big Ben joined him. Ben dropped his arm and they both turned and began walking away.

"Next time you see her, tell her I miss her," was the last thing I heard Coyote say that night. He and Ben turned past the stacks and disappeared as unexpectedly as they had arrived, leaving me frustrated, angry, and determined to finally make a fucking decision for once in my life.

The opportunity I was waiting for came in mid-May, just two weeks before graduation.

CHAPTER FORTY-THREE

May 1990

I had just finished my final exam in a throwaway music course. It was early in the evening, and I was crossing the North Quad just as the sun dipped below the rooftop of the liberal arts building. As I dropped my gaze back to the path, I noticed a man standing about fifty feet in front of me, looking in my direction. It took me a few seconds before recognition set in.

I walked up to him.

"Agent Barrillo."

Barrillo nodded. "Hello, Harden."

"I assume you came here to find me."

"Your assumption is correct."

I hooked my thumbs in the straps of my backpack and looked around. Mostly for Coyote.

"Sorry I haven't given you much over the last couple of months. I've been kind of busy."

He waved it off. "I need to talk to you," he said. "You have a few minutes?"

I did, but not many. I was supposed to meet Emma in about a half hour.

"A few."

"I drove here all the way from Albany just to see you. Let me buy you a drink."

"I don't turn twenty-one for another three weeks."

He laughed and put a hand on my shoulder. "The government has bigger things to focus on. Come on."

He walked me to a small parking lot adjacent to the university chapel and prompted me to get into a gray Ford Escort with government plates. The interior was spotless, and as he navigated us to the north side of town, music from a classical cassette tape filled the car. My throwaway course had at least taught me something: I was listening to a Bach fugue.

Barrillo seemed to have a place in mind, and minutes later he pulled up to a small Italian restaurant that I had never been to in all my time at Wyland. This part of town was mostly frequented by locals—too far a walk from campus and too uninteresting for those with cars.

We occupied a small booth near the kitchen and each ordered a Heineken; the waitress never even asked me for an ID. I realized my date with Emma would have to be postponed, and I was going to ask the waitress if I could use the restaurant's phone, but Barrillo never gave me a chance.

"Some of the info you've sent me has been useful," he said.

I hadn't given him much. Hell, I'd barely seen Coyote after he and Ben stalked me with baby masks in the library. "That's good."

"But there's not a whole lot we can use."

"Use how?"

"Against his father."

"I told you before. Coyote's never told me anything about his father, and I haven't asked."

"I know," he said. "But now I need you to. I need you to get Coyote on tape."

"Why is that my job? You work for the FBI, not me."

"Look, Harden, when I first approached you, this was kind of a fluff case. Sure, we've had our eye on Alastair Martin for a long time, just as we do a ton of different RICO guys out there. Some take more priority than others. I got assigned his primary detail after doing a stint in securities fraud, and I've been fortunate to dig up a few new things."

"Because of what I wrote?"

"No, of course not." He held up a placating hand. "Not that we're not grateful for your work, though." His tone sounded as though he was about to hand me a junior certificate of bravery made out in crayon.

Barrillo leaned over the table. "I want you to understand that anything I discuss with you is confidential and subject to criminal punishment if discussed with anyone outside of the Bureau. You understand that?"

"I understand."

He leaned back. "Alastair Martin is up to something, and we think it's somehow related to what Coyote is doing. I think the father needs the son, and this . . . *Revelation* is part of some other plan."

The idea stunned me. "Up to what?"

"I could be coy and tell you I'm not at liberty to discuss that. The truth is, we don't have a goddamn clue. Though I have some theories."

"Such as?"

Barrillo managed a tight grin. "I think Alastair Martin realizes what a charismatic and brilliant son he has, and the idea of founding a new religion as a way of creating a tax-exempt and protected shelter for him to launder money occurred to one or both of them at some point. Sometime over last Christmas."

Right before Coyote called and came to drag me back to school, I thought.

"Whoever came up with the idea first, I have no idea."

"Jesus."

"Or someone pretending to be him." Barrillo sipped his beer.

I thought back to my original paper, the one that had sparked Coyote's interest so much. Was that the reason he was so excited? Was he searching for a new way to launder money with his father, and my paper triggered the whole operation?

I told Barrillo about the essay.

"You never mentioned that before."

"I didn't think it was important."

He thought for a few seconds. "It's not," he concluded. "But it is interesting."

"Somehow, I feel guilty," I said.

"Don't. They would have thought of something else eventually."

"So he's worked with his father all along? He never really cared about school?"

Barrillo shrugged. "Who the hell really knows? My take is that Coyote's a rich son of a crook who was too smart to think he'd want to follow in his father's footsteps. But he lacked the patience to make a go at anything else, so he eventually decided to put his brain to use making a big pile of illicit cash into a bigger pile. I think he's bored. I think he likes the challenge."

This man just summed up Coyote perfectly.

"And Jacob?"

"I don't think Jacob has the foggiest clue about what's going on," Barrillo conceded. "I think Coyote takes his role very seriously, and he is truly committed to getting as many members as possible. I imagine he thrills at having everyone hanging on his every word, doing the things he tells them to do."

"What . . . what about the things they've done?"

He arched his eyebrows at me. "Like what?"

"The . . ." I felt stupid for saying it. "The levitation. The tree."

I received a patronizing smirk for my question. "Please, Harden. Grow up." His next sip finished the bottle. "That family has enough money to buy all the special effects they want."

"So why do you need me?"

Barrillo rested his elbows on the table and leaned in. "Because technically they haven't done anything illegal, at least not that can be proven. We know that Alastair has been to campus twice to meet with his son in the last month."

"He has?"

"Yeah, he has. I'm guessing that once Coyote . . . *legitimizes* his church, or whatever the hell he's creating, they're going to apply for a protective religious status with the government. Granted, that process can take some time, but it would be much easier to make a move against them before they even start it."

This was sounding too fantastic to be real. "But it's not even a religion," I said. "It's barely anything. It's a bunch of—"

"—lost college kids trying to find the meaning of life," Barrillo interrupted. "I know, I know. But don't think it can't be done, Harden. Look at Scientology. That's a helluva lot wackier than what your buddy is doing, and look how big that's become. But we're still early in the game. We just need some real proof. I'd bug his house, but we don't have enough for a warrant. That's where you come in."

The waitress came by and dropped off another round of Heinekens for us, unsolicited. My first one was still half-full. When she left, Barrillo continued.

"If they're smart, which they both undoubtedly are, they have to make sure they do things the right way. You know how he asked you to be his secretary—to write everything down?"

"Yes."

"Smart. They'll need as much documentation as possible.

Legitimate documentation. They need your notes as a way of showing what they're doing is real and not a scam."

"But it *is* a scam."

He wagged a finger at me. "But not the way you've written about it. You've been presenting it the way he wants it. Flowery but unbiased. Supportive. Believable. Your notes give credence to what he wants the rest of the world to believe. He needs you, Harden. You are in a position of power here."

I wanted to feel used, but I didn't. This was just another layer of brilliance I had to credit Coyote with. Then something occurred to me.

"Does any of this make me culpable?"

Barrillo arched his eyebrows. "Thought it would be a while before your mind jumped there. But, short answer: not really. If I were a real prick, I would tell you yes and hold it over you, knowing you couldn't afford any lawyer who would tell you I was full of shit." I noticed that Barrillo had loosened up considerably since he started drinking, and I wondered what another three or four beers would do to the man.

"But you still need my help?"

"I do. *We* do."

"And you want me to tape our conversations?"

He nodded. "How often do you see him?"

As little as I could. "Hardly ever anymore."

"Maybe start paying him a few visits—use that time to record your conversations with him."

That's exactly what I didn't want to do. "My tape recorder is a little big. He might see it."

"No. Not with that. I'll leave you with something a lot smaller—harder to find. I want you to get him to say something, anything, about his father."

This was going from bad to worse. "How the hell am I going to do that?"

"We've compiled some talking points—I'll give those to you. Probably won't work," he admitted, "so don't push too hard. Our case doesn't hang around you, but since you're already close with him, there's a small chance he'll say something wildly incriminating, and we can move things along much faster."

I felt my body slouch in the booth. "This whole thing seems . . . I don't know. Not what I would have expected from the FBI."

Barrillo smiled. "You mean it seems like we're flying by the seat of our pants?"

"Exactly."

Barrillo shrugged. "I will admit this is a little unconventional, but we also know when to take risks. This is a risk, but a calculated one. Like I said, probably nothing will come from it, but if you're game, you could make a real difference here, Harden."

Then something occurred to me.

"Do you think Coyote's father loves him?"

"What are you thinking about?"

Now it was my turn to chug the rest of my beer. The bubbles filled my throat, almost making me gag. I set the empty bottle down and said, "What if I was able to get Coyote to talk about a crime he committed a long time ago? It's something he's already told me before, so it would be easier to get him to recount it rather than me suddenly asking him about his father for no reason." I shifted in my seat. "Could that get Coyote arrested?"

"What crime?"

I ignored his question. "If his father loves him, wouldn't he do anything to get those charges dropped? Like plea to the crimes you suspect him of?"

Barrillo thought for a moment. "You watch too much TV,

Harden. Yes, I suppose that's all possible, but the crime would have to be significant."

"It is."

"What's the crime, Harden?"

"If it's all the same to you, I think I'll keep at least something to myself for now."

CHAPTER FORTY-FOUR

I graduated. It was a humid, rainy day in early June, and those of us receiving our $60,000 pieces of paper wore black gowns that, after mere minutes of soaking up rain, bled purple tears onto our clothes underneath. As I stood between Derek and Emma, I looked into the crowd and saw my father watching me. It was the first time in three years he'd come to the school to see me, but any bitterness I might have felt over that was erased the moment he shook my hand after the ceremony and told me he was proud of me. I think he was telling me the truth, and, though I didn't know what the hell I was going to do with an English degree, I was damn proud of myself, too.

At the reception following the ceremony, Derek's mother—whom I'd met on other occasions—pulled me aside to ask what was up with Jacob and that other roommate. *What is his name? Wolf?* I corrected her on Coyote's name and assured her that, while I saw Jacob from time to time, I had no idea what was going on inside his mind. She assuredly had received the same information from Derek, but she still gripped at her chest and told me in a performance worthy of at least a Daytime Emmy how she was *so relieved* Derek and I didn't get caught up in *all that weirdness.*

I agreed, gave her a half-hug, and then turned to Emma. She was standing next me, waiting to introduce my father and me to her parents.

Weird moment. Emma and I weren't exactly hiding our relationship, but we weren't shouting it from the rooftops, either. Derek knew, as did a few of Emma's friends, but there was still this weird fear of Coyote. We never even saw him anymore, but just knowing he was close somehow kept us from being as free as perhaps we would otherwise be. Graduation was what we needed to finally move on with our lives, and Emma and I were planning to go far away from Tillman.

Apparently Emma hadn't told much to her parents about either Coyote or what he was doing, but Derek's mother was quick to fill them in. Emma's father, a raspy-voiced man with a small paunch and rimless glasses, turned to his daughter.

"This is the man you dated?"

"Just for a little while, Dad."

Emma's mother, who, should the old maxim hold true, had looks that boded well for Emma's middle age, was equally distressed.

"How come you haven't told us about all this?"

"It's not important," Emma said.

"So they're trying to start a religion? As a joke?"

"I don't think it's a joke anymore," I said.

"Clearly not," Derek's mother said. "They dropped out of school for this. I've known Jacob since he was a freshman with Derek, and it just breaks my heart to see him throw his life away like that. God, to think it could have been Derek . . ."

My father, not one usually to join a conversation, broke his silence and said, "I spent a few hours with Coyote earlier this year, just as he was itching to start this whole plan of his. I didn't get a good feeling from that boy at all. Not a bit."

Emma's mother turned her attention from my father back to

Emma. "But you're not involved with him anymore, are you, dear?"

Clearly Emma hadn't told them about me. This would have to change soon, considering our plans.

"No, Mom, I'm not."

"Well, thank goodness. You certainly don't need *that* right now."

Everyone collectively nodded and *mmm-hmmmed*, and in the following silence it suddenly struck me that everything was good.

I don't know why that sense washed over me, but it did. Perhaps it was how easily this group of people churned and discarded the stories about Coyote, but everything that I had been consumed with and scared of suddenly seemed insignificant. There was nothing to fear, and Coyote was merely one of those eccentric people you meet in your life that warrants the occasional stories to your friends when you're older.

I felt a weight slowly lift from my chest, as if waking from a bad dream and realizing it was, in fact, just a dream.

Everything was going to be fine. Derek would spend a few more weeks on campus before going home to work with his father. Emma and I were planning to go to San Francisco. She had a management-trainee job lined up with some fancy Hyatt out there, and I'd find work. It wouldn't pay much, but we'd be happy. And Coyote and Jacob would become interesting, albeit pathetic, footnotes to our lives' histories.

That would be that. I was certain of it.

I lightly put my hand on Emma's back, keeping it there even under the weight of her father's gaze.

All was good.

CHAPTER FORTY-FIVE

I turned twenty-one a week after graduation, and the next day Emma was going to leave for San Francisco. I had just bought my plane ticket and was planning to join her a week later.

I finished my last shift of my last day at the library, and as I walked away from the stacks I realized it was the most steady job I had ever held. I was glad to see I had it in me. I could commit to something for a long time, see it though.

One last trip to Benny's. It was just after nine o'clock, and the moon was hiding behind clouds that had choked the sky all day. The air was thick and meaty with summer, as it always was in June, and I breathed it in, wondering what the air in San Francisco tasted like. Salty, I imagined.

I had this life in front of me I could only see in bright, momentary glimpses, these flashes of colorful bursts like fireworks exploding behind the tops of trees. I couldn't see much, but I was excited by what was out there. And I liked that I really didn't know what was going to happen next. Soon it would all start.

I reached down and tapped the front of my jeans, feeling for the recorder Barrillo had given me. He was right—it was small. The microphone taped easily to my chest and ran down to a control unit I had chosen to place inside my underwear. Not very comfortable, but surely much more so than strapping that damn Walkman to me.

Coyote was going to be there tonight, at my invitation. I needed him alone for enough time to get him to say something that would help Barrillo out.

I pulled out my ID—my *real* one—as I approached the bar, wielding it as proudly as had I been holding Excalibur herself. The bouncer, whom I suspected of letting me slide with the fake ID all this time, smiled and nodded his head as he checked my card. "Happy birthday," he said, letting me by. It seems weird that I never knew his name, and he had always known me as William Green from Minnesota. But tonight, I was me.

The air in Benny's was slightly less stifling than the air outside, but the smell was much worse. This, of course, I had grown accustomed to over the years, but it always seemed to me that Benny's was a deep cleaning shy of being a moderately decent place. But I guess not making the effort was also part of the bar's charm.

Derek and Emma were sitting at a table waiting for me. I got a happy birthday from both, a handshake from Derek—who was wearing his trademark *ANOTHER SHITTY DAY IN PARADISE* t-shirt—and a deep hug with a squeeze from Emma. There was a pitcher of beer already on the table and three shot glasses filled with, I guessed, tequila.

After we settled in, I dropped the news.

"Coyote's coming tonight."

They both looked at me as if I told them I just set fire to a daycare center.

"Why is *he* coming?" Derek asked.

"Because I invited him." *And because I need him here*, I didn't add. No one knew about my relationship with Barrillo, and I intended to keep it that way for the time being.

"Does he know we'll be here?" Emma asked.

I nodded. "Look, if it's awkward . . ."

She shot me a look that conveyed more words than she could have spoken, and I knew exactly what she was feeling.

They hadn't spoken since they broke up. Emma wanted nothing more to do with him, and I don't blame her. But there was a reason I wanted all of us together in that bar.

I needed to see Coyote and Emma together. I needed to see her reaction to him. I needed to remember what he did to her and how he made her feel, because I needed to hate him again. That sounds terrible. It's immature and selfish, but I'm not trying to justify it.

My hate had been wearing off, slowly but not without notice, and I was starting to feel my resolve to destroy him weaken. I was leaving for a new life with Emma in a week, so I had only a limited time to make a last push to put an end to what he was doing. Once I was gone, I was gone, and I knew I wouldn't look back.

"Yeah, Harden," Emma said. "It's awkward." Her look wasn't hateful, but rather questioning, as if saying, *Why would you do this to me?* God, that made me feel shitty.

"Is Jacob coming?" Derek asked. I couldn't tell by his expression if he wanted him to come or not.

"I don't know," I said, which was the truth. "But I would doubt it."

"Harden . . ." Emma said.

I held my hand up. "Look, it's my birthday, okay?" I tried to give her a look that said *I'll explain later*, but I don't think it worked. Barrillo swore me to secrecy, but once I told him I was moving, he said I could tell Emma when we had left the state. In a week I could explain everything to her, but for now she had to love me enough to do what I asked of her.

"Fine," she said, not quite pouting but clearly not pleased. I had to stay focused. Using the cover of the tabletop, I reached under my shirt and put two fingers down the front of my jeans, a move I had practiced many times in the last few weeks. I turned the recorder on and hoped the ambient noise from the bar wouldn't wash out the audio.

Seconds later, Coyote walked in the door. Alone.

He looked like the same old Coyote from our early days together, from when he robbed me of my tooth, but I knew better than to judge anyone, especially Coyote, on the kind of clothes or expression they wore.

I saw Emma flash Coyote a look of disgust, and that alone was enough to make me hate him all over again.

"A reunion of sorts," Coyote said, standing next to our booth. Derek and Emma sat across from me, and I saw them both look up at Coyote. Neither of them wore a welcoming expression.

"Hey, Coyote," I said. "Thanks for coming."

He shook my hand. "Harden, wouldn't miss it for the world. Happy birthday, man." As I shook his hand, he pulled me up and gave me a hug, which was strong and sincere. I don't remember ever having hugged him before.

He released me and turned to the table.

"Look," he said. "I know this is uncomfortable, okay? I mean, here I am with the girl who broke my heart and the guy who nearly broke my jaw." His smile was gentle and welcoming. "I want to apologize. I know things have been weird with me. I know I'm an intense person. My ambitions . . . well, sometimes they take me over. I know I have lost your friendships." He was looking directly at Derek and Emma now. "And I don't expect to make up for everything over a drink. But I just want to sit in peace with everyone here, just for a little while, okay?"

My gaze went to Emma. Her look of anger had changed to something else. Did she miss him? My stomach turned as I considered that possibility.

"Okay," she said.

Derek said nothing.

"Good," Coyote said. He waved to the waitress, whom I recognized from the last time Coyote and I were here together. I wondered if she remembered him levitating, or if she had discarded that memory as quickly as it took for the next night's worth of drunken idiots to fill her bar.

The conversation idled until the waitress returned and set Coyote's shot in front of him. He pulled out a hundred and handed it to her.

"Bring the bottle, will ya?"

Another nod. "Keep your feet on the floor this time, Dumbo."

Coyote ignored her as I smiled. Then he raised his glass, prompting us all to do the same.

"To Harden," he said. "A truly selfless friend."

My shot glass hovered for a moment. I stole a glance at Emma, who didn't look back at me. We all downed our tequila and, as the liquid slid down my throat much easier than it had four years ago, I wondered what this night had in store for us.

"When are you going to get a job, Harden?" Derek asked me with a thin smile.

I shrugged.

"You'll find something," Emma said, then winked.

"I have no doubt," I said, smiling at her.

"We're growing," Coyote said. "We could use your help. It won't be much longer before we need to organize with a full-time staff. I think we could pay you a competitive wage."

That almost made me laugh. "What kind of job would you want me for?"

"I'm going to need a chief operating officer," he said. "Someone to keep track of members, dues, bills, that sort of thing. You're organized, you're creative, and you know me better than anyone. You have no other plans. Seems like a perfect opportunity."

Derek leaned in. "You're charging dues now?"

"Fifty dollars a month."

"For what?" Emma asked.

Coyote shifted his gaze to her and quickly scanned her face. Assessing her. "I know you guys think what I'm doing is bullshit. And maybe at some point it was. Maybe . . . maybe that's how I always presented it. But what I'm doing is real. Legitimate. I need to collect dues to provide that legitimacy, at least to those on the outside looking in."

"How are you legitimate?" Derek asked. He squinted, which he always did when he started to get pissed off.

The waitress dropped the bottle off and Coyote refreshed everyone's glasses before he answered.

"Six months from now you won't even recognize the Revelation," he said. "We'll have over a thousand members. We'll have official government recognition in the form of tax-exempt status."

That wasn't even close to answering the question, I noticed.

Derek's mood started to change. He wanted to engage Coyote.

"But what does your . . . whatever the hell it is . . . even do?"

"Church of the Revelation. And what we do is give people hope."

"Hope?"

"That's right."

"Hope of what? Learning how to uproot trees?"

Coyote barked a short laugh and looked at the table.

"That's not how it works, Derek."

Derek dismissed his comment. "Because none of it's real."

"Oh, it's very real."

"How? How is it possibly real?" Derek straightened in his chair. "Explain it to me. Explain to me how you can perform a couple of parlor tricks and call it a religion. Explain to me how you can take someone like Jacob and derail his life so easily."

"Jacob is happier now than he ever has been. You wouldn't know because you haven't talked to him in months."

"Take it easy," Emma said. I wasn't sure which one of them she was talking to.

"It's not a religion," Coyote said, his voice soft. "It's not a cult. It's a . . . methodology." Coyote was the first to take his second shot, tilting it back with ease. "I'm telling you, Derek. It's not bullshit. I've discovered something and I want to tell people about it." He glanced sideways at Emma. "The hard part is finding people who are willing to listen. *Really* listen. Open their minds to new possibilities."

I felt an anxiousness creeping over me, the kind that makes you want to walk away from an argument rather than weather the futility of carrying on. But I couldn't help myself.

"Coyote, your whole experiment was based on something I wrote. It was an experiment from the beginning, because you were bored and you wanted to see if it could be done. How can you tell us now that it's a real thing?"

"Harden." Coyote spread his hands in a pacifying gesture. "I'm not here to convince any of you. I just came here to buy you a drink, man."

"He asked you a simple question," Derek said.

Coyote looked over at Derek and gave him the exact look he had given to that Colombian right before he leaned in and threatened to kill him. "I'm not asking any of you to believe in what I am doing. I'm just telling you it's real." He lightly tongued a drop of tequila still hanging on the edge of his shot glass, eying Emma as he did. "You can choose to follow whatever path you want to take. I've found mine."

Derek's words squeezed through a tight mouth. "Jacob's parents have driven up here three times, and he's refused to see them each time."

"Yes," Coyote said, seemingly disinterested. "I know."

"He's broken their hearts," Derek continued. "They're thinking about getting the police to investigate."

Coyote shifted his gaze to Emma. "Breaking a heart is not a crime," he said. "It's merely a shame." Emma dropped her own gaze to the table.

"Yet you think Jacob is better off now than he was seven months ago?" Derek asked.

Coyote didn't seem to be bothered by the inquisition. It was as if he was in control of the conversation, choosing which pieces he wanted to engage and which he wanted to parry away. "Jacob is a believer," Coyote said to Derek. "Just as I hope Harden here will one day be. As for you and Emma . . ." Coyote shrugged. "I don't think you could ever open your minds enough to see all the things Jacob can now see."

Emma started to say something, but Coyote cut her off. He leaned across the table to Derek.

"You know, we have a word for people like you, Derek. We call you Andalusians."

"What the hell does that mean?"

Coyote leaned back. "They were the first ones killed in the Spanish Inquisition in 1481. They were the original doubters." Coyote settled back and waited for a reaction, the part he always seemed to like the best.

I couldn't tell if he was joking or not. "So part of your *methodology* is to torture and kill people who disagree with you?" I asked. It was time for me to down another shot, which I did with no hesitation.

Coyote nodded. "We have a special set of rooms for just that purpose. Not here, of course. In another state." His gaze set upon each one of us, intense but brief. Then he broke out his famous Coyote smile. "Jesus, lighten up, everyone. I'm only kidding."

"I *so* don't get you," Emma said.

Derek abruptly stood. "You are so full of shit, man. I'm out of here."

I reached out with my hand, knowing it wouldn't do any good. "Derek, come on."

He turned to me. "Happy birthday, Harden. You'll have to get drunk without me."

Then Emma stood. "Yeah, I think I'm calling it a night, too."

She gave me a quick but telling look, and I knew exactly what she was thinking. If I loved her, I would go with her and Derek.

But I couldn't.

I was wearing the wire, and I needed Coyote to talk. I couldn't leave. Not yet.

"Well, aren't I just a big fucking buzzkill?" Coyote said. For a moment I feared he'd offer to leave and let everyone else stay, but he didn't budge.

I looked up at Emma, trying to tell her so many things without speaking and failing miserably. "I'm going to stay here a bit longer," I said.

Her eyes widened just a bit and then her face relaxed into the pantomime she had developed during our secret affair. "Suit yourself," she said. She leaned in and, to my surprise, gave me a small kiss on the cheek. "Happy birthday."

"Thanks."

Without saying good-bye to Coyote, Derek and Emma walked out of Benny's.

After they left, Coyote poured us another shot and told me to drink up. I did and he followed suit, and, with the bottle of tequila still two-thirds full, he peeled another hundred from his wallet and dropped it on the table like it was a used tissue. Two hundred dollars for a stupid bottle of Cuervo and tip.

"Take a walk with me," he said.

It was the last thing I should have done, but it's exactly what I did.

CHAPTER FORTY-SIX

The rain started coming down ten minutes into our walk. It was a light summer rain, the kind that did little but wet the roads and relieve some of the pressure that had been building in the pregnant air all day. It certainly wasn't enough to deter Coyote from his path, which as far as I could tell was a direct route down the western slope of campus toward the downtown area. I only asked him once where we were going. When he didn't answer, I didn't ask again.

For the most part I walked alongside my former roommate, though when the path narrowed I walked behind him, which I'm sure secretly pleased him. It occurred to me that following him blindly was exactly what he sought of me. This walk was a metaphor, and though I didn't want to help fulfill any fantasies he had, I needed Coyote to talk before I went in my own direction.

I began to bait him.

"Does it bother you that you've lost your friends?" My words were spoken into his back as I struggled to keep up with him.

"I haven't lost anything," he said, not bothering to turn around.

"What about Derek and Emma?"

"Derek was never a friend," he said. "He was always threatened by me, so I never let him get close. And Emma . . ."

I wiped rain from my face. "Emma what?"

"Emma isn't lost. Not yet, at least."

"What does that mean?"

He finally turned. "Emma is like you." It was dark, and a nearby streetlight illuminated half of his face, the raindrops giving him a waxy, jack-o'-lantern expression. "She wants something, but she isn't sure what exactly that is. You're both searching so hard and wanting so much, but there's a door in front of each of you that you refuse to open."

"I have no idea what you're talking about."

He put a hand on my shoulder, just as he had that night at the library. It didn't seem friendly. He seemed to be holding me down. "I know you don't, Harden. That's the problem."

He turned and kept walking. I didn't want to follow anymore. I wanted to turn in my own direction—anywhere but his—and lose myself in my own life. In a few days I would be gone, I reminded myself. Gone from this. Gone from everything except Emma. But tonight I needed to focus.

"The boy you killed," I said. "Do you think he opened a door he shouldn't have?"

Coyote turned and faced me, his one illuminated eye showing surprise.

This is it, I thought. *He's going to talk about it.*

I was suddenly worried that the rain had soaked though my jacket and pants and into the recorder. But I couldn't let that distract me. I leaned in, hoping for the best audio.

Yet Coyote said nothing. Instead, he slowly wagged his finger at me and gave me a grin that, for all my efforts, I could not interpret.

Did he know what I was doing? How could he?

Then he turned, once again. "We're almost there. Then you'll understand."

The rain picked up, as if what had previously been coming down was only an overture. I flipped up the collar of my Army jacket, which only served to drip water down the back of my neck. Coyote turned right down a small side street lined with hundred-year-old houses, and after a block I saw where he was taking me.

The Tillman Cemetery rested on a sloped piece of land that couldn't have been more than a couple of acres, yet it seemed to hold the history of the world within it. The plots ranged in years and condition. I couldn't imagine it was still open for business; there was simply no room left. What amazed me most was the abundance of mausoleums: intricate, carved chunks of granite rising several feet above the ground, each proclaiming a simple Anglo-Saxon surname at the top. Tillman never seemed the place where anyone had enough money for such an elaborate decaying bed, yet here were these markers of history proving otherwise.

The cemetery was dark; no artificial light guided us. The moonlight filtered just enough through the clouds so I could make out the shapes closest to me, and none of them seemed inviting. I instinctively inched closer to my guide, though I wondered if I was safer with the ghosts.

Halfway through, Coyote stopped and turned to me.

"There are over six hundred bodies in here," he said. "Six hundred people buried over a period of a hundred and twenty years." He had to raise his voice over the rain, which by now had soaked through to my skin and chilled me. Coyote raised his finger. "Not one person in here was well known. Not a single name would be familiar to you, Harden."

I waited. I glanced around me, but didn't want to take my eyes off him. There was something wrong with Coyote, and it wasn't the tequila.

"They lived their lives for shit, Harden. They might have been happy, they might have raised normal, productive children. They might have fucked beautiful women and eaten unimaginably exquisite food. But in the end, here they are, and no one remembers their names."

"So that's it? You just want to be remembered?"

Coyote shook his head. "You don't get it, Harden, do you?"

"Get what?"

"I don't want to just be remembered, Harden. I want to *be*."

"Be what?"

"Harden, you need to feel what it's like. I can open that last door for you. Once you go through, you will never want to go back."

"You're not making sense."

"You just haven't allowed yourself to understand."

I pushed my fingers back through my hair, squeezing the water out as I did. "Why do you need me, Coyote? Why is it so important to you?"

As soon as I asked the question, the answer blindsided me. It was so simple.

Coyote was talking nonsense on purpose.

He didn't need me to see anything. The truth was that only a handful of us knew Coyote was full of shit, and no one more so than me. His whole grand experiment was based off something I had created, and now that it was potentially turning into something much larger than all of us expected, he didn't want anyone unmasking him.

Jacob had followed him because he was too stupid to see Coyote was nothing more than a slick carnival barker. Coyote was hoping I, too, would believe he'd discovered a new form of existence, and here he was, soaking wet in the middle of a cemetery at midnight, testing me. He wanted to know which direction I was going to go.

I became uneasy. I didn't want to be here anymore.

"What if I don't go with you?" I asked.

"You have to, Harden. It's no longer a choice for you to make."

"Or what? I'll end up like the boy in the woods?"

He cocked his head and gave me another grin, his lips crooked and waxy in the wan light.

"That's the second time you've mentioned that tonight. Why is that? Is there something you want me to say, Harden? Is there something you need to learn from me?"

My pulse raced and my face flushed despite the chill of the rain. I wasn't even sure the recorder was working at this point, yet I had decided one more time to broach the subject, and I had just aroused his curiosity. In a bad way.

"I . . ." I didn't know what to say. "I've just been thinking about it a lot, that's all. It . . . it haunts me."

"You don't know what haunting is, Harden. It's time now, okay?"

"Time?"

"It's just time."

Coyote was suddenly gone, and I could barely make out his figure running down the crooked cemetery path, down the hill, and toward the sleepy street at the base of the cemetery.

I ran after him. I was so close. He hadn't said anything yet, but I could feel it. Just a little more time was all I needed. I suddenly wanted this more than anything. I wanted Coyote to be caught, exposed. Humbled.

Seconds later I caught up with him. Coyote had exited the cemetery and was now standing in the middle of the street, his arms held out wide. As if responding to a command directly from him, the rain suddenly started to come down in sheets. I was drenched and stood on the curb, my back facing the short cement wall that encircled the cemetery. I shouted out.

"What are you doing?"

There were no cars to be seen, and only a handful of houses dotted this quiet side road that connected the university to the downtown area. Coyote spun around in a tight circle, his arms still outstretched.

"Get out of the road, Coyote."

I knew he heard me over the pouring rain, but he didn't pay any attention. We were on a tight bend at the base of the hill, and a car traveling in either direction wouldn't see Coyote until it was almost on top of him.

Especially at night. Especially in the rain.

He wanted to convince me. He needed me to join his side. One less liability. But what was he doing? How was he . . .

Headlights came. I saw them before I heard the car.

A small car. Traveling from campus. It just rounded the bend.

Going fast. Too fast for these conditions. Probably a student.

"Coyote, get the fuck—"

Then I heard the tires catch what they could of the asphalt, which wasn't much. Coyote didn't move an inch. He had been facing up the road the whole time, as if he knew exactly when the car would be coming.

I was about to watch him die. I couldn't move. I couldn't breathe. I wanted to do something, but there was only time to helplessly watch it all unfold.

The car veered sharply to the left—missing Coyote—and came right at me. It was the last thing I had expected, but now I was the one about to die.

Instinct finally pushed me off my feet into a dive to my right. At the same time, the driver must have spotted me and pulled to the right. If the car had turned in my same direction, I would have been crushed between the front fender of the car and the cement wall behind me.

The front tires slammed into the curb and exploded. Yet the car barely slowed. In the split second before it hit the wall, a million thoughts went through my head, not the least of which was that it was a small car. Coupe. The kind you bought your kid for college. The kind that didn't stand up well to a cement wall.

The sound of it all was horrible.

CHAPTER FORTY-SEVEN

The car smashed against the concrete wall, crumpling like a massive beer can under a heavy boot. The wall didn't seem to budge at all.

"Go to a house and call nine-one-one!" I shouted toward Coyote as I raced to the front of the car. I didn't know what I could do, but I had to do *something*. Stinging rain streaked my vision, making everything a desperate blur.

I looked back toward Coyote, who walked toward me like a gunfighter knowing he was going to win. There was no hurry to his stride, but goddamn if there wasn't purpose.

Why won't he get help?

I turned back to the car and yanked at the driver's door. It was bent, but after using both hands and all my strength to pull on it, it cracked enough for me to pry it halfway open. I was terrified of what I was going to find on the other side.

I heard the moan as I bent down and peered in.

A woman. No. A girl. Maybe even younger than me.

Her wheezing confirmed she was alive, but in the washed streetlight I could see that the steering column had bent directly into her chest.

She turned her head toward me.

"*Help . . . me.*"

I gulped the air, smelling rain and piss. She must have lost control of her bladder shortly after she lost control of her car. I didn't smell gasoline. Good sign.

"It's okay," I said, hoping I was a good liar. "You're okay. We're getting help."

I straightened from the car and a fresh wall of rain pelted my face. Coyote was still ambling toward me.

"Why aren't you getting help? She's hurt! We have to hurry!"

I felt her touch me, and I lowered my head back into the car and found her reaching out, grabbing at my arm, turning as much as her pinned torso would allow. She wore a thin shirt, long-sleeved. Dark stains covered what looked like white fabric, and as much as I wanted those stains to be nothing more than shadows, I was certain it was blood. Her nails weakly scraped my forearm.

"You're going to be okay," I said.

"Please . . ."

Stop wasting time. Get her out.

But I couldn't. For all I knew her chest was crushed. Didn't they say not to move the victim unless absolutely necessary? And what if the steering column was the only thing keeping her organs inside her body? How was I going to help her? How were we—

I spun, ready to release all my fear and frustration on Coyote. The only people who could help this girl were paramedics, and we had to call them. Why wouldn't Coyote call?

A hand pushed me against the car. Hard.

Coyote then grabbed my shoulders, yanked me around, and punched me in the face. A flash of pain shot through my head, heating my body against the rain.

I tried to fight back but was helpless to do anything. He flipped me again as if I were nothing more than a rag doll, then pinned me on my stomach to the soaking ground. The collapsed front tire rested just inches from my face.

"Wake up, Harden!"

A fist slammed into my lower back and seemed to push a kidney right though my skin. I howled through the pain, and then thought immediately of the recording device. *He's going to find it, and then he'll kill me for sure.*

"What the fuck!" I screamed. "Get off of—"

He cut me short by pulling my hair back and leaning into my ear. I could smell the tequila on his breath.

"You're alive now, aren't you? Feel it, Harden. *Feel it.* This is what I was talking about."

I didn't feel alive at all. I felt asleep. It all seemed to be happening on another plane of existence, one in which I had no control at all.

He yanked so hard on my hair I was certain my scalp was going to rip completely off. God, I wanted to hurt him back. I've never wanted to hurt someone in my life as much as I wanted to hurt Coyote in that moment. I almost forgot about the girl dying in the car just feet away from me.

"You want to know what it was like to kill that boy in the woods?" Coyote said into my ear. "It was the best feeling in the world, Harden. I consumed him. He was mine for the taking, and I *took.*"

Was the recorder still on, and was it capturing this? I couldn't do anything but hope, and the next thing I knew I was on my feet, but only because he had yanked me effortlessly off the ground. I didn't understand how the hell he was so strong. Maybe he *did* have some kind of power.

Coyote dragged me to the passenger side of the car, where the door appeared intact. He yanked it open and shoved me inside. Next to her. For a second, my cheek touched hers, and her skin was cool wax. I heard her shallow, raspy breaths. She smelled of mints mixed with the coppery fumes of blood.

Coyote squeezed his face inside the car with us. His body pressed up against mine from behind, blocking me in.

He grabbed my right hand. It happened so fast. Everything was happening *too fast*.

He pressed my hand against her mouth, covering her lips and nose. I tried to pull back, but I couldn't. Goddamnit, why couldn't I move my hand? He was too strong.

The girl's eyes grew so wide they seemed to breach their sockets. She tried to flail underneath me, but she couldn't move.

"Stop!" I screamed.

"Feel it," he replied. Coyote was right there. He was everywhere. He pressed harder.

I think I screamed. I don't remember. I do remember feeling the girl's teeth beneath my fingers. She was trying to bite me.

"*Feel it*, Harden."

I pulled and pulled, but my hand was glued to this girl's face. She stared at me with a look that will haunt me forever. Not even a look of fear as much a look of *why are you doing this to me?*

Then she started to die. Her body shook and heaved under my weight. I was suffocating her and I couldn't remove my hand.

I felt her tongue on my fingers, desperately trying to burrow between them, seeking even the smallest of air holes.

I'm sorry, I wanted to scream, but that would have made everything real. This wasn't real. This couldn't be real.

In the dim light, I could see her eyes begin to roll. A heavy wetness rattled in her lungs.

Coyote pressed harder on my hand. His knee pressed into my lower back. I never felt so helpless in my life.

"You're killing her," he said in my ear, inside my head. "Your face is the last one she will ever see. You are the last moment of her existence. *Understand* that, Harden. You're not her murderer. You are *God* to her."

"Please stop," I pleaded, aware I was now crying. But Coyote was a boulder I could not move.

Blood welled in her eyes, and two dark tears rolled down her cheeks and stained her neck.

Then she was gone.

Her eyes stayed open, but she was gone. The moment a person dies is unmistakable. In an instant, she was nothing more than a bloody doll.

She was dead, and I killed her.

Coyote released his weight and yanked me back from the car. I collapsed on the curb and immediately threw up. The rain showered over me but it could not wash away what had happened.

I looked up and he towered over me, fists balled, hair hanging in wet, ropey strands over his face. I thought he was going to kick me, but instead he merely turned away, perhaps thinking I was only a shell of a man, no longer—and perhaps never was—any kind of threat. Maybe he was right.

Coyote removed his soaking shirt and wiped down the outside of the car door. Then he reached in and wiped anything that we had touched.

That was when I charged at him.

Everything I had left I put into attacking Coyote. I wrapped my arms around his legs and managed to lift him off the ground, slamming him hard onto the street. If a car was coming, we'd both be run over, but I didn't care. I wasn't just going to hurt him.

I was going to kill him.

I could tell I caught him off guard, but he quickly adjusted to my attack. He slammed his elbow into my ear and I thought my head was going to explode. With the speed and strength of an Olympic wrestler, Coyote was then on top of me again, pinning my stomach to the street and my hands behind me, his knee in my lower back. I struggled and fought him, but I couldn't do anything. I was a little boy, helpless under the weight of an older, stronger man. All I wanted to do, for once in my fucking life, was fight back, and even if I died inflicting my own harm, at least that would be something. I did not want to die as simply as a bug being stepped on.

"You're a part of this now, Harden. The police will come soon, and you killed her. You can go or stay. If you go, you go with me." He pushed my bones deeper into the asphalt. "If you stay . . . well, good luck to you."

His weight suddenly lifted.

I turned over, and saw Coyote running up the hill through the cemetery. In a few seconds he was gone, lost among the dead and their homes.

I only waited a few seconds before I ran after him.

CHAPTER FORTY-EIGHT

The rain mixed with my sweat as my feet slapped the hard pavement beneath me. Up through the cemetery, onto Watkins Road. Behind a house, onto another street. I wanted to stop. I wanted to turn around. Go back. Wait for the police. But I didn't know how. It was as though once my initial instinct to run was acted upon, my body couldn't rewind. There was no other course.

And then I saw Coyote in front of me. It was dark, and he had a good lead, but I just made him out in the moonlight.

The chain of events from the last few minutes flashed through my mind.

Coyote knew he could cause a car accident. He knew someone would eventually drive down that road, and it would swerve to avoid him. He knew the wet pavement would cause the car to lose control. The moment Coyote realized I wouldn't join him, he decided to kill someone and implicate me in it. It was the only way to keep me on his side. It was the only way to control me.

He had bet his life on it, and he was right.

I had run away. I was a coward, and he had predicted all of it.

I stopped.

I gulped at the thick air, trying to drink it in. I tasted the sweat on my lip, salty and warm, mixing with rainwater.

I thought of *her*. I thought of her eyes. Dead, vacant eyes.

Suddenly, Coyote stopped and turned.

I struggled to hold still, almost hoping he couldn't see me. I don't know why, but I didn't want him to see me.

But he did. He looked right at me. I couldn't see his face, at least not clearly, but I knew he was watching me.

I thought I saw him shake his head. I could almost hear his voice in my head.

Don't do it.

He was reading my mind, I thought. He knew. He knew what I had to do.

I thought of my father. I could see him, watching me, as if he were dead and looking down upon me. It was such a strong sensation I almost looked up, though I knew he wasn't there. Yet I could feel his gaze pierce me, and inside I could hear his judgment. Would I do the right thing? Or would I continue to be a disappointment to him? Was this the moment, he wondered in my head, that I would find what he found? Salvation? Was this the crisis I needed?

Do it, Harden. Go back to her. Get help. Tell the truth. Whatever road you start walking down now, you'll be on it for quite a while. Choose the right one.

Coyote kept watching me. I could only see his outline. A scarecrow hoping for company at the back of a barren field.

This was my future. I could see it as clearly as I could still see the blood of that girl in my mind. This was the rest of my life. Right now.

I spit on the ground, jettisoning bile from my mouth. I reached down and patted my crotch, feeling the recorder. Everything still seemed to be in place. Whether or not it had captured anything was a different story; I would have to wait to find out.

As I turned, I knew Coyote would keep watching me. I didn't care. I began walking back to the car. Soon the police would be there, and I would tell them everything that happened. Explaining things would go a lot easier if the device had recorded any of the last few minutes.

I heard footsteps behind me, growing louder.

Faster.

Harder.

I turned.

Coyote was no longer human. He was an animal. Suspended in midair.

Reaching.

Clawing.

He knocked me off the ground.

I heard a crunch as my head hit the pavement. Pain seared through me, but I didn't lose consciousness.

I tried to stand, but he pushed me back to the ground and kicked me in the ribs. I lost all breath and desperately tried to suck in fresh air, but it wouldn't come.

Then there was another sensation.

A prick in my skin. The sting of a needle.

A sensation of cold in my chest.

Then everything went black.

PART III

CHAPTER FORTY-NINE

Harden woke in the cell, as he had done countless times before, cold and hungry, soreness seeped into his bones, and a rancid taste in his mouth, the flavor of rotten meat. None of this was new. Yet there was something different this time. He could feel it.

He eyed the scar on the back of his right hand. It was healed over with only a thin red snake of a line across the bones. He slid his hand under his shirt and felt the stitches. Or where the stitches had been. They'd removed them some time ago—maybe a week? Now a series of raised bumps replaced the open stomach wound Bill had been so happy to give him.

The scar felt the same to him.

Since the game, the other Baby Face had been the only one in contact with Harden. The man talked very little. Bill seemed to have disappeared. Maybe Bill had been fired. Maybe Bill was dead.

Harden stretched along the floor, feeling the pain in his joints. He didn't know how much longer he could last. Since the day the second Baby Face had Tased him, Harden had thrown himself into his writing. He would never leave here by escape—two painfully failed attempts made that clear. He had to write to live. It was a long shot, but it was his only hope. He didn't have the strength for anything else. His book was nearly done.

He wondered what Coyote thought of his latest chapters.

Harden hadn't been harmed since the day Bill cut him. That day seemed like months ago. Perhaps it was. He wondered if Emma was still alive. He thought about that a lot. Maybe more than anything else.

Harden rolled over and opened his eyes. He had no idea how long he had slept. He never did. This time, though, it felt like he'd slept for days. He scratched at his beard, which was at least two inches long. He fucking hated his face covered in hair, but, as with everything else in this situation, there was nothing to be done.

Again he felt the sensation of something *different* in the cell, but Harden couldn't tell what it was. Something had woken him, and it wasn't the cycle of either the sun or moon, because he had no concept when one was up and the other was down. His gaze first caught the typewriter. He hadn't put his last bit of manuscript by the door, he remembered. Instead, fatigue had overcome him, and he'd bedded on the dirt floor without even removing the last page from the machine.

But it was gone. Gone, too, were the other pages, once neatly stacked on the desk.

Harden's eyes opened wider and he tried to force alertness on himself, but it was like trying to see clearly through a pair of glasses that weren't yours.

They'd never removed the pages when he was sleeping. They'd always made him stand in the corner before collecting the pages. When did they come in? How had he not heard them?

The answer came to him as a dull ache in his left arm. He looked over and saw a small bruise just below his shoulder. In the center of the bruise was a very small hole, nearly imperceptible.

They injected me again.

He moved his gaze to the dirty lightbulb and focused until the image finally became sharp. His body was weak and his mind torpid, but this small exercise made him finally feel awake.

He felt a sharp urge to pee. He struggled to his feet, shuffled to the corner, and relieved himself in the bucket.

I've been out a long time, he thought.

He zipped, turned, and that's when he saw something he wasn't sure was even real.

The door was open.

Not much. Just an inch or so, enough to create a vertical slat of light that widened as it pierced the dull grayness of his home. But it was open.

He would have run to the door if he could, but only slow, steady movement kept him from falling. It could be a trap. They could be waiting on the other side with the Taser, just to destroy his hope. Harden didn't care anymore. He had given up hope, so he had nothing to lose. He just directed himself to the light and didn't think much about the consequences.

He reached the door, brushed his greasy hair out of his eyes, and peered through the small opening, seeing nothing but the wall on the other side of the hallway. He strained to hear the faintest noise, but there was only silence.

Harden opened the door.

He took a hesitant step out into the light, waiting for a blow to strike him at any moment. But none did, and the only assault came from the intensity of the fluorescent bulbs above him. His eyes struggled against the piercing brightness.

He turned and looked back inside his cell, seeing it as the Baby Faces had seen it—from the outside. In that moment Harden decided if he was going to die, it wasn't going to be back in there. If they found him in the hallway, he would try to kill them. Knowing he most likely couldn't, he would ask them to finish him off. Anything but being put back in that room.

Movement on the floor of the cell caught his eye.

Charlotte.

Whether the spider had seen the open door and was also trying to escape, or if she had finally decided to bite Harden, she was heading directly toward him. He hadn't seen her in days, maybe weeks, though every time he closed his eyes to sleep he would wonder if she would come out to crawl on him. Inject him with her poison, just because she could. When he woke, Harden would often spend the first minute or so delicately searching his body and clothes for signs of her.

She kept coming toward him. Straight line. Full speed. Harden stood and watched until she nearly made it to his foot. Then he softly raised his shoe and stepped on her, crushing her beneath his toes.

And that was that.

When he lifted his shoe and saw the smeary remains, he felt a faint surge of energy. Harden had, at last, defeated something.

He turned and looked down the hallway. The door of the other cell was open, as was the door at the far end of the passage, revealing the stairs behind it. It was as if the prison wardens had just abandoned their posts. He had to look for Emma.

As he got closer to her cell, he heard only silence. He didn't know if he could bear looking inside. What if he found her in the same state he had discovered Derek? The thought was too awful to consider, yet it was the only thing he could think about. Still, he had to look.

Oh, please, God.

His legs nearly buckled in relief when he saw the cell was empty. No Emma. No table, chair, or even bucket. He looked at the dirt and found not even footprints on the hardened earth. Thin lines stretched in haphazard patterns on the soil, as if lightly raked. None of this meant she was safe. But at least he didn't find her body.

Harden left the cell and made his way toward the stairs.

CHAPTER FIFTY

He'd been here before, centuries ago it seemed. He had been about to walk up the stairs then, but instead he went to the other cell and discovered Emma. That was as close to freedom as he had made it.

As he put his foot on the first step, he wondered how far he'd get this time.

Fluorescent lights buzzed overhead as he listened to his weight press on each riser. His ascent was slow, and he expected at any moment a Baby Face to open the door at the top and kick him back down the stairs. The muscles in his legs had grown weak enough for him to burn with every step, and he knew he wouldn't have the energy or the power for any kind of fight.

One step at time. The old wooden stairs creaked under whatever weight he still had. Halfway up, he took a moment to rest.

Finally, he reached the top. Harden placed one hand on the round doorknob and wondered what he would do if it was locked.

It wasn't. It turned easily in his hand, and the sound of its mechanics seemed to echo in the stairwell. He pushed the door open a few inches.

A kitchen.

A kitchen?

Holy shit, he thought, *it's just a kitchen.* An old one, small and simple, something out of another era.

Harden opened the door all the way.

Then he started to cry.

CHAPTER FIFTY-ONE

The normalcy of the house overwhelmed him, but what triggered his weeping was the sunlight. Real sunlight, streaming in through dirty windows and faded, laced curtains. Harden hadn't seen sunlight in a long time. He walked through the kitchen and into an open living room, which was small, simple, and sparse. In the vague sense, it reminded him of his father's house. Functional, spartan, depressing. The air was stale, and even had a touch of rot to it.

Then he saw the body.

There, beneath the windowsill, laid out flat on the wood floor. Peaceful, almost.

Harden knew exactly who it was.

Bill.

Bill, the man who liked to answer questions as long as the person asking was willing to pay a price.

He was in his underwear, his skin as white as copy paper. A jagged wound erupted from his chest, and blood had pooled and congealed around the body.

"I didn't want to do it."

Harden spun and nearly lost his balance.

Across the room, a man was sitting on a tattered green couch. Harden had no idea how he missed him before, but there was no mistaking who it was.

Ben. Big Ben the frat bouncer. Friend of Coyote. Child of the Revelation.

He was casually cleaning blood off a hunting knife with a bandana. Harden turned his head, looking for a weapon, but there was nothing he could use. Certainly not before Ben sliced him to pieces.

"Don't worry," Ben said. "If there's one thing I do well, it's following orders. And my orders are to let you go. Unharmed."

Harden found his voice.

"Where's Emma?"

Ben seemed to consider whether or not to answer.

"She was taken out yesterday."

"Taken by whom?"

"Others like me."

"Where did she go?"

"Couldn't say."

"Can't or won't?"

"Doesn't seem like you'd end up with the answer in either case."

Harden tried to swallow but found only cotton on his tongue.

"Who do you take your orders from?"

Ben looked up, mid-wipe. He didn't answer.

"Were you the other Baby Face? Bill's partner?"

The wiping resumed. "I was."

"Why did you kill him?"

Wipe wipe.

"Because I was told to. Like I said, I follow my orders."

Ben stood and sheathed the blade in a scratched leather holder fastened to his belt.

"I'm leaving now. Wait ten minutes after I drive away and then you can start walking."

"Where are you going?"

Ben took a set of keys from his pocket. "Away."

He started walking toward the door.

"Wait . . . wait a minute."

Big Ben stopped.

"What does Coyote want with me?"

"I have to go."

Harden took a step toward him, unafraid. "You owe it to me. After what you did to me, you owe me answers."

Ben scratched the back of his neck. "I'd say it's up to me to decide who I owe and who I don't. I don't owe you anything, Harden."

"I need to know why," Harden said. "Why he did it. Why he wanted me to write."

Ben chewed on this question for a moment, seeming to decide whether or not to answer.

"Let's put it this way. Coyote thought he knew Bill. Just from a few basic things Bill wrote down, Coyote thought he had him pegged. And he did, for the most part. Bill was a normal-seeming dude who, underneath a mound of fat and muscle, was actually a fucking psychopath who got erections watching people bleed." Ben tapped the side of his head. "Coyote got that about him—he *saw it*. Knew how to use his talents. But he didn't know Bill couldn't be totally obedient. He thought Bill would know not to play games. Not to talk to you. But Bill couldn't control himself, and Coyote didn't see that coming. Bill died because of that."

"Bill died because he disobeyed," Harden said.

Ben shook his head. "You don't get it, do you, Harden?" Ben took a step toward him and Harden felt himself tense. "Bill died because he was *unpredictable*."

"Like me."

"If I had to guess, I'd say Coyote needed to *learn* from you. You were consistently unpredictable, and that made you worthwhile."

"Yet he let me live."

"I don't think he's done with you. Maybe there's another act to this. One that he's got all planned out for you. And when you see him again, you can ask him all these questions yourself."

Finally, Ben pivoted and reached for the door. He opened it and Harden could feel a rush of air—*real air*—enter the room. The scent was instantly intoxicating.

"Don't ever think you're safe as long as Coyote's alive," Ben said. He placed one foot—clad in an old cowboy boot—just over the threshold to the outside world. "And don't think she's safe either, because she certainly is not."

Harden started to speak, but Ben raised a hand.

"No more questions. Ten minutes. Then you can leave. Then you'll be a free man, depending on how you see it."

Ben walked outside and shut the door behind him. Moments later, the sound of a car rolling on dirt and rocks slowly faded until Harden found himself alone in a silence to which he had grown well accustomed.

Harden had no watch, so he had to guess at how long ten minutes would last.

The house was old. Barnlike. Small. Next to the kitchen was a small living room with nothing in it except a tattered couch and an orange floor lamp, its brightly glowing bulb highlighting the dirt and grime on the faded hardwood floors.

The walls had been plastered several times over, the most recent layers cracking and peeling like makeup on a decaying clown. Harden turned back to the kitchen and saw something he hadn't noticed on his first scan. On the counter, partially hidden behind a large cardboard box, sat a computer monitor and a fax machine.

Harden pressed the power button on the monitor. The indicator glowed green for a moment before turning red. No source. A keyboard and mouse rested next to the monitor.

He looked down and saw the computer. Its power was off, but Harden knew better than to even bother turning it on. On the floor next to the computer was the system's hard drive, the black central nervous system that contained all the data. Harden counted seven holes that someone had neatly drilled through the box.

He eyed the door to the left of the living room. That was the exit. To where, he didn't know, but it went outside, which was a better option than inside. He didn't think he could wait a whole ten minutes.

One more minute, he told himself.

Harden quickly checked around for a phone, finding none.

Then he turned his attention momentarily back to the cardboard box on the kitchen counter. He looked inside.

His manuscript.

He pulled out the pages, smelling the dirt, sweat, and blood that had embedded into the fibers. Everything he had written since his first day was there. Then he looked at the fax machine and understood.

This is how they were getting the pages to Coyote, he thought. *Which means Coyote is nowhere near here.*

Where the hell am I?

The impulse to run suddenly overwhelmed him, and Harden did one more thing before acting upon it. He opened the refrigerator, finding only a half-empty gallon of milk. He opened the cap and took four large gulps, thinking he'd never tasted anything so good before. In the cupboard next to the refrigerator, Harden discovered three PowerBars.

He put the milk and the PowerBars into the box with his manuscript, picked it up, and walked directly out the door Ben had left open.

A farm.

He was on a farm. Nothing but decades-old trees and long-abandoned crops filled his view, and Harden decided with little effort it was the most beautiful thing in the world. He was outside. He was free.

Harden felt a few more tears fill his eyes as he started to walk.

CHAPTER FIFTY-TWO

The air was thick and wet, and a squadron of buzzing insects circled Harden's head as he made his way down a long dirt road. He turned and looked at the house. It looked so simple. So normal. Soaking it in, it was hard to believe that house had been his prison.

There were no cars, though tire tracks were still visible on the dusty path that stretched for a seeming eternity alongside acres of crops disguised as weeds. Harden no longer cared about staying out of sight. He didn't want to veer off this path and get any more lost than he already was. Wherever he was, Harden knew he was alone, and it sure as hell didn't look at all like Tillman, New York.

His initial joy at seeing the sun quickly faded as the rays beat down upon him without mercy, preying on his blanched skin and weakened muscles. He took a greedy swig of milk and tore into a PowerBar, devouring it in seconds.

Less than a minute later he collapsed to his knees and vomited. His body simply wasn't ready for any food different than what he'd been eating for so long. He stayed on his knees for a few minutes, wondering how long it was going to take to find someone. Or for someone to find him.

After wiping his chin, Harden resumed his walk. There was only one direction. Straight ahead. He didn't care how long he had to walk. It was just what he was going to do.

After what felt like miles but was likely less than one, the road ended in a "T" and Harden had to make his first real decision. Right or left on another dirt road, this one with faint tire tracks in each direction.

Harden looked at the sun and decided it was afternoon, which told him where west was. He went right, which was west.

Another eternity passed. The crops faded into trees, some of which showed faded sprinklings of orange and red.

I was taken here on my birthday, Harden thought. That was June. *Jesus, how long was I in there?*

Something bit his neck and Harden slapped at it, peeling his hand away to discover a fat mosquito smeared on his fingers, its blood mixed with Harden's. He wiped it on his filthy pants and kept walking.

He suddenly wished he wore a watch. He never had, but it seemed desperately important to know the time. He needed to be connected to something, even if it was just knowing the hour of the day. A watch with a calendar would even be better.

He fantasized about that for a bit, and then he started thinking about food. Real food. Hamburgers. Pizza. Homemade lasagna, with some spicy chorizo cut up and mixed in. Beer. An icy Rolling Rock in a bottle.

He flirted with a fantasy about how everyone was going to react when they found out Harden was alive, but he forced the thoughts away. He couldn't go there. Not yet. He had no idea where he was, which meant he wasn't safe. He wasn't rescued. He was still lost—the only difference now was he was outside rather than inside. For all he knew he could be fifty miles from the nearest interstate or town, which meant he'd have to sleep outside. He had no idea how cold it got at night, and he had nothing to keep him warm. He might be free, but he was far from safe.

He had just started to digest this thought when he saw another road.

Actually, the first thing he saw was a stop sign, the familiar red octagon beaming at him like the face of a long-lost friend. It was a hundred yards away, give or take, staked into the ground where the earth sloped gently upward.

He stopped and stared at the sign. As he savored it, something even more beautiful whisked by. A car. A car had just sped past the tiny intersection, the small gray blur traveling north at a million miles an hour.

Harden started to run.

The milk sloshed in the container with every pounding step, and the pages threatened to bounce right out of the box as Harden half-ran, half-stumbled his way to the stop sign. As he reached the sign, panting and sweating, he saw what he knew would be just over the rise.

A road. A real fucking road. Asphalt and everything. It was a two-laner, with a faded procession of white stripes stretching in each direction as far as he could see. There was even a street sign, giving Harden the first clue of his location.

County Road 7.

It didn't mean anything to him, but it didn't matter. It sounded like the most important road in the world, and he knew people liked to drive on important roads. The car he had seen was well out of sight, but where there was one, there would be more.

Harden wasn't going to take any chances. He wasn't going to stick out his thumb and hope someone would stop for a hitchhiker who looked like death.

Harden placed his box in the middle of the road and then sat down next to it, waiting for the next car to come barreling by.

It didn't escape him that this was exactly how Coyote had caused that poor girl's death.

CHAPTER FIFTY-THREE

He watched the sun creep along the sign as he waited.

And waited.

He couldn't believe no one else had passed along the road, but that's exactly what happened. Nothing. The most important road in the world seemed to be closed for business. It had likely been less than a half hour, but in Harden's mind there would never be any cars to pass this way again. He just started to think about walking when he heard the engine.

The truck was far away but visible. Heading south. Harden's instinct was to jump up and start waving his arms, but that was too risky. The driver might swerve around him, thinking him insane. No, Harden had to hope that the driver would stop for someone who looked badly in need of help.

He stretched his body along the middle of the road, his torso bisecting one of the painted stripes. He watched as an old white pickup truck rumbled closer, showing no signs of slowing. It would either stop or it would run right over him.

As it barreled toward him, Harden wondered if this was a really stupid decision. He could just start to make out the outline of the driver when he decided to reach up with one arm, a zombie rising from the grave.

The driver finally slowed.

Instead of getting out, the driver pulled the pickup alongside

Harden's body and rolled down the window. A perfectly normal-looking man. Midforties. Denim button-down shirt. Nicely combed hair, with a few streaks of gray just above the ears. A look of hesitation on his face.

"What the hell you doin' in the road, son? You hurt?"

Harden wanted to jump up and hug him but didn't want to scare him off. He slowly sat up.

"Please help me. I've been . . . I've been held captive and I just escaped. I don't know where I am."

"Captive? What do you mean captive? Like a prisoner?"

"Back there," Harden said, pointing off in the distance.

"Only thing back there is Nathan McHurley's old house, and that place has been abandoned for years."

"Farmhouse," Harden said. "It was a farmhouse. They kept me in the basement. Large basement. Locked rooms."

"Maybe I should call the police."

"Yes, yes. Please call the police. I need help. Please, call them. Call anyone."

"Okay, then, son. Calm down and get your ass out of the middle of the road. No one comes down here much, but you don't want to get run over." He checked the rearview mirror and lifted the handset of a CB radio. "And stay where I can see you. I got a gun nice and handy here so don't try anything stupid."

"No. No, sir. I won't." Harden moved to the other side of the truck. As he did, he noticed the license plate for the first time.

Iowa.

He yelled at the man through the closed passenger window. "Is this Iowa?"

The man waved him off as he spoke into the CB. When he finished, he rolled down the passenger window.

"What's that now?"

"Your plate says Iowa. Is that where we are?"

"Holy shit, son. You're either stoned, stupid, or telling me the truth. Goddamn yes, this is Iowa. Carlyle County." He stared at Harden a moment longer. "You really didn't know that?"

Harden shook his head. "Last place I remember being was in New York."

"*New York?*"

"Yes."

"Well, the police are on their way. I'll sit here and wait with you, but forgive me if I don't invite you inside my cab. Stay where I can see you, and keep your hands at your sides."

"Yes . . . yes, sir. And . . . thank you."

"Well, wouldn't be right if I didn't do something." The man turned his head and spat a wad of something out onto the road. Turning back, he said, "Name's Walter Hornsby." He offered a small and not unfriendly nod.

Harden nodded back. "Harden Campbell."

The man blinked, then drilled his gaze deep into Harden's face.

"The student from New York?"

Harden nodded, his excitement growing. "Yes. Wyland University. You've heard of me?"

The man finally grinned. "Hell, the whole country's been looking for you and a couple other kids." He reached over and opened the passenger-side door. "Get in here. I can't believe I just found myself a bona fide celebrity."

CHAPTER FIFTY-FOUR

Eighty-four days.

Harden still couldn't believe it. Eighty-four fucking days he'd spent in that cell. For eighty-four days, people all over upstate New York were looking for three kids who had just graduated from Wyland University. The search now continued for Emma and Derek.

Harden took a sip of his water and placed the plastic cup back on the tray suspended over his hospital bed. The cold water made his stomach growl, and he yearned for real food. But it was only his second day in the hospital, and his doctor told him he was malnourished and had to work up to consuming larger meals. Another couple of days, the doctor said. In the meantime, all sorts of fluids and nutrients raced through an IV tube into his arm, making him have to piss every half hour.

The last two days had been little more than a blur. Walter Hornsby took a picture of Harden using a beat-up 35mm camera he kept in his truck while they waited in Walter's truck for the police to show up, telling him he was going to send the photos to any news agency willing to shell out for it. It was Walter who told Harden how long he'd been missing, and the news stunned Harden into silence as they waited. Eventually a squad car came, followed by an ambulance and, for some reason, a fire truck. Harden was taken on an endless journey until he ended up in Cedar Rapids, where he was admitted to a hospital with the word "Memorial" somewhere in the name.

There he was poked and prodded by a team of doctors who examined every bit of his ravaged body. In Harden, the physicians discovered a cornucopia of ills, including malnutrition, anemia, broken teeth, fractured ribs in various stages of healing, cuts along both sides of the face, and poorly sutured knife wounds to the back of his right hand and lower abdomen. Not pretty, one doctor had told him, but nothing that couldn't be fixed. More than once he was told he was lucky to be alive.

The doctors eventually gave ground to the police, who poked and prodded Harden even more. It didn't take long for the reality to strike everyone fully.

Here was the missing kid. All the way from New York. Kept prisoner in an old farmhouse in Iowa. Who had done this to him?

Clues to that answer came from Harden's manuscript, the bloodied, typed pages he'd been carrying when he was rescued. But that manuscript ended with the chilling scene from Harden's twenty-first birthday in June. There was nothing in the pages about what happened to Harden after that night. How he got to the cell, and what happened to him there. The police asked many questions, but Harden simply told them he would only speak to Agent Mike Barrillo from the FBI. His allowance for trust was narrow.

Thanks both to Walter and a medical staffer who gained access to Harden's medical chart and recognized his name, word of Harden's sudden reappearance spread. In a few hours, swarming reporters from networks and newspapers descended on the hospital. The doctors closed access to their patient, and even the attempts to reach Harden by his hospital-room phone were thwarted. That was okay by

Harden, who wanted nothing to do with them. There was so much to tell, but not to these people. He just wasn't ready to talk about it.

All he wanted was to talk to his dad, eat a burger, and get some sleep.

Reston Campbell took the first flight out and saw his son about eighteen hours after Harden had been found. Harden had never given thought to how much, if at all, he loved his father, and vice versa. But seeing his father's tears and hearing his voice crumble into exclamations of gratitude to God and Jesus revealed what Harden had always hoped to be true: the father and son, in fact, loved each other immensely. The reunion ended with the doctor insisting on rest for Harden and his father promising to be back first thing in the morning to see "my little boy." Harden had never heard his dad use that term before, even when Harden had been a little boy.

He stared at the clock on the wall, its illuminated hands telling him it was just after eleven at night. Harden managed a weak smile. He was happy to know the time once again.

Seconds later, his door slowly opened. Harden tensed, still associating an opening door with bad things happening.

His doctor stepped into the room. "Sorry to bother you, Harden," he said. "I know it's late and you need to sleep."

"Can't," Harden said. "I've been sitting here awake since you last left."

"I've been talking to the police. They've been tracking down the man you've been asking for." He looked down at a piece of paper in his hand. "Mike Barrillo?"

"Yes," Harden said. "Agent Barrillo. FBI."

"FBI. Yes. Right."

"Did they contact him?"

"No. Well, that is, not exactly."

"What do you mean?" Harden sat up more in his bed.

The doctor looked uncomfortable. "Harden, you see, the thing is—"

"The thing is *what?*"

He sighed. "There is no Mike Barrillo with the FBI. The police have assured me they checked thoroughly, and no one with that name, or any name like that, works there. Are you sure you have the name right? How do you know him?"

Harden's head was spinning, not with disbelief at the nonexistence of Mike Barrillo, but as his own stupidity.

Of course Barrillo's not real, at least not a real FBI agent. He was Coyote's plant all along.

He wasn't in the theater that night to question Coyote, Harden realized, but to question me. *The actor playing Barrillo got me to tape Coyote, but I'll bet it was our own conversations being taped and being fed back to Coyote. More information to use against me, data with which to judge me, to* consume *me.*

Coyote knew everything all the time. When I wrote about Barrillo, he wasn't shocked or scared, he was laughing his ass off at my naiveté. He probably couldn't believe I was so stupid to actually think a real FBI agent would want to enlist the help of a dopey college kid.

Harden thanked the doctor and told him he would talk to the police now. He'd tell them anything they wanted to know, though his understanding of the truth was suddenly blurred. The police would search for Wiley Martin, though Harden already knew Coyote had likely disappeared again, and wouldn't be found unless that was part of his plan.

Coyote had a plan for everything, had a reason for his every move. And his last move was to take Emma and disappear somewhere, while setting Harden free.

This was calculated, Harden now realized. This wasn't a move by a man fearful of the police closing in on him. This was Coyote's way of telling Harden to come and find him. Harden pictured Coyote's face, and this time he saw fangs. *Come and rescue Emma, your secret love. The woman you stole from me.*

Coyote didn't really let Harden free after all. He just let a little slack out of the leash as he pulled Harden deeper into the dark forest.

CHAPTER FIFTY-FIVE

The criminal forensic examiners found Derek's body buried under three feet of loose dirt thirty feet behind the old farmhouse. Although an advanced state of decomposition had loosened the flesh and sloughed most of the skin from his face, identifying him wasn't very difficult. It was Derek, and the wounds Harden described to the FBI were consistent with the ones found on the corpse. Death by exsanguination as a result of knife wounds, the medical examiner concluded.

The FBI appended the kidnapping charge with murder, naming Wiley "Coyote" Martin as the primary suspect. Initially, the story came only in small bursts of incomplete information, infuriating the public, who, suffering a slow news cycle, demanded to know the most intimate details of what had happened at that tiny college in New York.

Before long, however, the story came together. Harden followed it loosely in the paper and on the news from his father's house in Owen, though he refused to grant interviews himself. It was enough that he had to repeatedly talk about his experience with investigators. He didn't want to relive it all with entertainment and news reporters who promised him cash and celebrity. Harden wanted none of that. All he wanted was to find Emma, which neither he nor the police were any closer to doing.

In the end it didn't matter. The media had enough sources inside the FBI to show the alleged trail of destruction Coyote had left:

Coyote started a bogus cult for the assumed sole purpose of establishing a credible religious institution in order to shelter his family's illicitly gained income. His father had been thoroughly questioned, but that yielded no clues to the whereabouts of either Coyote or the woman he abducted. No charges had yet been filed against Alastair Martin.

Coyote duped hundreds of would-be believers with fierce words, intense charisma, cheap parlor tricks, and, as it turned out, drug cocktails, rendering some of his followers nearly catatonic.

Coyote had demonstrated criminal negligence in the death of Cassidy Parker, the nineteen-year-old sophomore who smashed into the brick wall surrounding the Wyland cemetery.

Coyote and his Children kidnapped three Wyland students, murdering one and torturing two others.

A Child of the Revelation simply known as Big Ben had killed one of the Revelation's own: Bill Stuggart of Olathe, New York.

No one knew who Ben really was, and no one would ever find him. Big Ben simply vanished.

Jacob was not named in the arrest warrant, but was rather being treated as another potential victim of Coyote's. No one had heard from Jacob since June.

No one else from the Revelation was talking, and despite Bill's body and the treasure trove of other evidence at the farmhouse, nothing linked Coyote directly with any of the crimes. Even a record from the fax machine at the farmhouse showed all the pages from Harden's manuscript had been sent to a phone number registered to a man named Simon Wolff, who turned out to be completely fabricated.

None of it really mattered, though. Not to Harden.

Only one question gnawed at him. In those biting hours, usually after midnight but before dawn, when sleep felt like a burden, a chore to be postponed to another day, and when the sounds of a house made the whole world feel manufactured, only one question gnawed though Harden's body like a cancer.

Was Emma alive?

CHAPTER FIFTY-SIX

It had been three weeks since Harden walked out of the farmhouse, feeling the sunshine for the first time in months.

Now he was safe, but he was far from being the person he once was. Despite his youth, Harden aged immeasurably over the past three months, and he no longer obsessed about his future. As long as the future existed, that was good enough for him.

His father looked up at him from across the table, the two men separated by plates of eggs and chipped mugs half-filled with coffee. The coffee was weak. That was the way his father took it, and so that was the way Harden made it.

Harden took a deep breath and said something he had never uttered to his father in all the years of his life.

"I love you."

Reston Campbell blinked.

"Well, hell, Son, I love you, too. You know that, don't you?" Reston fought to maintain eye contact.

"Yeah, I guess I do." Harden didn't know why he had said those words suddenly to his father. He supposed because it was a statement of fact, and it seemed a bit silly to keep such things a secret. "Kinda wish I said it more growing up." He then amended his comment. "Or at all."

"Me, too, Harden. Me, too." Reston finally dropped his gaze and focused on his eggs. Harden looked out the dirty window and stared at the dead grass that was the front yard.

"Empty today," he said. "First time that's happened."

His father chewed. "They'll come."

Harden wasn't so sure. The media had made daily encampments outside the residence, hoping for a brief moment with the young man who had so far refused to tell his story publicly. Harden remained inside the house, though occasionally Reston went out to pace the front porch, cradling an old shotgun in his arms like it was a newborn kitten. This kept the reporters on the other side of the chain-link fence, and even the most tenacious of them refrained from yelling out questions. After a few days, the herd thinned, and Harden hoped he had seen the last of them.

"You can stay here as long as you want, you know." Weak sunlight highlighted the leathery creases in his father's face. "Maybe find a job here in town. Or . . . or do your writing. Whatever makes you happy."

Harden smiled. It was just ten months earlier he sat at this same table and watched as Coyote insulted his father. Harden was ashamed to remember agreeing with Coyote at the time, but that sentiment was now gone. He wanted it to stay that way, which is why Harden knew he couldn't live here forever.

"I need to figure out what I want to do, and I'm not sure this is the best place for that."

He father nodded and muttered, "Ayuh."

"But I want to stay for a little while, okay? You know, rest up and figure some things out."

Now his father returned the smile. "Long as you want. Like I said."

"But today, I'm going outside. I'll walk to the store—get some groceries."

"Now wait a min—"

Harden cut him off. "Dad, I'm going crazy in here. Remember

what the doctor said? Don't stay in confined spaces too long?" He swept his arm in front of him. "This place is a pretty confined fucking space. No offense."

"Language, Harden."

"Sorry."

"What about the reporters?"

Harden looked outside. "I think they're gone. To be safe, I'll wear a ball cap and go out the back."

Reston mulled it over. "Want company?"

Harden shook his head. "No, thanks. I think I want to be alone. Just for a bit, okay? You make a list of what we need, and I'll take care of everything else."

"Okay, Harden," his father said after a silent moment. "If that's what you want."

Of all the things Harden was unsure of, it was the one thing he did know he wanted. He wanted to be in a world without walls, if even just for a brief walk to the store.

CHAPTER FIFTY-SEVEN

The day fought to maintain its relevancy, a difficult thing to do in a town where indifference took a backseat only to Steelers football.

It was an intense sun for mid-September, and the heat sat on Harden's skin like an unwanted blanket. His skin was still sensitive to sunlight, and his dark sunglasses didn't keep him from constantly wincing against the glare. Still, he was outside, and he promised himself he would never take an open sky for granted again. He reached the sidewalk at the next cross street and pulled up on the brim of his ball cap.

The grocery store was in the opposite direction of his old elementary school. Not having to walk past it was another thing for which to be thankful.

He made an errant kick at a broken piece of pavement, sending the piece tumbling a few feet into a thatch of weeds. He was just a block away from the store when he heard the footsteps behind him.

Harden turned at the sound, then froze when he saw the man walking toward him.

Agent Barrillo smiled.

Well, not Barrillo. The man who played the role of Barrillo.

There was perhaps thirty feet separating the two of them, and that distance narrowed by the second as Barrillo kept walking and Harden stood still, his legs unwilling to do as his brain commanded, which was *run*. Moments later, Harden knew it was meaningless to try to flee. He simply wasn't strong enough and would be overtaken by the man in seconds.

Harden scanned the ground and saw a rock resting against a discarded piece of wood. The rock wasn't enormous—about the size of a fist. But that was big enough. Harden lunged for it, picked it up, and held it at shoulder-height.

"What the fuck do you want?" He kept the rock hoisted, knowing in reality his aim was poor and a rock was no match for a weapon if Barrillo had one.

Barrillo halted and held up his hands. "Whoa. Take it easy, Harden. I just want to talk with you a moment."

Harden cocked his arm back a bit more. A drop of salty sweat fell from his forehead onto his upper lip. "I'll call the police."

"With what, that rock?"

"Just leave me alone."

Barrillo took one step forward. "So, I'm assuming at this point you know I'm not with the FBI. Sorry, buddy, I was just following orders. Though I have to say I'm pretty pleased with my acting. You fell for the act hard."

Harden waved his arm holding the rock.

Barrillo didn't seem intimidated in the least. "Look, Harden, if it makes you feel any better, I had no idea that sick fuck was going to do what he did—it certainly wasn't part of the plan. I was just playing a small role, and I didn't even enjoy doing that."

"Where's Emma?"

"Well, now, that's exactly what I wanted to talk to you about. Put that rock down and we'll discuss."

"No," Harden said. "You'll tell me right now."

Another step closer. Harden hoisted the rock higher.

"Don't be afraid, Harden."

"I didn't say I was afraid."

"Then put the rock down."

He kept it raised. "Coyote tried to kill me. I'm not putting the rock down."

"I don't work for Coyote, actually. I work for his father. There's so much you don't know, Harden. You don't even know my name."

"I don't care what your name is."

"Sure you do. It's Vincent. Really, no bullshit. I won't tell you the last name."

"Tell me where Emma is or I'll smash this rock—"

In three fast strides Vincent was on him, his movements so fast Harden only had time to cock his arm back to swing the rock. Vincent swiftly punched Harden's arm just above the elbow, and Harden howled in pain as the rock fell harmlessly to the sidewalk. Then Vincent's hand was around Harden's throat, his fingers squeezing against his trachea.

"You ever hear of a honey badger, Harden?"

Another squeeze meant Vincent wanted an answer.

"No," Harden rasped. He could smell the sweetness of Vincent's cologne.

Vincent smiled. "A motherfucker of an animal. Lives in Africa, south of the Sahara. Small thing, you know? Twenty, twenty-five pounds. Like a little dog. *Small.* They look like big skunks."

He lightened his grip just a fraction, and Harden said, "Do they?"

"They do, Harden." Vincent was almost laughing. "They really do."

Harden felt the burn of fresh air scraping against his barely open windpipe. "Fascinating."

Vincent shook a finger at him. "No, Harden. That's not fascinating. That's just how they are. Many animals are much more interesting in terms of looks. Take the zebra. Or platypus. Hell, the platypus wins the strange-looking contest hands down against the honey badger." Vincent tilted his head. "No, Harden. The fascinating thing about the honey badger is its ferocity. The honey badger has no natural enemies because nothing will tangle with it. You know why?"

"I assume you're going to tell me."

"Because it's one angry fucking animal, Harden." The pressure on Harden's neck was back. "An animal without regard to its own safety. It will launch itself at you without fear of consequence. It doesn't think. It just attacks, sinking its tiny, bacteria-ridden teeth into anything that pisses it off." One more firm squeeze and now all air to Harden's lungs was cut off. "I am Alastair Martin's honey badger. The sooner you understand that, the more productive this little talk will be."

Vincent leaned in and Harden saw the crazy in his eyes, a crazy that was never there with Agent Barrillo. Vincent released Harden with a shove, sending him to the sidewalk. Despite the pain from impact, Harden was thankful to be breathing again.

The rock was nearby, but Harden did not reach for it. The idea of defending himself lost purpose when Vincent opened his jacket and flashed the gun tucked in the waist of his pants. Harden wanted to stay on the ground but forced himself to stand. No matter what happened next, he would be on his feet for it.

"Tell Coyote to let her go. He has no reason to keep her."

Vincent swiveled his head, eyeing up and down the empty street.

"Let's go for a ride, Harden. More privacy."

"No."

"Yes, Harden."

"If I get in a car with you, I'm not happy with my odds of getting out of it alive."

Vincent shook his head just enough to register his obvious disappointment, then removed the gun from his waist. Harden tensed and started to turn, his impulse being to run. But it took only a fraction of a second for logic to kick in. *I'll never make it.*

Then Vincent did the last thing Harden expected. He grabbed the nose of the gun and handed the grip to Harden.

"Take it," Vincent said.

Harden didn't have to ask why. He snatched it from Vincent's grip and immediately pointed it at Vincent's head.

"It's not loaded, G.I. Joe. What am I, new?"

Harden did not listen to him. He'd listened to him before and all he'd been told were lies. His finger tightened on the trigger.

"Plus the safety is on," Vincent said, sighing. "No bullets, and safety is on. Now put that thing away and let's go for a ride."

Harden kept the gun at Vincent's head. He was now certain the gun was useless in the moment, but it felt good to aim it like this. "Why would I go anywhere with you?"

Now Vincent reached up and lowered Harden's extended arm until the gun pointed at the sidewalk.

"Because, Harden, I'm going to tell you where to find your girl. And then you're going to use that gun to put a bullet into the head of my client's only child."

CHAPTER FIFTY-EIGHT

Harden sat next to Vincent in the front of a white Mercedes C-Class as they crept through the familiar streets of Owen, winding about in no particular direction for a few minutes. Harden thought they were at last headed toward the interstate, but when the car veered into the empty parking lot, Harden felt his chest tighten.

Vincent had driven them to the elementary school.

"Why are we going here?" Harden asked.

Vincent took a moment before answering. "Privacy," he said. He looked at Harden. "We were a little obvious on the street. Is there a problem?"

Harden struggled to fight off memories of his childhood. "This whole thing's a problem," he said.

Vincent knows, Harden thought. *He knows because Coyote knows, because he read every page of what I wrote in that cell.*

The car pulled into a slot near the back building. Harden looked past Vincent's suntanned face and spotted the old swing set he used to play on. He went there a lot by himself—especially *afterwards*—and he used to imagine swinging hard enough to fling himself all the way to another city. It was one of his many escapist dreams that never came true. Rust now covered the chains of the swings, and the rubber seats crackled like elephant skin.

"I don't like it here," Harden said.

Vincent's voice was soft. "This will just take a moment, Harden.

I have a proposition for you I need you to consider. Then I'll leave you alone."

Harden barely heard him. He was staring out the front window, the sunlight outside muted by the dark tint on the glass.

The room was three windows over from the left-side wall of the building. Room 4A.

Just over there, less than a hundred feet away.

"I don't want you telling anyone about this."

The voice jolted Harden. Vincent's hand now rested on Harden's forearm. Harden jerked his arm free.

"Don't touch me."

Vincent pulled his arm back. "Take it easy, Harden."

"Tell anyone what? What don't you want me to tell anyone?"

"About this meeting. It wouldn't be good for either one of us."

"I don't make those kind of promises," Harden said.

"It's not a request, Harden. You're going to do exactly what I say, and you're not going to mention any of this to anyone. Not the police, reporters, your father, *anyone*."

"Or?"

Vincent shrugged. "Or we burn your daddy's house down with him in it. Is that clear enough for you?"

Harden didn't think Vincent was lying now. He nodded.

"Good," Vincent said. "Now look. Mr. Martin's son has issues with power, which really shouldn't surprise me. I've known the little shit since he was two. But I didn't realize the extent of it until he disappeared. He called me the day before he disappeared. Not his father. Coyote called me. He called me because he knows I can talk to the old man. Be the voice of reason, if you will." Vincent leaned forward and Harden could see crow's feet around his eyes, something he'd never noticed when he knew the man as an FBI agent. "Coyote told me everything. He even made me a copy of your story."

"My story? You mean my school project?"

"No," Vincent said. "Your *story*. What you wrote in those three months he held you. That's how I know how motivated you must be to find your girlfriend."

"So you know—"

"Everything. I'm actually surprised Coyote shared that with me, because it shows how deeply he strayed from his father's instructions. But I think he wanted to use your story to apologize, to confess to me so that I might convince his father to absolve him of his misdeeds. Unfortunately, Mr. Martin is not so forgiving."

Harden's mind tried to put everything together, but this was a puzzle missing a few key pieces.

"What do you mean *his father's instructions*?"

"Harden, don't you get it? Coyote was working for his father. The whole Church of the Revelation thing? That wasn't just some vanity project. It's a front for the family business. Harden, most of the shit I told you about Alastair Martin? It's true. My boss is . . . well, I'll just say not all of his business dealings are completely within the limits of the law."

Harden's look must have been obvious: that first glint of understanding before total realization took form.

"Alastair needed Coyote to do two things for the family business," Vincent continued, ticking off his fingers. "One, create a tax-free entity. And two, be a distraction. The idea of Coyote starting a church was brilliant and crazy."

"So the Revelation is all bullshit?"

"Well, of course it is, you know that. But Coyote got carried away. Maybe he was surprised how effective he was as a church leader. I suppose he liked the idea of people doing whatever he told them to. What was supposed to be a distraction became a major shit storm. Fucking kid."

"Why did you need him to be a distraction?" Harden asked.

Vincent shot him a cold stare. "Now, Harden, you don't really want to know that, do you?" He smiled, flashing his teeth just a little.

Honey badger.

"No," he said. "I don't suppose I do."

"Good answer."

Harden turned over the gun in his hand. "Why do you need me?"

"Coyote's . . . *activities* have put a lot of pressure on Mr. Martin's business affairs." Vincent scratched mindlessly at the leather on the car seat. "I know he killed your friend, or at least had him killed. I know he has your girlfriend." He paused. "I know what he did to her finger. He's become more of a problem for us than a solution."

"Yet you trusted him with the family business," Harden said.

"What we asked of Coyote was simple. Coyote expressed interest in joining the family business, and his father was willing to try him out. Having a son for a business partner can either be brilliant or disastrous, and Mr. Martin decided to test the waters with him. For the most part he executed proficiently. But then he got carried away, proving to be an unreliable employee. He became . . . unpredictable."

Unpredictable. Just the thing that had gotten Bill killed.

"Now I've been tasked with cleaning up this mess," Vincent continued. "And you need . . ." His voice trailed off.

"I don't need anything from you."

"Yes, you do, Harden. You need to find your love. And I know you want to. I read what you wrote about her. About your secret affair. Your fear of Coyote finding out."

Harden leaned in toward Vincent.

"*Where is she?*"

"He took her, of course. I don't know what he has planned for her, but I don't imagine it's good."

And then it hit Harden. It all suddenly made sense.

"He wants me to find him," Harden said. "It's why he set me free. Why he took Emma. He's not done with us yet."

Vincent took this in for a moment and then shrugged.

"Perhaps," Vincent said. Then he considered a moment longer and smiled to himself. "Son of a bitch."

"What?"

"Maybe you're just right. Maybe he's a step or two ahead of all of us."

It took Harden only a second.

"He told you where he was, didn't he?" Harden asked. Again he looked at the empty gun in his hand, considering its heft, the coolness of the grip. "He told you, knowing you would tell me. So I would come to him."

Vincent turned his gaze out the window, toward the school, to the empty swing with rusted chains rocking gently in the breeze.

"Son of a bitch," he said again. "I think you just may be right."

"You came to tell me where to find him because you want me to kill him."

Vincent nodded. "He's become a liability."

"But he's waiting for me."

Vincent considered this. "That's a very real possibility. But we don't have a choice, Harden. You can kill Coyote and save your girlfriend, be a hero. No one would be surprised by that story. You'll say that Coyote called you and told you where to find him, threatening to kill Emma if you didn't come alone."

"Or you could just kill him," Harden said.

"Yes, Harden, we could." Vincent pulled a pack of Marlboro Lights from the center console and used a brass lighter to light one up. He took a long inhale and as he held the smoke in his lungs he rolled down the window. Smoke snaked from his nostrils as he spoke.

"That was the idea, Harden. Once Coyote told us where he was, his daddy wanted me to pop him. But I convinced him to have you do it. Not just because that kept our distance from it."

"Then why?"

Vincent pointed the tip of his cigarette at the school. "You went to elementary school here, didn't you, Harden?"

Harden said nothing as he felt his skin chill.

"I know what happened to you here. It was in your manuscript. All your secrets were in there, and you told them all to Coyote. Why did you do that?"

Harden stumbled to find his words. "It's . . . what he wanted. He wanted the whole story. It was my only chance at getting out of there."

"He wanted to know your vulnerabilities," Vincent said. "He wanted to know what makes you scared. What you would be willing to fight for, or how easily you'd agree to do what you were told." He took another long, slow drag on the cigarette, and the smoke in the car swirled around Harden's head. "You know what I saw in those pages, Harden?"

"What?"

"I saw a kid too scared to fight for himself. Too willing to please. I saw a follower, Harden."

"Fuck you," Harden said. "You have no idea what I've been through."

"The worst kind of itch is when someone is right but you can't admit it, Harden. Time to scratch that itch. I told my boss you should do the job. That you *earned the right* to do this job. Harden, don't you *want* to kill him? See the expression on his face as you pull that trigger?"

It was what Harden wanted more than anything in the world, and his expression must have revealed his feelings.

"I thought so."

Harden pressed his palm against his forehead, as if pushing away all the memories of pain from the last three months. Suddenly he felt all of his injuries at once: his ribs, his head, his mouth. The knife wounds in his hand and stomach. It suddenly overwhelmed him, and he thought it was only a matter of seconds before he threw up.

"If he's expecting me, what kind of chance do I have?"

"Honestly, I'd say somewhat slim. I have no way of verifying Coyote's even at the location he told me. And if he kills you, we'll have to eventually go after him ourselves, which we'd prefer not to but it's doable. But I'm giving you this chance, Harden. If you don't want to take it, I suppose you could just go on your way and forget about this conversation." He flicked the butt of the cigarette out the window. "So what's it gonna be?"

Harden didn't answer, but he kept holding onto the gun. He supposed that was all the answer that was necessary.

CHAPTER FIFTY-NINE

Sleep didn't come that night. Harden twisted in the thin sheets of the bed in which he grew up, listening to the familiar creaks and groans of his father's aging house. He told himself he would stop looking at the old night-table clock once it showed two a.m., but that was a promise quickly broken. At just after four in the morning, he got out of bed and started packing.

He didn't have many clothes at his father's house, but what he did have he stuffed into a plastic grocery bag that he knotted tight. He walked quietly into the kitchen and picked up his father's battered leather wallet off the counter. It smelled like grease. Inside, Harden counted eighty-six dollars. It sickened him to take all the cash, but he had no choice. He couldn't chance using a credit card. He hoped his father would understand.

It would be about a six-hour drive, he figured, assuming he kept to the speed limit. He'd have to stop for food and gas, but that should be it. He wouldn't tell anyone where he was going.

Harden pressed his ear against the closed door of his father's bedroom, hearing the deep, rhythmic snores from inside. He then crossed the hall and went back to his room, where he lifted the mattress and pulled out the gun Vincent had given him yesterday. It was heavy. Vincent said it was a Beretta nine millimeter, untraceable. He'd taught him how to release the safety and fire. It was a simple piece of machinery. One clip, fully loaded. No more ammo than that, but that should be enough.

Vincent had then given Harden an address where Coyote was supposedly hiding out. Would Coyote actually be there, and if he was, would Emma be there as well?

There were so many unanswered questions to this plan, so much uncertainty. Harden was assuming all the responsibility and, even if he succeeded in killing Coyote and saving Emma, he would still have to deal with the police. They would want to know how Harden had tracked down Coyote. They'd want to know where he'd gotten the gun. What would Harden tell them? Vincent made it clear if he told them the truth, they would take their anger out on his father.

Can't think about that, he told himself.

Just find Emma. It's the only thing you can do right now. Worry about the rest later.

The last thing Harden did before leaving the house was write his father a note.

Dad -

I'm sorry and I love you. Just remember those two things, please?

I need to go away for a couple of days, but I will be back. I will explain everything then, but I can't explain now. Don't call the police. Just wait for me, okay?

Don't be mad at me. Try to have faith in your son. I need you to do that for me, now more than any other time.

I love you. Harden.

After leaving the note on the table next to his bed, Harden opened his bedroom door and crept down the hallway to his father's room. His father's heavy breathing continued, the rhythmic rise and fall he remembered as a boy. At no time was that sound more comforting than when Harden had a childhood nightmare and had crawled inside the bed next to his old man. That was so long ago.

He knew where the keys were. They would be in the pocket of

his dad's jeans, crumpled in a ball next to the bed. Reston Campbell was a fiercely religious man but not a tidy one. Harden took long and slow silent strides to the jeans and fished the keys without much effort. The keys jingled like a bell on the collar of a waking cat, and Harden froze for a moment, making sure he hadn't stirred his father awake.

He hadn't.

Harden stood, looked in his father's direction one last time, then left the room.

He went to the front of the house and slid into his father's 1978 Dodge Challenger. Reston had bought it with nearly 150,000 miles on it, and Harden knew his dad loved the car. He didn't want to take it but had no other choice.

He started the ignition—the engine purred a bit before coughing up a small hair ball—and backed onto the street. Pointing north, Harden flipped on the headlights and crawled down the block. He considered stopping and changing license plates, just in case his father reported it stolen as a means of trying to get his boy back home. But Harden didn't have a screwdriver handy.

He told himself he wouldn't be gone long enough for it to matter, anyway.

CHAPTER SIXTY

The Challenger rumbled along the interstate at precisely the speed limit. Harden had no reason to suspect he would attract attention except for the fact he was now the subject of a national news story, and word of him disappearing once again would create a stir.

What would his father do when he woke? Would he call the police? His father hadn't even wanted him going out for groceries, so who knew how he would react to Harden suddenly stealing his car and his money and disappearing? If he did what Harden fervently prayed he would, Reston Campbell would remain quiet and patiently wait. Harden put the odds of that happening at about 1 percent.

He pulled the sheet of paper from his front pocket and unfolded it. Though he'd already memorized the directions Vincent had given him, he studied it one more time. He'd heard of the lake where Coyote had his rental house. It wasn't too far from the Wyland campus—about forty minutes north—and one of his professors had a summer vacation home there. Harden had never been to the area.

Harden gripped the steering wheel more tightly as he thought about Emma and what might have happened to her. Or be happening to her at this exact moment. Maybe she was screaming for help. Maybe she was bleeding.

Harden cracked the window and let the cool air distract him. It smelled like morning, when the air sat heavy on the earth and only moved reluctantly when something pushed its way through it. He looked out the passenger-side window and saw the sun peeking over a cluster of interstate fast-food restaurants, each of which had a line of cars at the drive-through but hardly any parked in the lot. He spied a coffee shop and was tempted, wondering if the jolt of caffeine was worth the risk of stopping.

I'm probably overthinking this.

Yes, my picture has been on national news, but the story only lasted a few days after I was found. The cycle has turned, and now the country's attention is on to the next story. No one will recognize me.

Temptation gave in at the last second and Harden had to veer more sharply than he wanted to make the exit. It wasn't until he was slowing down on the off-ramp that he noticed the cop behind him.

Fuck.

He tried to slow without braking too hard, but he wasn't used to how sensitive the Challenger's brakes were and the car jolted abruptly. The cop came up fast on him, and Harden shifted his gaze between the rearview mirror and the stop sign looming before him. His stomach turned over as he waited for the squad car's lights to sparkle and dazzle behind him, but nothing happened. He turned right at the stop sign. The cop followed him.

He debated rolling through the parking lot of the coffee shop and heading back to the interstate, but thought that would appear too suspicious. He pulled in to an empty slot next to the store, and the cop, to Harden's dismay, pulled in the one next to him.

Harden got out.

The cop did, too.

Harden went for the door of the coffee shop.

Locked. The damn place wasn't open yet.

"Couple more minutes, should be," the cop said.

Harden cursed himself. *Why did I stop here?*

"Oh," Harden mumbled, searching for words that sounded neither suspicious nor inane. "Guess the clock in my car is fast."

The cop approached Harden's car and ran over the lines of it with an appreciative gaze. Harden guessed the man in his early forties and, given the officer's physique, was probably not tasked with much more than paperwork and school vandals in whatever sleepy Pennsylvania town this was.

"Nice car. What year?"

"Um . . . seventy-eight."

The cop *mmm-hmmm*ed, as if he had guessed as much.

Harden's mind whirred. He thought about how his driver's license wouldn't match the car's registration. How his dad was now already awake and panicking that both his son and car were gone. How he didn't know the first thing about Challengers, and that's all the cop would probably want to talk about as they waited for the coffee shop to open.

But the cop said nothing more about the car. He looked from the Challenger to Harden himself and said, "You look familiar. You from around here?"

Don't lie, Harden told himself. He knew the tags on the Challenger would say exactly where he was from.

"Nope. From Owen."

"Owen, huh? Been down there once or twice. Didn't stay too long."

"Not much to stay there for."

A faint smile from the cop, who seemed fixated on Harden's face. Harden felt himself grow hot.

"I know I've seen you before. You come up this way often?"

Harden wasn't sure which direction to go with his answer, and as he was deciding, a teenage girl with blond hair, black roots, and a green apron unlocked the door to the coffee shop. Harden tried not to look desperate to go inside, as much as he was. He pushed the door open and turned back to the cop.

"I go up to school in New York, so I always drive through here. Got a ticket around here a couple of years ago. Maybe that was you."

The cop nodded and looked up at the sky, as if the recollection was going to fall on his head. "Maybe that's it."

Harden didn't wait to extend the conversation. He slipped inside and ordered a large coffee. The cop followed and waited in line behind him, then stole a few sidelong glances as Harden moved to the end of the counter to receive his drink. Harden took his drink and attempted to sneak out of the store without any more interaction, but the cop asked him a question as Harden walked by.

"What school you go to?"

Harden's mind simply froze. He could not think of an answer other than the truth, and then he just blurted it out.

"Wyland."

As he left the store and got back into his car, Harden hoped he hadn't just made a big mistake.

CHAPTER SIXTY-ONE

He didn't want to do this during daylight. He pulled the Challenger over in an empty parking lot outside a grocery store forty miles from his destination and napped in the car. Sleep didn't come easily, and when it did, it only came in bursts, punctuated by nightmares. His dreams were too close to reality. He saw himself as helpless. Helpless to stop Mr. Kildare. Helpless to get out of the cell. Helpless to save the girl in the car by the cemetery. Helpless to save Emma.

The sleep finally sucked him in fully and didn't spit him back into consciousness for several hours. He woke confused, weak, covered in sweat. He looked at his watch: just before ten p.m., much later than he wanted. He drove to the nearest McDonald's, used the drive-through, and devoured a Quarter Pounder and a Coke in about three minutes. Afterwards, he went inside and used the bathroom, keeping his head down as he passed the front counter.

It was nearly midnight when Harden finished navigating the series of country roads that twisted through the valleys of upstate New York. Harden had never been to Ulysses Lake before, though he knew it wasn't far from Bradford College, where a lifetime ago he'd gone with Coyote and Jacob. They went to pick up non-lesbians, but they ended up paying a hooker to drink with them in a hotel room while Coyote told them all how he'd murdered a boy in the woods on a camping trip.

Did all of that really happen, or was it a false memory induced by his time in captivity? Ever since he walked out of the cell and into that farmhouse, Harden struggled to clearly remember things that occurred in the months before his abduction.

He looked out the car window into the night and saw a conspicuous absence of light, knowing that was the lake. He knew he had several miles left before approaching the house Coyote rented, so he pulled over and double-checked the torn map page Vincent had given him.

27 Hollow Way.

It looked like Hollow Way was only a stub of a road, one that jutted out from the lake like a stray whisker on a freshly shaved face. Harden had no idea whether Coyote's was the only house on Hollow Way, but given how few houses he saw in general, it was a good bet.

He rolled his window down a few inches and breathed in the lake air. Since getting out of the cell, he sucked in the outside air a lot.

Smells like camp, he thought.

Harden reached out and touched the butt of the gun in the seat next to him. It didn't feel reassuring.

It felt dangerous.

CHAPTER SIXTY-TWO

Harden slowed and drove past the road once without stopping. He was right—there was only one house on Hollow Way. Even in the moonlight Harden could tell the house was large, maybe three levels, with a back deck extending into a pier. He saw lights in three windows but no movement. No car out front. No idea if anyone was even home.

He drove about another half-mile before pulling the car over onto a dirt shoulder. There would be no fast escape if something went wrong, but Harden couldn't chance parking anywhere Coyote might see him.

He stepped into the still and cool night, and, despite his nerves, it felt good to stand. As he shut the car door, he made sure the safety of the gun was on and then gently nestled the weapon into the waist of his jeans. He had a sudden vision of shooting himself accidentally, so he removed the gun and tried to check the safety again under the weak light. He couldn't see well enough, so he felt for it instead. Up. Down. Safety is up, that's what Vincent said. Okay. Good.

Safety was on.

The gun went back into the waist of his pants.

Harden locked the Challenger and shoved the key in his jeans pocket.

The house wasn't far, and Harden started to walk.

His feet rolled small pebbles as he walked. He heard them crunch beneath his favorite pair of sneakers. His only pair of sneakers, actually. His t-shirt left his arms exposed to the cool lake air, and a flirting breeze raised goose bumps on his skin.

Something splashed nearby on the lake. Small, but enough to make a sound. Fish, probably.

A smattering of lights appeared in the distance, across the black expanse of water. Houses on the other side. Far away. Maybe a mile?

Harden stopped walking for a moment and listened.

He thought he could hear something like music in the distance, very soft, like someone talking to you in a dream. It didn't seem real enough, so he decided it wasn't. Just his nerves.

Focus.

He walked on. As he reached a slight curve in the road, he finally saw the house. He could see the dark outline of its roof against the moonlight, and from this angle he only saw lights on in two windows. Either the third window wasn't visible from this viewpoint, or someone had turned off a light.

As the house grew closer, Harden wondered if there was a security system in the house. Would he just try to open a door and see what happened? He had the entire drive up here to figure out a plan, but he was now realizing he hadn't a clue how to go about any of this. And the uncertainty was terrifying.

He stopped again and listened. He heard music again, and this time he was certain it wasn't his imagination. It was coming from the house. It sounded . . .

Not right.

Somewhere, way out there, a dog barked. Twice. Then silence.

He pressed the button on his watch to illuminate the digital dial. 12:37 a.m.

He hadn't felt so alone since he was in Coyote's cell. Here, he had all the heavens above him yet still felt trapped in a tiny box.

His pace slowed as he got closer. He felt himself hunching over, almost creeping as he neared the place he'd come so far to find.

The music grew louder from the house.

He took a dozen more steps.

Close now. Close enough to hear . . .

It wasn't actually music, was it?

Maybe.

More like . . . all the sounds in the world. Played an instant at a time, strung together.

Sounds. Just sounds. *All* the sounds. It didn't make sense.

He was less than a hundred feet away and the goose bumps washed over him again, covering his arms like a rash. It suddenly felt like too much. Way too much.

He desperately wanted to be able to call someone. The police. His father. Anyone who could come and help. He wasn't ready for this. But he was far from a phone, far from anyone who could help.

Then he heard the scream.

CHAPTER SIXTY-THREE

A woman's scream, cutting through the night.

Emma. Oh my God. That's Emma.

The second he heard her, Harden abandoned all thoughts except getting inside that house. He had found her, and he was not leaving here without her. He hunched down and scurried toward the house, moving as fast as he could while still trying to be quiet.

There was no wind now. The night was still, and Harden braced himself for the next scream. It didn't come, and the silence was even more agonizing.

There was no streetlight. Under the moon, Harden could just make out the first few feet of Hollow Way. The main road dropped off toward the lake. There was probably a more covert way of approaching the house from the shoreline, but there wasn't enough light. He could stumble. Fall into the water. Make too much noise.

No. He had to go down the dirt path of Hollow Way.

Closer now. The sounds grew louder. He thought he heard the words of a familiar movie line, but wasn't sure.

Sharp, jagged sounds. Too many to take in.

So close.

The house loomed in front of him. He could feel it watching him, like a lion patiently eyeing a rodent.

It's just a house, he told himself. *Just a house.*

Harden approached, holding his hands in front of him, just as he had done that first moment he'd woken in the cell. Feeling for whatever was waiting for him in this unfamiliar, evil place.

The porch light was on. Had it always been on?

He thought so. But ... maybe not.

He stopped in a shadow cut by the light, just beyond the edge of the porch.

Go around back. Must be another door. More windows.

The sounds grew louder. It sounded like someone had the television on full volume and was changing the channel every second.

Harden crept around the lakeside edge of the house, where the land seemed to spill over into nothingness. He touched the house for the first time, felt the flaky paint from the old siding scrape off in his fingers like dead skin. The ground shifted under his feet, and the rocky soil threatened to give way at the steepest point of the slope.

Keep going, Harden. She's in there.

The noise was much louder. Coming from a nearby room. Music. Static. Words. A scream, but not from Emma. From something else. Almost like an animal's scream, a monkey.

Harden felt for his gun and thought about taking the safety off. His brain told him it was the smart thing to do, but his fingers didn't listen. They were frozen in place. Another step.

Take out your gun, Harden.

Another step. Now he heard words inside. They were clear. A movie?

"Time is time is time. Don't you know that?"

"Dead eyes. Like a doll's."

Another cut in the sound. Harden's ears were assaulted by machine-gun fire.

Then the sound of a car crash.

A baby crying.

Water running.

Harden stopped breathing. He felt the muscles in his arms tighten into knots.

What is happening in there?

Then he saw the window. Light flickered around the edges of interior drapes. A fissure of light shot out from the middle of the windows, where the drapes didn't quite close together.

Harden took out his gun and felt for the safety. The metal was cool and smooth, the gun heavy. He slid the safety off.

Another step. Toward the window. Toward the crack.

At the window, Harden got on his knees. A sudden memory jolted him. He thought of the water balloons in their apartment back at Wyland. Harden, Derek, and Jacob all fell beneath the sightline of the window after firing a round. Not Coyote. Coyote looked out the window, daring anyone to challenge him.

Music now. Acid rock. Screaming lyrics.

Laughter.

A cartoon.

"One lump or two?"

He slowly rose, nose first, toward the crack in the light.

His eyes took a second to adjust.

When they did, he saw her.

Emma.

She was strapped to a chair on the far side of the room, facing him. Her eyes were open, but just barely.

She blinked once as she continued to watch rapidly changing movie clips playing on a vinyl projection screen on the other side of the window.

Emma.

Harden felt time stop. He couldn't take his eyes off her. She was dying, he knew. He had to stop it. He had to—

Coyote ripped open the drapes and smiled down at him.

CHAPTER SIXTY-FOUR

There. Again.

On his face. Something touching. Crawling.

Probing.

"Charlotte," Harden said. He swiped at his face, remembering the black widow from the cell. Was he in the cell? What had happened? Was everything a dream?

Harden opened his eyes.

"Hey, buddy."

Coyote crouched over him and lightly drew his fingertips back and forth across Harden's face. It was almost loving. Harden tried to move but couldn't. He looked down.

He was strapped to a chair, and it all came flooding back to him. He was in the lake house. He had seen Emma through the tiny opening in the curtains, and she was strapped down, watching some random series of scenes projected onto a screen. The sound was so loud, but her eyes showed only the faintest glaze of life. Then Coyote appeared like a phantom. It all happened so fast.

Now it was silent.

"What are you—"

"Shhh." Coyote stroked Harden's upper lip with his finger and Harden recoiled.

"It's not quite time for you to speak."

Harden moved his head enough to take in the room. The music

was gone, but a projector on the floor fired out images like bullets onto a white screen nearly the size of the wall. So many images, each lasting no more than a second or two. Bodies from ancient war footage. Animals attacking each other in the wild. Lights from a nightclub. A naked baby crying alone in a metal crib.

Harden moved his head to the other side. Emma stared at him. Duct tape now covered her mouth, and her eyes were halfway rolled up into her head.

At least she was alive.

Harden tried to remember what had happened after Coyote appeared in the window.

It flashed in his mind, bits and pieces of a struggle. Harden had jumped backwards, just enough to lose his footing and balance. He had tumbled down the slope next to the house, falling hard and twisting his ankle. He reached for his gun, but it was no longer there.

Coyote had sprung from the house and pounced on his prey, delivering a forceful blow to Harden's face. And then?

Pain in my arm, Harden remembered. Sharp. Brief.

Needle.

Harden looked down and saw the puncture wound in his forearm.

He'd been expecting me. Just waiting. Watching. Knowing I would come.

"Fast acting," Coyote said, as if following the events in Harden's mind. "Doesn't have to go in a vein. More like a muscle relaxer, really. Not nearly as strong as what we used on you before taking you to Iowa."

Harden could feel his adrenaline overcoming the effects of the drug. He was alert but confused, like waking up and not remembering where you are.

"I knew everything," Coyote said. He offered one of his winning smiles, but this time Harden didn't see his mask. Coyote's face offered no sense of comfort or assurance. It was ugly and evil. "I wrote the end of the story for you. I knew how it was going to end the whole time."

"What . . . what are you talking about?"

Coyote gripped the back of Harden's chair and swung him around to face Emma, then Coyote moved to stand directly between them.

"I knew exactly how this was going to play out. I knew Vincent would find you and have you come here." He smiled down at Harden. "Did Vincent go into the whole honey badger thing?"

Harden nodded, and Coyote chuckled. Then the smile turned into something else. Something dark.

"He killed my mother, you know. My father killed her. Staged it as a car accident."

Harden kept his voice level and calm. "How do you know that?"

"It's obvious, looking back on it. She wanted to leave him—I knew that for sure, even as a kid. And she knew too much. She was a liability, so he killed her. Which is why I knew he'd have no problem getting rid of me, either. *Which is why I told them where I was.*"

Harden looked at the veins bulging from Coyote's arms. "Because you wanted to die?"

Coyote smirked. "Because I knew he'd send you to find me. You don't think I let you out of that cell just to be a nice guy, do you? I didn't want it to end there." He looked around the room. Emma's face was streaked in sweat. She looked as if she was losing her struggle with sanity. "I wanted it to end *here.*"

"Why?"

Coyote turned and looked at Emma as he spoke. "Because I wanted to be *right*. I knew you would come for her, and predicting a person's decisions made of their own free will is a drug I can't get enough of, Harden. I could have killed you both in Iowa. But that's not much of a game."

Emma started screaming beneath the tape. It sounded like she was being strangled.

"It's okay," Harden said, craning his neck to see her around Coyote. "You'll be okay." Though that wasn't remotely true. She had already lost a finger to Coyote.

Coyote placed his hands on his knees and leaned into Harden's face. "Maybe she will be," he said. "That's going to be up to her. It's *you* I'm more worried about at the moment."

Harden looked at him. "I called the police," he said. "They're coming."

"Really? With what? You have a car phone in that old Challenger of your father's?"

He really does know everything, Harden thought.

"Twenty minutes ago. Before I came here. I used the phone at another house here on the lake."

"Oh, yeah? Which house? What did it look like? Describe the person who opened the door."

He didn't even give Harden time to answer, which didn't matter because Harden already found his throat locking up searching for a response.

"You're transparent, Harden. And you know what? That's the beauty of you. You're pure and transparent. You're a good guy. You would've made a great husband someday. A great father. But now that's not going to happen, because you wanted to be the hero. You didn't tell anyone you were coming here, mostly because that's what Vincent probably told you to do, I'm sure. And that's what you do, Harden. You take orders." Again he ran his fingers though Harden's hair, which made him shudder. "But you also wanted to be the one to kill me, didn't you? Here I am, the man who opened your eyes to the world, and you want to kill me."

"You didn't open my eyes to anything. You nearly killed me already."

Coyote shook his head. "No, Harden. In that cell, you became alive for the first time in your life."

Harden looked over at Emma, who just stared back and forth vacantly between the two of them, a strand of sweat-stained hair pasted to her forehead.

"Let her go. Take me instead."

"That's how you really feel, Harden? Like you could just sacrifice yourself for her? Or is that what you're supposed to say in a situation like this?"

"I've never been in a situation quite like this."

Coyote swept around Harden's chair. "True. Fucking invigorating, isn't it? You see? This is *life*, Harden. Can you feel it pulsing through you?"

"I don't . . . I don't understand."

"Harden, I never asked you to understand me. I only wanted you to do every single thing I asked of you, but you didn't. You should have, but you didn't."

"That's why you took me. Put me in the cell."

"You needed to learn."

Harden strained against the binds. "Why not kill me? Why go to all the trouble?"

Coyote jabbed a finger at him. "Trouble. You're right. It was *a lot* of trouble. I had to get other people involved. Drug and transport you, Emma, and Derek. It was a *lot* of work."

"So why—"

"Because I had hope. I wanted you to write. That's what you do, you know? You're a *good* writer. You probably had a real future in it."

Had was the word on which Harden focused.

"I wanted to see what you had to say, and then, in all truth, I was probably going to kill you. But . . ." Coyote wagged a finger at him. "You surprised me."

"Yeah?" Harden felt the energy slipping away from him and he shook his head to try to focus. "And how did I do that?"

"You wrote about *her*." Coyote stepped to the side and pointed at Emma. Harden tried not to look at her face; there was too much pain in it. "About the two of you," Coyote said. "I'm the smartest person I know, but I have to admit I didn't see that coming."

Just like you didn't see how insane Bill was, Harden thought.

Harden lowered his head and spoke to the ground. It gave him a momentary chance to rest, but more importantly he could avoid Coyote looking him in the eyes as he spoke. "I don't think you're nearly as smart as you think you are."

"Is that so?"

"I think you're a fraud with a lot of money."

"Fraud? I had no training in any kind of magic or illusions, and I practiced for weeks to get down the levitating act. That's dedication."

"So you're a dedicated fraud. Big deal. And the tree on that video you showed? Cheap camera tricks."

"Not cheap at all, actually."

Now Harden looked up. "And you have access to drugs. Not too hard to gather a large following if you drug all of them."

Coyote leaned in and Harden could smell his sweat. "Don't underestimate me. Everything I did I *earned*. Drugs? Yes, I used drugs on some of them. Poor Jacob. He'll never be the same again. But do you know how much studying and practice I had to do to figure out exactly the right methods to apply? Which people would be the most susceptible? Who would be the most likely to convince the others to listen to me? It wasn't easy, Harden. And it's not like I had any help or ample time."

"Yet you still failed."

"Failed? Oh, I don't think so. What you didn't know the whole time was the reason for it all. You thought it was because I was bored and needed a challenge."

Keep him talking, Harden thought. "So why did you do it? Why did you start the Revelation?"

Coyote shook his head. "I think you know about all of that by now." His voice dipped into a whispered baritone. "You talked to Vincent."

"He told me you wanted to play with the big boys, but you took things too far. He said you were a liability."

Coyote smirked as his neck muscles tightened against the collar of his shirt.

"I'm not a liability."

"Yes, you are. That's why you went into hiding. You're scared of them."

"I told them exactly where I was, didn't I?"

"Because your need to predict my actions is greater than your concern for your own safety. Actually, that's not even really true, is it? You're not scared, because you think you're in control of everything."

"I am," Coyote said, though his expression betrayed the slightest hint of uncertainty.

Harden continued. "Vincent said your father gave you a simple job and you fucked it up. He said Alastair was glad he didn't tell you more about what he was really doing."

Coyote wagged a finger. "Now, Harden, you're just trying to piss me off here." His words were controlled, but there was an edge to them. "Dad wanted a tax-exempt entity, and we were so close to getting it."

Harden kept going, trying to push Coyote harder. "Yeah, until you turned into a murderer. I'm surprised your dad even gave a shit, considering your dad seems just like you. Rich, smart, and bat-shit crazy. Besides, why would you even want to help your father if he killed your mother? Or is that just another thing you think but don't really know?"

Coyote bent down and leaned into Harden's face. "You don't know anything about my family."

"I know your father wants me to kill you. He doesn't give the slightest shit about you. Just wants you dead. Erased."

Coyote threw his right fist so fast Harden didn't have time to brace himself for the blow, not that he could have done anything more than close his eyes. The knuckles connected on the left side of Harden's jaw and snapped his head violently to the side. Pain seared through his face, and he was certain more teeth were lost, just like the first time he had met Coyote.

"We're not making progress here, Harden!"

Harden spat. Blood spewed from his mouth, but no teeth. "Your dad was using you as a distraction," Harden managed to say, "and getting a tax-exempt entity wasn't even that important. You were just a decoy—something to turn the eyes of the feds off him long enough for him to do whatever illegal shit he had to get done. But you fucked it all up; you went too far with everything. Vincent said he called you a loser."

Another fist cracked across his face, and Harden felt instant burning and swelling.

"You might want to consider changing the subject now, Harden." He nodded toward Emma. "The next time you make me angry, I take it out on her. Now, you care to share with me what you think my father is planning? Aside from my own murder, of course?"

Harden tried to shrug but couldn't. His vision was blurred in his left eye. "I have no idea. You think Vincent would have told me that?"

Coyote squinted, trying to read the truth off Harden's face. "No,

I don't suppose he would. If my father didn't tell me, he certainly wouldn't have allowed Vincent to tell you. Not that I give a shit about the bullshit empire my father thinks he has. He's small. Very small. And when I'm done here, maybe it'll be time for me to tell him what I think."

Keep him talking about his family, Harden thought.

"How do you know he killed your mother?"

"Don't try to distract me, Harden."

"Is that why you did what you did at the cemetery? With the girl in her car? Did you hope to kill someone there because that's what your father did? Was she your . . ."

"*What?*" Coyote nearly shouted the word. Harden looked over and saw Emma shaking her head, telling Harden not to goad him. "First *deliberate* murder? You must be confused, Harden. It was you who killed her, not me."

"You held my hand over her mouth."

Coyote grabbed Harden's throat and squeezed just hard enough to limit—but not completely block—his air flow. "You're not responsible for anything, are you? You're happy enough to ride any wave, then you jump off whenever it suits you. Well, Harden, tonight you are going to take responsibility. You will *claim* the words you wrote. Here. *Now.*"

Harden could see it in his eyes. The unhinging. The look of a mouse who's run on a wheel for so long it's on the verge of death, yet doesn't know how to stop.

A low moan came from Emma, and then a long, high-pitched hum came from her throat, like a bird stuck on a note. She was drifting away. Far away.

Coyote lunged to the corner of the room and picked up the gun Harden had been carrying. Vincent's gun. Coyote waved it above his head.

Keep him talking.

"All this so you could kill me here? I still don't understand why you didn't just kill me in the cell."

Coyote stopped his waving and kept his hands above his head. "Well, Harden, I'll be honest with you." Then Coyote pointed the gun at Emma, who didn't react at all. "*She* saved your life."

Harden looked at her and tried to will her back into the realm of lucidity, but she was far gone. What had Coyote done to her?

"That so?"

"I wanted her to come with me. She said she would do it voluntarily if I let you go."

Harden squeezed the arms of his chair, testing the tape. It was tight. "She doesn't look like she's here voluntarily."

"But she came here willingly with me. I didn't have to knock her out."

"What a gentleman."

"That's not to say I haven't had to do a little experimenting on her. She's rather willful."

"Is that why you cut her finger off?"

Coyote held the gun up and studied it. "The finger was a lesson about vanity. When a beautiful woman loses a body part, she loses much of her identity. She becomes more inhibited. More subservient. I would have cut up her face, but that would have made the sex less enjoyable for me."

Harden felt a wave of nausea roll through him. "You raped her," he whispered.

Coyote did a two-step around him and then leaned in from behind and whispered in Harden's ear. "Now that sounds more like *your* words, doesn't it?"

"What do you mean?"

"You seem to have a thing for sexual abuse. First, your unfortunate childhood experience. Then all that business about me raping Emma on the night she broke up with me."

Harden wondered where this was going.

"Only," Coyote continued, "that's not what happened, was it? Because I would certainly know, wouldn't I? I was there. I never touched her that night. We didn't even break up that night."

"It's what she told me," Harden said. "I just wrote what she said."

Coyote's breath warmed his ear. "Or maybe you made it all up."

Made it all up. Those four words scared Harden more than anything else Coyote had said.

Harden changed the subject. "Why did you really let me out?"

"I told you."

"Emma wasn't the reason. Not really."

Coyote crossed his arms and stared down at Harden. The gun's nose bobbed loosely in the direction of Emma's head.

"You keep surprising me," Coyote said. "Just when I think you don't know anything, you say something smart. Okay, why do you think I let you out?"

Harden spit a glob of blood on the floor then took a deep, long breath. As he exhaled, he tried to relax every muscle in his body.

"I think you let me out to kill me here. You had no idea about Emma and me. You, the man who knows everything, who can predict people's behavior from only knowing them a few minutes, had no idea his roommate was fucking his girlfriend."

He waited for another blow, and when it didn't come, Harden kept talking.

"You must have been furious when you read my story."

"She means nothing to me," Coyote says.

"Of course she does. Maybe you don't care about her, but you care about the *concept* of her. You see her as a possession, and the idea of someone taking something of yours was unacceptable."

Harden looked over at Emma and saw her close her eyes. He didn't know if she was dying or passing out, but fear spiked through him. She was so close. *Right there.* And he was helpless to do anything. The only control he had was through his words, and he had no idea if what he was saying was doing anything but solidifying his and Emma's deaths.

The projector played on, the images silent.

A shark attacking a seal.

A still photo of a concentration camp.

A circus car full of clowns.

"You let me out to see if I would come for her," Harden said. "Like you said, you wanted to control the end of the story. You knew I would come, and now that I've reenforced your power of perception, you're going to kill us."

"You died a long time ago, Harden. You both did."

But Harden knew this wasn't true. If he hadn't written about their secret relationship, they'd both already be dead. And if Emma hadn't pleaded for her lover's life, Harden would have been killed back in that dirty farmhouse cell. They had bought themselves time, though that time looked to have finally run out.

"You really love her," Coyote said.

Harden looked away from him and over to Emma. She was clearly drugged, though with what Harden had no idea. Drugged and forced into sex. Forced to watch this show, these images, the blaring sound, for God knows how many hours on end. And for what purpose? He could only assume to slowly suck all hope away from her, to make her some kind of zombie. To break her down into something that Coyote could completely control.

But somewhere Emma was still in there. And Harden could find her if he could just get out of these restraints.

"Yes," Harden said. "I do."

Coyote lowered his head and shook it just a little, a parent dis-appointed—but not surprised—by his child's actions. Then Coyote left the room, and when he returned a few moments later, he was carrying a buck knife, its long, charcoal blade smooth and sharp on one edge, serrated on the other.

"Let's find out how much she loves you."

CHAPTER SIXTY-FIVE

All Harden could picture was more of her fingers falling to the floor, one by one, as Coyote sawed away and Emma just stared straight ahead in her catatonic gaze.

"*Don't touch her.*"

"Don't worry," Coyote said. He leaned into Emma and cut through each shackle of tape, freeing her arms and legs. Then, in one quick movement, he ripped the tape from her mouth, making Harden wince. Yet Emma didn't react at all. Her body barely seemed able to hold itself up in the chair, and her head lolled gently to one side.

"She's shutting down," Coyote explained. "Happens every night. She gets a nice specialty cocktail in her, then I show her some of my homemade movies while I whisper sweet nothings in her ear." Coyote looked back and gave Harden a wink. "Then, right about now, we usually head into the bedroom. Or, I should say I drag her there. But not tonight."

Harden stared wide-eyed at Emma and tried to will her muscles with his mind. *Run.*

Yet she was like a stuffed animal set down in a chair, a lifeless afterthought.

"What happens tonight?" Harden asked.

Coyote placed the gun in Emma's lap.

"Tonight we see who she loves more."

Harden stared at the gun. Emma still didn't move. The gun sat in her lap, the barrel pointed directly at Harden.

Coyote's voice was soothing, as if he were speaking to a child. "Pick up the gun, baby."

Emma didn't move her gaze, but slowly her fingers found their way to the butt of the gun. She put her right hand—the one with all its fingers—limply around the grip.

"Good, love. *Good.*"

Harden didn't understand. "Shoot him, Emma. *Shoot him.* Get us out of here."

"Don't listen to him, darling." He leaned over and stroked her hair, then ran his fingers through it until knots prevented them from going any further. "You know who you're with now. You know who is taking care of you."

Harden saw her fingers squeeze the gun with a little more force, but still she didn't lift it.

"Emma, Jesus, listen to me. Coyote's going to kill us. *Shoot him.*"

Another long note escaped her lips, a high, warbling moan directed at no one.

Coyote turned and walked up to Harden.

"This is how you get people to believe, Harden. I've mastered it. Your whole concept about starting a religion? It's not hard at all. There's no revelation. It's all *power of suggestion.*"

He turned back to Emma and lowered his voice, his tone suited for a lullaby.

"Emma, I want you to pick up the gun now, please."

Emma flicked her eyes up for the first time and looked at Coyote. It wasn't a look of fear. It was a look of understanding. Then she lifted the gun a few inches above her lap.

"There you go. Good girl."

Harden felt the panic rising through his chest. "Emma, he's brainwashed you. *Don't listen to him.*"

Coyote walked back and stood next to Harden. Emma held the gun with what looked like barely enough strength to keep it in her hands, and it pointed back and forth between them. Harden tensed at the thought of a bullet exploding from the barrel at him; Coyote didn't seem concerned in the least.

Coyote reached out and put a hand on Harden's shoulder.

"Now, Emma, you have to make a decision. You need to kill one of us. Harden has written a long and eloquent tale about how the two of you are lovers. If you truly love him, then you must kill me."

Emma flicked her gaze to him for the slightest of moments as he spoke, her head tilted gently to the side. A ribbon of drool snaked out of the corner of her mouth.

"But if you don't love Harden, then you must kill him, because he has come here to steal you away from me. All this . . . this time we have spent together. It is so good, isn't it? Haven't I shown you how I can take care of you better than anyone else? Isn't that what you really need, Emma? To be taken care of?"

He didn't say *but if you love me*. He said *if you don't love Harden*.

Harden strained against the tape. "Emma, don't do this. I love you. Do you understand that? I *love* you. Just like I told you in the cell that day. Don't listen to him."

Emma's singular note resumed again from the base of her throat, as if calling for help deep under mud. The gun now pointed at Harden.

"I'm the only thing that's real here, Emma." Coyote's voice was hypnotic. "You must cling to what's real, because everything else will just leave you numb. You must feel, Emma. *Feel* it."

"Emma, wake up!" Harden thought raising his voice might snap her out of whatever state she had ventured in to. "Wake up! You need to shoot him, Emma. Your . . . your family. They're all looking for you. They need you. *I* need you. Shooting him is the only way we'll get out of here alive. Please. Oh, God, please, Emma."

She seemed to consider this, and for a brief moment Harden thought he saw a spark of her old self in her eyes. A twinkle of recognition. A flash of defiance. The gun tilted toward Coyote.

"Yes," Harden said. "Good. Good. Now pull the trigger, Emma. You can do it."

Harden knew Coyote could lunge and likely snatch the gun from Emma's grip, but he didn't. He was completely confident in his power of suggestion.

Though his voice took on a sharper edge. "Emma, love, listen to me. We have so much left to do. Do what is right. Kill Harden. Don't let him steal you away."

"*Emma.*" Harden tried to get some momentum, spilling out the words as fast as he could. "He's scared now, do you hear it? He thinks he's invincible. He's only doing this because he's so convinced in his ability to brainwash you that you'll do anything he says. But you're strong. *You're strong.* I can see it in you. You're in there, Emma."

Harden didn't know what else he could do. He couldn't believe there was actually a chance at getting out of here alive. They were *so close.*

"He's not that smart, Emma. Coyote thinks he's won. Don't let him win. This is our only chance. He'll kill us both if you don't do something *right now.*"

"Shoot him, Emma." Coyote's voice had turned commanding. "You must kill him now. I'm running out of patience."

Emma seemed to be waking from a paralyzing sleep, her gaze now darting rapidly between the two of them, the gun waving without focus. The guttural sound grew in her throat, a scream that so desperately wanted to come out but couldn't.

"I love you, Emma," Harden said. "*I love you.*"

"He doesn't, Emma. He doesn't care about you at all. Don't let him convince you otherwise."

Emma's eyes bulged. Her shoulders shook. The death-rattle moan was finally turning into a terrifying scream.

"I love you."

"*I* love you."

"Kill him, Emma. Set us free."

"Kill him."

"Shoot him!"

Emma's scream fully erupted and it tore through her as she stood. Her body shook as she placed her left hand around her right, her fingers all wrapped firmly around the gun. The stub where one finger had once been pointed directly at Harden.

"Please don't do this, Emma."

"*Do it.*"

"No, Emma. Listen to me!"

The screaming suddenly stopped.

Emma gasped for air.

A tear fell from her left eye and rolled down her chin.

She steadied the gun as she finally spoke, repeating the same three words over and over, both an apology and a declaration.

"I love you I love you I love you I love you I—"

Then she fired.

CHAPTER SIXTY-SIX

A sledgehammer slammed into Harden's chest. The force of the bullet's impact knocked him backwards in the chair, spilling him to the ground.

The chair was on its side and his body still strapped to it. He tried to lift his head, but it weighed a thousand pounds. But he could move his eyes, and it was easy enough for him to see the blood pumping sideways out of him and pooling onto the floor. His whole body was in a vice, slowly being squeezed into a flat piece of nonexistence.

He heard crying. Then hysteric laughter.

Coyote's voice. Close.

"Good girl."

They were behind him. He could only see the projection screen, which silently flashed the images of death, as if mocking him.

A soldier stepping on a land mine.

A house in flames.

A pig in a slaughterhouse, its throat peeled open.

Harden knew he was dying the moment he stopped caring.

He didn't wonder why Emma had chosen to shoot him instead of the man who would surely kill her. He didn't wonder why he didn't just drive for help rather than come to the house. He didn't miss his father. He just wanted to sleep, because sleep would make the pain go away. He was so, so tired.

He closed one eye, the other one watching the life ooze beneath him. The blood was warm on his skin, but his body started to shake with chills. Heavy fatigue. A spike of nausea.

Sleep. Just sleep. It's okay.

Emma's crying grew distant, the sound fading into another world. Laughter. Light, the kind at a cocktail party. Far away.

Harden closed his other eye.

The light in the room became heavy, liquid, a sea of opacity. Images didn't matter. Shapes had no meaning. There was only sensation, and even that was fading. This wasn't like sleep. This was the end. Harden had never been so certain of anything as this truth. He had tried and failed. His best wasn't good enough, but that no longer mattered.

More laughing.

The fading image on the screen showed a girl eating cotton candy. Her dress was green.

Then a foot in front of him.

Coyote. Knife in his hand.

Reaching down.

Cutting.

Harden waited for the pain, but felt none.

His body was suddenly free, but not from life. From the chair.

On the floor. Coyote had cut off his restraints.

Then, Coyote was in his ear. Inside his head.

"I'm the last voice you will ever hear. How does that feel?"

Harden couldn't answer if he wanted.

"All that life of yours. So many years. *Gone.* You have maybe a few minutes left, and then you'll be nothing for the rest of eternity. And you never did anything with your life."

If only he could suck in a deep breath, but Harden sensed he would never feel air enter his lungs again. Then he felt his arm being yanked. Pulled.

Dragged.

His body was sliding across the floor. He turned his head.

He saw Emma.

Emma saw him.

She was crying.

The gun was on the floor next to her chair.

Harden's body slid along the floor as Coyote dragged him toward the door. In his mind, Harden could see the smear of blood being left in his wake.

"Let me get rid of this mess, baby."

Harden was sliding on the floor past her. Closer to the door. Coyote was going to dispose of him.

Harden willed himself alive a few more moments.

Hand reaching out. He tried to touch Emma. He couldn't.

She bowed her head as he passed her.

He was then sliding next to the gun, but he wasn't at an angle where he could reach it. In seconds his opportunity would be gone. He had to stop moving.

"Youuu . . . ." he groaned.

He stopped. Coyote kept his grip on Harden's arm and looked down at him.

"I what?"

Harden summoned all his strength to talk, and for a moment he actually felt the pain leave his body.

"You were wrong," Harden managed to say.

Coyote let Harden's arm drop to the floor, then squatted down and leaned into Harden's face.

"What was I wrong about? Tell me, Harden."

Harden reached out, knowing the gun was close. He stretched his arm as much as he could, then finally felt the nose of the gun. Dull, cold steel.

"You believed everything I wrote. Back . . . in the cell. You believed all of it."

Coyote didn't even pretend to play down what Harden said. His eyes narrowed—part confusion, part anger—as he said, "What did you make up?"

Harden's fingers flicked against the tip of the gun, and he was able to spin the handle toward his hand just a bit before the gun left his reach completely.

"You're so . . . so sure of yourself. So certain of your ability to read people," Harden said. His words came in sputtering gasps, and he was certain his death was near. But he would not die here without taking Coyote with him. "But you can't see the truth right in front of you."

Coyote's breath warmed Harden's face. A beautiful, hot wind on his freezing cold skin.

"Tell me."

Harden moaned and stretched, hoping Coyote wouldn't notice him reaching for the gun. His fingers found it and in one swift motion, he pulled it close to his side. Coyote was too close to him to notice.

Then Coyote said, "You never were with her, were you?"

Harden heard Emma sobbing to herself, somewhere an eternity away. His left hand spidered over the gun, twisting it so he could grip the handle. He had never practiced shooting with his left hand.

Coyote stood and smiled. A genuine, goddamn smile as big as the sun.

"You never were even with her at all! Well, Harden, I have to give you credit. You—"

He didn't get the rest of his words out. He stopped talking when he saw the gun pointed at him, the gun Harden had used all the strength he had left in his body to level at Coyote's head.

It lasted just an instant, but an image came to Harden. It was the image of the boy in the woods, the one who had so wanted Coyote's walkie-talkie. That boy died because he didn't know the true nature of Coyote. He underestimated him, didn't think he would fight back. Sometimes people control you, make you promise to do what they say, make you promise to keep the darkest of secrets as they steal away bits of who you are, flaying you one thin layer at a time.

But sometimes, you fight back.

Harden pulled the trigger.

The bullet caught the top of Coyote's head, which snapped back as if pulled by an invisible wire. A chunk of his skull flew off and hit the wall, then landed on the floor just before the rest of Coyote's body hit the floor.

His eyes were open, and they stared directly into Harden's. But they saw nothing. Harden knew Coyote was dead, because for the first time, there was nothing to see in his eyes. No joy, menace, lust, greed. Just frozen, clouded marbles, as empty as the glass eyes of a doll.

Harden's arm collapsed to the ground, and he knew he would soon join Coyote in death.

He no longer heard Emma crying.

As he closed his eyes and considered that killing another human would be the last thing he did before leaving this earth, Harden thought he heard something.

Very distant. A door opening.

Footsteps.

Somewhere, in the ether of his consciousness, Harden's last memory that night was of a voice. Soft. Male.

"Sweet mother of Jesus."

EPILOGUE

Whatever happens, say we are lovers.

That's what I had scratched in the dirt floor of the cell, in the brief moments they put Emma and me together. She had nodded, and then I told her aloud I loved her. It was all an act, but it felt good, like some kind of release. Truth is, I think there was some kind of love between us then. Even if we were doing it all for show, it wasn't a difficult acting job to pull off.

It seems a thousand years ago I last saw her. Actually, it's only been about six months.

Six months since I killed Coyote in the lake house. Six months since I nearly bled to death on the floor next to his body. Six months since a local cop burst into the house and saved my life.

His name was Walter. I have since bought him a very nice case of beer and shared a half-dozen with him as he told me how my father had called the police the morning he found my letter. The police put out a *be-on-the-lookout* alert, and the cop I ran into at the coffee shop finally remembered where he'd seen my face. That narrowed down my direction and position, and Walter had been patrolling the lake when he'd seen my parked car. When he ran the plates, he found out whose car he'd just found, so he called it in before getting out to look for me.

Well, he found me, and thank God he did. Later, the doctors told me if Walter had shown up ten minutes later that would have been it for me. As it was, they had given me a 20 percent survival rate for my first three days, all of which I spent in a coma. That 20 percent became 50, and eventually, over a period of a few weeks, 100.

I had many visitors in the hospital, just as I had when I first escaped from the farmhouse in Iowa. This time it included real FBI agents, who told me there was apparently no major crime Alastair Martin was planning, at least not that they could tell. The working theory was that Alastair convinced his son to start the church as a "first step" in working with the family business, a small, organized crime family with its reach primarily within West Virginia. Coyote, it was assumed, was told to use the church as a tax-free means to launder money. But the FBI thought in reality the father wanted the son to fail, and that failure would diminish Coyote's ability to eventually usurp power over the business from Alastair. Well, I suppose the father knew the son well, and guessed Coyote would become addicted to anything where he was able to control people. Maybe Alastair thought he succeeded, but he hadn't planned on me telling everything I knew to the feds. Both Alastair and Vincent were arrested and awaiting trial for a number of charges, and I get the pleasure of testifying, whenever it gets to that point. They are even reopening the case of the death of Coyote's mother, looking for a link back to Alastair.

Yes, they threatened me. Threatened to burn my father's house down with him in it. But I've finally learned something from all this, a trait I should have picked up from my father years ago. Life's too short to spend it being afraid.

I'm writing my book now, the one that started in a small cell occupied by just a black widow and me. Actually, I suppose it all started with that essay I wrote about religion. That's some kind of metaphor for religion itself, I think. A small, simple idea, which in the wrong hands leads to very bad things.

Three months ago I was contacted by a major publishing house who wanted the rights to my story. They offered me a ghostwriter, but I told them I wanted to write this myself. It should be my voice, my words. They offered me a healthy advance, at least healthy for the likes of a kid from Owen, Pennsylvania. My dad didn't owe a whole lot on his house, but now he doesn't owe anything. I bought a small car for myself, a used Audi with 63,000 miles on it. But most importantly, I don't need to worry about finding a job, at least for a little while. It's given me time to write, to reflect on everything that's happened. It didn't take me long to realize that I needed therapy, and not just because of what happened to me this past year, but also what happened to me as a seven-year-old kid. I'm twenty-one, but my therapist says I've seen more than a lifetime's worth of pain. That's good, because now it should be smooth sailing from here on out.

If only things were that easy.

After I got out of the hospital and once the media attention died down a little, I spent some time with Derek's family. Sometimes, when I'm feeling sorry for myself, I remind myself I'm lucky to be alive. Seeing the pain on the faces of Derek's mother and father is a miserable affair, and it makes me wonder if I would ever even want to have kids. They have an anguish that will be with them always, a dark stain that goes with them everywhere they go, clouding every happy moment, heightening the sting of the painful ones.

I haven't seen Jacob since he disappeared, though I understand he's back living with his family. I've tried, but he doesn't want to see anyone. I've heard he might have permanent damage from the drugs Coyote gave him, but that could just be a rumor. I don't think he had any part in what happened to Emma or me, and I don't hold any bad feelings against him. I don't think I could even if I wanted to; I just don't have the space for that kind of thing anymore. Maybe one day we'll sit down and have a beer together, though most likely I will never see him again. I suppose either of those scenarios is okay by me.

I'm nearly at the end of my book, but there's one loose end.

Emma.

After the night I killed Coyote, both Emma and I were rushed to the hospital. I was in more critical condition, but my wounds were ones that could heal. The abuse she endured went beyond the physical, though there was no small amount of that. The drugs Coyote had been using on her seeped deep into her brain, leaving her in a catatonic state for nearly a week. When she came out of the state, she was prone to fits of screaming, uncontrollable shaking, and endless hours of weeping. Coyote had consumed her, and what came back up was weak and damaged, just like everything else he had touched.

After three months she had healed; not entirely, but enough to move on with her life. I haven't seen her yet, but we've spent hours on the phone together. She called me first, wanting to tell me she had no recollection of shooting me that night, and that she never would have chosen to do that. Of course I believe her. She had been brainwashed by Coyote and was able to only respond to his voice at that point. She very nearly killed me, but I would never blame her for anything. We were both victims, and she has only four fingers on her left hand as a grisly reminder of that fact.

Right now I'm in a sad little town called Redemption, Kansas, sandwiched between endless miles of fields that I'm guessing grow wheat and corn in the summer, but are barren, frozen landscapes in January. This place is barely a speck on my Thomas Guide map. I'm staying the night in a motel here, and will stay only as long as I need to get enough sleep to drive many more hours. There's a quiet desperation to this town, where the few faces I've seen seem wrinkled not by years of smiling but by worrying, as if for decades they've all been told something horrible is just around the corner. I'm a stranger here and feel unwelcome, and am glad to only be passing through.

I'm headed west. San Francisco, to be exact. What I wrote about Emma wanting to move to San Francisco was the truth, and a month ago she did exactly that. I last spoke to her a week ago, and it was the first time I told her I was writing a book based on my experience. She asked if she was in it, and I told her she was.

Funny thing is, Emma has never read what I wrote in that cell. All she knows is one time I asked her to say we were lovers, and she did. She doesn't know all the things I wrote about a secret love that never actually happened, about our first kiss, or making love in my apartment when Coyote was far away in the woods with Jacob. I wrote these things out of desperation, thinking that I could catch Coyote by surprise for once, and maybe then he would make a mistake. But rereading the words on my tattered and stained manuscript, I see more in my sentences than a ploy. I see something amounting to real affection—if not quite love, at least a serious crush. Maybe I've felt this way about Emma since the first time I met her at Benny's, when I imagined that the gaze from her bright green eyes lingered on mine just a little longer than anyone else's. That night, I thought she was the kind of woman men kill each other over.

So I'm driving to San Francisco and I'm going to let her read all the words I've written, and then I'll take life from there. Maybe we'll end up together, or maybe I'll just be another boy who's traveled a great distance for a girl, only to end up alone.

On this one, I'm going to be optimistic.

Redemption, Kansas
March 1991